Double Bridle

For permission requests, contact the author at:
Admin@RiiFinley.com

Cover art by Rii Finley:
iStock Photo 1323814024 Licensed.
iStock Photo 1445387866 Licensed.
Internal illustrations by Rii Finley
ISBN: 979-8-9995821-3-3
1st edition 2026

Content Warnings

This book is not dark; however, there are adult themes and mentions of topics that could be upsetting. Please read below before saddling up.

Warnings include:

- Talks of abuse
- Bullying due to a disability
- Mentions of murder (brief, non-graphic)
- Adult language

Explicit on-page sex scenes including:

- Relatives within the relationship (NO incest)
- Group sex scenes
- Vaginal felching
- DVP
- Triple penetration
- Degradation
- Exhibitionism (Light)

Save a horse, ride a trainer, a stable hand, and two fellow trainees while you're at it... Or however that song goes.

Get ready for a ride.

One

Leah

Rumbling fills the humid night air as my trusty Silverado barrels down the highway. Everything I hold dear in the world is loaded into this truck and attached trailer. We've been on the road for nine hours and have only stopped for gas and a single restroom break.

Tally has to be restless. She's never been fond of long rides cooped up back there. She'll be one ornery gal by the time we reach our destination.

We're just about there, T.

A nice, long rest stop would be amazing, but there's not exactly an abundance of horse-friendly hotels on the Gulf Coast. The absurd image that flashes into my mind makes me titter. Imagine being the housekeeper at a horse hotel. No thanks. I barely want to deal with Tally's massive road apples. No amount of money could convince me to clean up after others.

The final stretch of our journey is dragging on. Nearly twenty-four hours without sleep will do that to the best of us. At this point, I think I'm a little delusional—more than my family would lead you to believe. Fortunately, the roads are clear. Apparently there aren't tons of people trying to chase their dreams at four in the morning around here.

Slackers.

Life's short. Opportunities like this don't come along often. Hell, for a lot of people, they *never* do. Only a fool would squander a chance of this magnitude.

Is twenty-six too old for Olympic glory? Yes, if you ask my parents. The fact that I don't want to sit around and rot on the family ranch forever is a hard concept for them to grasp. The four behemoths I call brothers are more than content to do so; they don't need me withering away there, too.

According to my family, I'm foolish for spending part of my lottery winnings on the horse I've always wanted. And even more insane for deciding to pack up and move hours away, stay at a world-class training facility, and focus on what *I* want for once.

Too damn bad.

Hartbrook is home to some of the best trainers in the world. Months of research solidified my decision to board and train here. With six medals under their belts in the last four summer Olympics, no other training facility holds a candle to them. They don't have a gold to their name yet, but I plan to fix that issue—if Testy Tally doesn't break her trainer first.

A dimly lit little town greets me as I pull off the highway, tires on crumbly asphalt disturbing the silence. Down long driveways, single-story houses sit tucked into grassy yards. It's almost like I'm back home in Mississippi, but with palm tree-lined roads and, somehow, more humidity.

A quaint corner store marks the intersection I need—brick with stone embellishments, timely and rustic like the surrounding architecture. Turning onto the private drive is akin to entering an alternate reality. For a moment, I had second-guessed my GPS, fully convinced that all of my Googling was a lie. Unlike the patchy, worn roads I traveled down to get here, this one is immaculately paved. They must redo it at the first sign of damage.

Quality, that's what it screams.

If the entryway is this nice, I *know* the facilities will be everything I read about, and then some. Jolts of excitement zip through my body, invigorating me, fatigue long-forgotten. I can't wait to get unpacked. Tally had better love it here, because I already do, and I haven't even seen the place.

White fences line pastures. Trees canopy the road as we approach the entrance. Chest fluttering, I pull up to the keypad to punch in the security code. With a loud buzz, the wrought-iron gates pull back. Tears immediately fill my eyes. If heaven is real, this is it.

The clock on my dashboard reads five fourteen in the morning, making our travel time ten hours and fourteen minutes.

A shaky sigh breaks free as we cross the threshold to our future.

We made it.

My bubble bursts as the lights of the main house turn on and a disgruntled-looking older woman marches out the front door. Her gray hair is up in curlers, ice-blue eyes narrowed at me. A sky-blue silk robe breezes behind her as she approaches my truck in a frenzy.

"Just who in the world do you think you are?" she asks, voice a shrill screech in the early morning.

"Leah Porter, Ma'am. You must be Mrs. Hart." I tip my chin to her from my driver's seat, hoping to calm her blazing fury. I'm well aware of who she is, but I've got to play the part. Can't let on that I've stalked this place for months and know every staff member by name—down to the groundskeepers.

"Bah, you're not slated to arrive until tomorrow." Her uppity accent grows thick as she rights herself. It's as if—now that she knows I'm a paying client—she has to put on a front.

Too bad she's already shown me *exactly* why the rumors are true. No matter, I'm great at faking it till I make it. If I gave a hoot about acting, I'd have at least one or two Oscars to my name by now.

"My apologies, I was a wee bit overzealous. Turns out my old boarding contract ended a day sooner than I figured." The lie rolls off my tongue with ease, part of my carefully curated plan.

The woman at my window would never let someone like me infiltrate her prestigious training program. I'm eternally grateful that their background and identity checks are nonexistent if you have enough money.

"How unfortunate. However, we can accommodate, I'll amend your bill for the month to reflect the additional days lodging... alongside a convenience fee." Lifting her nose, she turns toward the wall of windows she calls a house, strolling casually up the pristine white driveway. "Find Grady or Parker, they're your contacts, or staff, whichever you prefer to call them. They'll assist you from here."

Who? Neither of those names rings a bell, which is only mildly concerning. "How am I supposed to know what they look like?" I yell.

If she hears me over the rumble of the engine, she doesn't give any indication.

Lovely. What a great start.

Is it unprofessional to show up a day early, unannounced? Yeah, I guess. But given the amount of money this place will be funneling out of my account every month, I'd expect a teeny bit of hospitality.

I'll be staying in cabin one-fourteen. Tally's supposed to be boarded in the stable across the drive from me. So, seeing as I have no choice but to self-orient, I follow the road signs and head toward my housing. The fact that this place is so large that it *needs* marked roads is ludicrous. Just the way I like it.

Dawn approaches, shining warm light upon the sprawling pastures. Horses graze peacefully, only momentarily bothered by my existence. Tally stirs in her trailer, whinnying to them as we pass. She's going to do well here. Where her people skills are lacking, my girl loves other animals.

I drive slowly, admiring how well-kept the land and facilities are. There's hardly a sign of use—or life—anywhere. Immaculately raked paddocks, hedges trimmed to perfection. Even the crisp, white siding on the buildings is spotless, free of any vines or moss—things from home I never thought I'd take for granted.

I knew coming in that Hartbrook prides itself on cleanliness, but this feels... clinical. Everything looks staged, like walking into a catalog. The grounds are large, and the further I go, the more the lodging appears to be empty... strange. Truthfully, it's probably for the best. I'm rowdy, and their normal clients are stuffy.

They're going to hate me.

Shaking my head, I rid myself of the negative thoughts. There's no time for insecurity or inferiority, I have goals and aspirations. While they're likely unattainable, that's never stopped me before.

As I cut the engine off, the stable door slides open. Hopping out of Ol' Trusty, I step around to the passenger side and pause.

So does *he*.

Haloed by the morning sun is a man who can only be described as a Grecian lumberjack. He's tall—*so* tall—sporting a rich tan that looks to be all natural, and hello, biceps.

My brain misfires. Part of me had assumed the door was automatic. The idea isn't far-fetched, given how unnecessary half of the amenities here are.

Nope. I was *very* wrong. Which, at the moment, I'm thankful for.

Focus, Leah.

Right, staring is rude. Say something, mouth.

"Hey there!" I call out, plastering on my best warm smile, eager for a reply... that doesn't come.

Instead, he dips his head, directing his gaze at the pavement as he strolls my way. The closer he gets, the more I want him to look up. With his face pointed down, I'm only given the chance to admire the sharpness of his cheekbones.

"I'm Leah. Are you Parker?" My voice sounds fake as I try to hide my accent, just in case he's as pretentious as the old hag that greeted me at the gate.

Stopping in his tracks, he lifts his golden gaze to me—brows pinched like I asked the dumbest question he's ever heard. A shake of his head accompanies the faint scowl barely visible through his deep brown beard.

"Ooookay..." I squint, pursing my lips.

What's with the silent treatment?

"Ah! Grady?" The faintest hint of twang breaks through as I approach him.

One distinct nod, and he carries on past me to unlock my trailer.

"Wait!" I step next to him. "Tally isn't too keen on strangers. She also doesn't like the trailer, so she's bound to be extra cranky." Sparing him a glance, I take note of his raised eyebrows, expression filled with surprise. "Trust me." I place my hand over his on the latch.

His eyes dart across my face, over to where we're touching, then straight to the ground. Pulling away, he clears his throat and runs his fingers through the long, nearly black mess of hair on his head. Stepping back a few feet, he nods for me to open the trailer.

Climbing inside, I carefully approach Tally and scratch behind her ear, right where she likes. Once I slip her halter on, I attach a lead and gently coax her out.

The man—who I'm going to call Grady, assuming he's not full of shit—stands with his mouth slightly open, eyes wide.

Yeah, take a good look.

Even after half a day cooped up, Tally is stunning. My girl doesn't believe in bad hair days. Her flowing mane and tail are strategically chaotic until I tame them for her. At almost sixteen hands, her withers are just a bit higher than the top of my head. Solid black, naturally, she gleams in the sun.

"Ever seen a Friesian in the flesh?" I raise my brows, patting Tally's neck. Grady shakes his head, letting out a low whistle of appreciation. "I figured as much. A lot of Dutch Warmbloods and Hanoverians train here, huh?" I pull a peppermint from the pocket of my jeans and toss it to him. With lightning-fast reflexes, he catches it, jerking his head back. "I'm assuming you're the stable hand that will be caring for her, yeah?"

He nods, still silent.

Awesome... just great.

"Well then, consider this a peace offering. It should help her hate you less." A mischievous grin splits my face as he audibly gulps.

Unwrapping the candy, he slowly approaches and extends his hand. Tally—the little harlot—lets out a low nicker, practically rolling over for him. As she takes the mint from his palm, more gentle than I've ever seen, he passes me a bemused look.

"She's a filthy traitor!" I huff. "Don't get too confident. She'll strike when you least expect it."

His lips twitch, trying to maintain the indifferent expression he's been wearing. Despite his efforts, two small bursts of air escape him.

Was that a laugh?

"Ha. Ha. You won't think it's funny when she puts you on your ass," I grumble. "Now show me the way to her stall. I'm beat and she needs some good rest, too."

He nods, turning toward the stable. Tally nibbles on the end of my braid as we trail behind him.

Inside the building is *way* too fancy for my blood. Everything here is so segmented. Unlike other facilities where there's one large central boarding stable, Hartbrook is more like a campground. There are about a dozen clusters of identical buildings—as far as I've seen, anyway.

Each has a stable with four large stalls, a tack room, and a supply room. There's a corral, private training arena, and pool for every group as well, along with six cabins—one for each trainee, another for the trainer, and a final one for the stable hand.

Some may call the layout "curated". I call it ridiculous. But, if this is what gets me a podium spot at the Olympics, so be it.

The secluded area I'm assigned to is the exception to their standard layout, with only five cabins. Yet the stable still has four stalls, so I'm not sure why that is. A trainer and stable hand who aren't listed on their staff site, a cluster of buildings that is intentionally segregated from the rest, and me, the unorthodox client. This smells funny, but who am I to question it?

We stop at Tally's stall. The door sign has her registered name on it, along with a—hopefully convincingly Photoshopped—picture of us at last year's World Cup. Grady looks between the picture and us a few times before shrugging.

I relax and try to hide the relief on my face. "Thanks, I'll get her settled in and head to my cabin. I already know which one it is." I force a smile through my nerves, turning away from him before it stops being convincing.

Grabbing a comb, I get to work de-tangling Tally's mane. It's down to her shoulder and usually stays fairly neat, but she was thrashing quite a bit on the way here. She's unbothered now, face buried in the feed bucket. My girl loves a snack.

Startled by commotion behind us, I whirl around to Grady hauling our gear into the storage closet.

"I would have gotten all that, you know." I plant a hand on my hip.

Expression flat, he sighs and points to the Hartbrook logo on the chest of his polo.

"Ah, fair enough. But still, I'm capable." I cross my arms.

He throws his hands up in surrender and walks out of the stable, shaking his head.

How have we had a whole conversation, but he still hasn't said a word?

Once I have Tally unpacked and settled, I head back to my truck for some of my bag before making my way to the cabin I'll call home for the foreseeable future.

Today is the start of the rest of my life.

Two

Leah

While my personal cabin is fully finished, everything inside has the appeal of a concrete slab. Gray, it's all gray... The couches, every curtain, each bare wall. Burial chambers have more appeal.

Kicking my boots off at the door, I haul my bags to the bedroom—also gray, but a lighter shade. How cheerful. The only things that aren't *some* shade of drab are the appliances. They're stainless, so close enough. Since I'm a day early, I have free time before training starts. Introducing myself to my peers would be nice, but decorating has been promptly moved to the top of my to-do list.

Foresight is one of my best qualities. For that, I'm immensely thankful. Most people would never consider bringing décor to a boarding facility. But me? I have trunks filled with a variety of trinkets and figurines. The benefit of being a closeted nerd pretty much ends there. Nonetheless, between them and my art supplies, I have more than enough to keep me busy.

Powering on my Bluetooth speaker, I connect my phone and open Spotify. Volume cranked, hair tied into space buns so they look like pink cotton candy poofs, I get to work. If I have neighbors, they're either going to love me or hate me. I'd like to think anyone who stumbles—or storms—in on me attempting to dance along to 90s boy bands would be entertained.

Bopping along to "Bye, Bye, Bye," I pull open the zipper on my large cow print suitcase. Mountains of clothes erupt from it. All of my favorite dresses had to make the journey. There's no world I'd want to live in where they don't exist. The occasional romper and overalls fill in the gaps for rainy or cold days.

Does Florida even get cold? We'll see.

My plush burgundy comforter is the next thing released from its luggage confines. Haphazardly tossing it over the bed, I move along to the sitting area by the large window. Throw blankets are pivotal to human existence, and I'll fight anyone who disagrees. I brought seven.

In my expert opinion, my favorite throw—cream-colored, decorated with little ivy vines—will complement the dark red on the bed perfectly. I drape it over the plush chair, grinning from ear to ear as I admire my improvements. The benefit of a monochrome, blank slate is that everything goes with it. A girl's got to look on the bright side, after all.

I dance my way to the kitchen, cutting the tape that seals the cardboard box on the counter. Mismatched dinnerware shines back at me in a kaleidoscope of colors, like beacons of comfort and *personality*. I file them away, appreciating the glass cabinet doors. The peek of life visible from inside livens up the space without needing any extra effort. My cow print apron finds its new home on a hook by the fridge. Sunny-yellow place mats on the round glass-top table provide the perfect pop of vibrancy to the dining area.

Hanging a few of my favorite watercolors fills in the gaps to bring the space together.

Music still booms through the cabin. I've been at this for hours. If the other cabins were occupied, someone would have broken my door down by now.

Solitary confinement means I can be as loud as I want, nobody is around to tell me otherwise.

Jackpot!

One final trip to my truck for things to add a little pizzazz to the living room, and I can call this done. The amount of chaos I've imbued into the space is amazing. As I lay the rest of my throw blanket collection along the couches, the first notes of "Livin' la Vida Loca" fill the air. Naturally, I burst into a full-on frenzy—whirling, spinning, shaking my hips—forgetting the world as I lose myself in the sweet musings of Ricky Martin.

As the beat stops, I strike a final pose and shake myself off, catching my breath. My hair is a wild mess. I'm sweaty, panting with a giant grin on my face. That is, until I realize I didn't close my door.

Leaning suggestively against the frame is a man—arms folded, one hip pressed against the molding, legs crossed at the ankles. Backlit from the sun, his face is cloaked in shadow, so I can't make out the expression hiding there.

He's lean, so definitely *not* Grady.

Some people would feel bad for disturbing his day, others might even feel embarrassed and scurry to stop the music. Not me. I casually press pause, letting my hands find their familiar perches atop my hips. Chest puffed, I return his silence.

Please don't be another silent mystery man.

"What a display," he says after a minute, voice deep but surprisingly light.

Oh, good, he talks. Still, that doesn't excuse his gawking.

I tilt my head, trying to get a look at his face. No luck. "Do you make a habit of watching people?"

"Only the cute ones." He straightens, knocking on the already open door. "It was unlocked, I took it as an invitation to introduce myself. Besides, I love a good party and expected an entire gaggle of women in here. Instead, I got one hell of a solo show."

"Wow, okay," I say with an exasperated huff, looking for more words. They're somewhere in the pudding my brain has devolved into.

"Can I come in?" He lets out a soft laugh.

"You're already halfway there, may as well." I shrug, strolling to the kitchen.

The door latches behind him, click echoing louder than needed. I immediately swallow down tingles.

Did I just let a strange man shut himself in this—suddenly very small feeling—cabin with me?

"Well, this is a pretty secure place. I'm also not *that* strange." His eyes, so blue they're almost colorless, sparkle when he chuckles, pillowy lips pulled into a half-smile.

I lean against the refrigerator, groaning into my hands. "Stupid mouth. I said the inside parts out loud again."

"You're not the usual type of clientele they take on here," he comments with a playful smirk. I'm definitely staring way too long, but it's *just* enough to commit his chiseled jawline to memory. "I'm Parker, your trainer," he interrupts my studying, destroying the fantasy life I started building for us in my mind.

My lungs stop working. "P-Parker?"

"In the flesh. Grady told me you were here."

"Grady?!" I squeak.

"Yeah, he said my new project had arrived. In fewer words, but still."

"He... talked to you?"

"Ah, my bad. No. He sent me a text."

"That sounds—wait. Your *project?!*" My face twists, lip curling.

"It's a long story. Mostly a tale of my shortcomings and why I need you." His mouth corner twitches despite the attempted humor in his voice.

My heart pounds rapidly, nerves prickling the back of my neck. "So I'm a pawn. For what? Are you going to use me for your own gain, make yourself look good, then discard me once I've finished being beneficial?"

"Uh, wow. Okay. There's an entire truckload of worms I don't wanna open. What I mean is, we both have something to prove. Your secrets are safe with me. I'd like to think we could be friends." He taps his fingers on the counter.

Friends. *Riiiight.*

I raise my chin, straightening my spine. "Good thing I don't have secrets."

"Of course not. Silly me for insinuating that you might. But, if you ever find yourself in need of an alibi, hit me up, Pinkie." He pulls a business card from his pocket, slapping it on the counter.

"Pinkie, how original." I roll my eyes. "Haven't heard that a million times from guys trying to take me home."

He chuckles. "That's the difference, I'm already in your home." I scoff, but the heat on my cheeks betrays me. "Fine, I'll get more creative. I appreciate a spunky lady. The pink hair is a bonus."

"Good, you'll love my horse then."

"Grady gave me a heads up, don't worry, I'll keep peppermints on hand for her." He circles the counter, leaning in close.

My stomach flips from his presence, only getting fuzzier as our eyes lock.

"What do *you* like?" Brows raised, head tilted a little to the left, he watches me with such intensity that my breath catches. No man should be this magnetic. I've been with a sinful amount—if you ask my mother. His aggressive confidence would usually earn a knee to the groin. But good god does it work.

My mind slips into a maddening spiral. "L-lemon," I squeak out.

"Lemon heads? Or lemon meringue pie?"

"Lemon heads are to die for," I reply, finally coming back to reality.

"Peppermints and lemon heads, got it. I'll stock up. Happy girls make for a good time."

Red alert, change the topic.

"How are you a trainer? They're all ancient. You must be twenty years old." It's obvious that he's older than that, but exaggerating to see his response is entertaining.

His face is expressive. He also absolutely enjoys my sense of humor. Every poke and jab rewards me with small smiles and little lifts of his eyes, which I need to stop staring into.

He's your trainer, Leah. You can't sleep with him.

"I'm twenty-nine. But thanks for the flattery." Leaning against the sink, he braces his hands on either side of himself, forearm veins bulging.

My lip almost bleeds from how hard I bite it. Does he know how attractive he is, or is this just the way he naturally acts? I guess I'll find out soon enough.

He raises a single eyebrow. "You good?"

"Yup. So, am I your only client?" Another change of subject, getting back on track before I leap across the kitchen and lick him. That would be a massive mistake.

"No, but I only have one other. She's a... special case, too." The slight frown that tugs at his mouth marks the first hint of negativity I've seen.

"Lucky you. A 'project' and a 'special case' all to yourself," I joke, hoping to bring his smile back.

"It's the price I've gotta pay to prove myself." He shrugs, pulling out his phone. "I'm famished, wanna get lunch with Grady and me?" When I go stiff, he winces. "Did he make a bad first impression? He can be a little rough around the edges, but he's a decent guy. Just don't ask him to talk to you."

"So he *can* talk?"

"Come to lunch and give him a chance to show you his personality. He's going to be very involved in our day-to-day routine, so there's no avoiding him." He motions to the door. "I'll text him. We can all take my car."

I shift on my feet, trying to think of an excuse that doesn't suck. "I'm sweaty and gross from unpacking."

"He won't care, neither do I. You look gor—" Clearing his throat, he tucks his hands in his pockets. "Good, fine. You look fine. We'll be waiting outside. Take a minute to get ready if you need it."

With that, he leaves, not giving me the chance to argue further.

Looks like I'm going to lunch.

My stomach growls on cue. I had planned on grabbing food soon anyway. Some attractive company can't hurt. Might as well get started on those introductions.

Jitters fill me, like there's an entire atrium coming alive in my stomach. I scurry to the bathroom to brush my teeth and apply fresh deodorant. As for my hair, messy space buns will have to do. It's far beyond salvageable. Not that it matters, they'll see me at my worst soon enough.

It's just lunch with my trainer and stable hand.

Rein it in.

A snort escapes me from the thought.

Pulling on a baby-pink dress with a scattering of small white flowers all over it, I stop at the full-length mirror to admire myself. The skirt flows loosely, landing mid-thigh. Buttercup sleeves flatter the fullness of my upper arms. That's right, I'm hot shit.

Walking with a spring in my step, I'm ready to take on whatever awaits me at lunch.

After I slip on a pair of cream-colored flip flops, I swing the door open, freezing at the sight of them.

Man, am I in trouble.

Three

Leah

Parker and Grady are standing next to a blacked-out BMW, each wearing a nicely fitted T-shirt with jeans that should be illegal. When I applied to train here, I was under the impression—thanks to my stalking—that all of the staff members are at least twice my age. At the moment, I don't know whether or not I'm glad I was wrong.

At the end of the day, my success is on the line, so I can't indulge, no matter how glorious they look. Hopefully, they're of the same platonic mindset.

Totally, definitely platonic. No attraction here. Nope.

"Look at you!" Parker's brows lift as he unashamedly admires me.

Platonic.

Grady, in all his silent, mysterious glory, joins him, face showing no clear indication of whether he appreciates my efforts.

Screw him. I don't need his googly eyes, anyway.

"I figured you guys wouldn't want to be seen with me if I was still sweaty and gross," I reply with a wide smile.

"With a body like that, you'll *never* have to worry about me not wanting to be seen with you." Parker winks playfully. Grady rolls his eyes, jerking his head toward the car. "Okay, you're right, we should get going. Our lunch break is only so long." Circling to the driver's side, Parker slides in and starts the engine.

My flip-flops slap against the soles of my feet, breaking up the awkward silence. Grady stands tall—as if someone his size could stand any other way. Face impassive, he gives me a faint nod and... opens the door for me.

He definitely catches the moment of surprise on my face, the pinching of his brows tells me so. I almost feel bad about it.

Almost.

"Thank you," I mutter, dropping into the leather seat.

Grady settles in behind us. As soon as he's buckled, we peel out of the driveway—too fast for the stuffy old money's liking, surely.

Nobody says a word for the first several minutes. I'm not sure what *to* say. Clearly, neither of them is going to start a conversation, so I let it be, watching the rolling hills pass.

Apparently sick of the silence, Parker taps a few icons on the dash screen and "Livin' la Vida Loca" begins to play. I gasp, staring slack-jawed at him. Red-faced, he bites his lips to hold in a laugh. I jab him in the ribs, and he grunts, sputtering out his withheld chuckles.

"You're a tease!" I poke him harder. There's no time for mercy in the presence of a sadist.

"Okay, okay, I'm sorry." Breathless, he shakes with residual little laughs, stopping the music. "I couldn't help myself. You looked real good shaking your ass to that song earlier. Grady's super sad he missed it." His gaze glides to the rearview mirror.

There's no hint of amusement, or any real emotion, on Grady's face. A small pout pulls at my lips and I return my focus to the world passing us by.

Parker is wrong about him, which is good news for me. I'm already going to have a hard time fighting off one of them, let alone both. Parker is a fun flirt, though, and I'm a sucker for good conversation.

We stop at a little diner in the center of town. The faded pink awning above the front door reads "Carrie's" in a black, swirly, retro-style font. It's quite homey—tan brick, large windows, old cement planters out front with vibrant pink flowers bursting over the top.

Lost in my admiration, I startle when my door opens. Grady stands with his hand extended, eyes soft but avoiding my own.

What's his deal?

With a slight quirk of my brows, I let him help me out of the car. The instant I'm upright, he tucks his hands into the pockets of his *very* nice-fitting jeans. Parker comes to my side, elbow bent so I can lock my arm with his. Grumpy Grady opens the front door for us, focusing intently on our linked elbows. For the first time, there's a slight change in his face. The tiniest flare of his nostrils makes my mind race.

I doubt he's interested or jealous. Maybe it's concern?

In an effort to ease his troubles, I offer a soft smile. His eyes land on mine, then immediately shoot straight to the floor.

Okay, then.

Vinyl booths fill the small diner—a mixture of pinks and blues with polished wooden tables. The floor is checkered, shiny black and white tile with little Coca-Cola emblems scattered about—vintage but clean. Records and neon Coke signs on the walls. An old-time jukebox at the back, lit up with a spectrum of colors, plays soft jazz music.

Our waitress approaches with a toothy grin. On brand, she's got a graying blonde beehive, Barbie-pink lips, and a frilly polka dot dress that sells the "I've been sent back to the fifties" vibe. "Howdy, fellas! The usual?" Her voice takes me by surprise, raspy with age, but warm. "I see you brought a lady friend. How sweet! Welcome to Carrie's."

Parker nods. "Of course we want our usual spot, Darlene."

Following her lead to a far back corner, a worn booth sits tucked away, nearly out of sight. Parker scoots against the wall, and I sit on the outside next to him as Grady takes the spot across from us.

She clicks her pen against the spiral-bound paper pad. "Same old drinks?"

"That would be amazing, you're the best." Parker flashes her a vibrant smile.

She returns it, then shifts her attention to me, brow quirked. "And for the miss?"

"Oh, just a cherry Coke, please," I reply.

"Amazing, what are we eating?"

Skimming the menu, I chew my lip, considering my choices. That is, until Grady reaches across the table and takes it from my hand.

"Hey!" I snip.

"He knows you don't need it. If you order anything but their award-winning chicken and waffles, someone will question your sanity." Parker nudges me with his elbow. "That someone is Grady."

"Three orders of Carrie's famous chicken and waffles, comin' right up," Darlene says with a too-wide grin, sauntering away.

As I glare at the mountain of muscle across the table, I'm made aware of how *close* Parker and I are. As in, our legs are pressed together, shoulders brushing. There's definitely enough room in this booth for him to scoot away.

Fine. If he wants to get so comfortable, I'm about to get *nosy*.

"So, who is your other client, and why weren't they invited to lunch?" I rest my chin on my hand, eyes boring into his soul.

The way he tenses speaks louder than whatever excuse he's about to give. My focus drifts to Grady, who appears more pissed off than usual, as if that's possible.

Interesting.

"I'm going to meet them tomorrow, you know. Oh my god! Are you married to them or something? Par—"

"No! Okay? I'm single, *very* single," he grumbles, staring a hole into the tabletop.

"Okaaaay. So what's with the kicked dog looks?"

Grady doesn't think I notice his change in demeanor, and is even more caught off guard when I turn to him with my head tilted. His lips curl inward, shoulders rising and falling on a sigh. Dark waves of hair sway as he shakes his head.

Looks like tomorrow will have to tell me what they're not.

Two can play this game. Or, I guess three. Folding my arms, I scoot as far as possible to the edge of the booth.

"Hey, please don't be upset, I just don't want to talk about her," Parker begs as our food arrives.

Darlene, oblivious to our little back-and-forth, beams. "If you kids need anything at all, wave me down. I'll leave you to it."

Talk about quick service. They must keep this stuff on the ready. Or, they saw us enter and knew to make it. Grady has an exceptionally large portion in front of him, so my money's on the latter.

"Thanks," Parker mutters, pleading eyes locked on me.

"So it *is* a girl, then. You have history with her, huh?" I pop a bite of crispy chicken into my mouth, moaning at the savory breading paired with a special syrup—maple, but spiced with a hint of something smoky. "This is amazing."

Eyes glued to me, one of them audibly gulps, but I don't know who. In slow motion, Parker brings his hand up to my lip, spurring excited flutters to bloom in my stomach. I shouldn't let him. This is terrible. But if he kisses me right now, I won't stop it.

Tongue ghosting over his lower lip, he leans in… and wipes the corner of my mouth. "You had a little syrup there." Chuckling, he licks the sticky sauce off his thumb.

With a ragged swallow, I nod, returning my attention to my food.

Why was that such a turn-on?

Duh, of course it was. There's *no* way he doesn't know he's hot, right?

Keep it together.

"Anyway, consider this lunch a very lax business meeting. Of sorts…" He turns in the seat to face me directly. The places we had been touching grow colder without his contact. "Grady is my best friend. I know that probably sounds strange, but I've gotten to know him quite well over the past few months."

The man in question shrugs with one shoulder, nodding in silent agreement. I have no clue where this is going, but the hair on the back of my neck is standing on end. Parker's face doesn't look like he's about to crush me, but I can't deny the tension filling the booth.

"What does your friendship have to do with me?" I lick more maple-flavored goodness off my lip, enjoying how those crystal-blue eyes track the movement.

Oh yeah, the attraction is mutual, alright.

Bad. Very bad.

Clearing his throat, Parker speaks up, "Well, I'm not going to put Hulk's business out there, but just know that I want to get us both out from under the thumb of Henrietta Hart." Their faces pull into matching grimaces.

"And where do I come in?" My nose crinkles.

They must have a telepathic link or something. Parker gives Grady a nearly unreadable look. They exchange a series of nods, eyebrow movements, a subtle grunt from Grady—the first sound I've heard from him—and Parker turns back to me.

"We want to open our own training facility. I almost have the funds saved for something small... but—"

"You want my money?" I cut in with a rough tone, rolling my eyes.

Of course that's it. Greed ruins everything.

"No," he fires back, hands raising in defense. "I mean, money would be helpful, but what we really need is to prove that we can compete with Hartbrook. I'm not some old-money, pedigreed trainer, nor am I a titled rider who has proven that I know my stuff. If we all work together to make you and Tally Olympians, it would catapult our reputation and make people more inclined to take a chance on us." The tone of his voice is almost sorrowful.

Whatever their reasons, these two do *not* want to stay here. Meeting Henrietta one time was enough to imagine what it must be like to work for her. The publicity would be a great kickstart for them, especially training a nobody. We all have everything to gain from this. But there's always a catch.

"So, you want me to make it to the Olympics, that's it?" I ask, neck tingling from the heat rising.

"Yes, which means we need to talk... if you're interested in helping." Parker tentatively places his hand over mine, relaxing when I don't pull away.

Stupid body, I *want* to move, but it won't. His touch is like fresh-baked muffins—warm, fluffy, sweet. There are no edges to this man. Sure, he's a stranger, but there's a genuineness in him, almost delicate in a way I'm not accustomed to.

Still, I know better than to let a pretty face pull me into a mess I didn't sign up for. I have questions, and he'd better give me the answers I want. "Why can't your other trainee help? Why does it have to be me?" I catch the flash of emotion in his eyes, but I'm not entirely sure what to make of it. "Well?" I press further. "If I'm going to be on board with this, I need to know why it has to be me."

He chews over the thoughts racing in his mind, looking across the table to ask permission to say... whatever it is that's eating at him. When Grady nods, Parker inhales deeply through his nose.

Squeezing my hand, he lets out a heavy breath. "She's... Henrietta's daughter, which would not be conducive to our plan. She—"

"Her *daughter*?!" I straighten in my seat. "How am I supposed to compete with Bridget Hart?!"

His eyes bulge, painfully large. "You... know who she is?"

"Yes, Parker, of course I do. She's dressage royalty! I don't mean this to sound bad, but why are *you* training her and not one of the seasoned professionals?" I try to keep my tone soft, but I'm still met with a slight pinch in his face.

"Because, even though I'm not proven, Henrietta knows that I'm the best trainer she has. Bridget needs help, and my methods are her best bet. She can't be a proper heir to the empire without proving she deserves it. That's why she had Bridget assigned to me as my only trainee. Then you applied and... things didn't add up." His gaze darts away before reconnecting with mine. "But, undoubtedly, Henrietta wants your money. So she threw you on my roster and told me to give you the bare minimum. But, I promise you that's not going to happen." He rubs at the back of his neck with his free hand. "Bridget also wants to marry me. In her mind, we'll be this power couple and can rule the dressage world together."

"She's pretty." I shrug. "Could be worse."

"Yeah, pretty fucking awful. Sleeping my way to the top also isn't my style. Plus, me getting with Bridget wouldn't do Grady any good." Lips curled, he looks across the table.

Grady sits still, with the same empty look on his face, staring at the spot where our hands are locked together. I hadn't even noticed until just now. Parker's easy affection feels so natural.

"So, what happens when I make it to the Olympics? You also do realize how crazy it is to think I'll do it in less than a year, right?" Surely I sound a bit confused, because I am. But I'm also a realist and don't want them putting their futures on the line for something so reckless. I have nothing to lose here, but they have their livelihoods at stake.

"I don't know. You can do whatever you want. I just... I *know*..." Words laced with confidence in the unspoken truth, he pins me with a look that shoots ice straight into my soul. "I'll never tell your secrets, but *when* you make it to the Olympics... if you let some specific information come to light. It could be an amazing endorsement of my abilities and techniques."

"So, you're blackmailing me?" I lurch my head back, tearing my hand from his grasp.

Forget everything I thought I was feeling for him. Manipulation must be his middle name. I like to think I'm a good judge of character, but he's had me fooled until now.

Grady is already kneeling at my side, blocking my exit from the booth. My wild eyes scan his face, ready to try and wrestle a bear if I need to. Instead of malice in his expression, I find a hint of... apology? Maybe reassurance? I don't know, but whatever is there calms me enough to give Parker a chance to explain.

Straightening, I peel my glare from Grady's soft, golden eyes. Twisting to Parker, I bark, "Ten seconds. Make them count."

"I... I didn't mean for it to come out that way. Anything revealed would be at your discretion. Grady and I are the only two who know. I swear that we'll never tell a soul. I'm sorry for being selfish and asking this of you. I just..." His voice wavers as he looks over my shoulder at his friend, affection glimmering bright in his eyes. "I want to get us out of here, and I want to help you achieve your dreams, regardless of what Henrietta Hart has to say. Give me the chance, please?" A tear slips down his cheek, lips quivering.

He's not telling me everything. But, he's sharing what feels safe. Whatever the reason for his desperation, it's larger than me. Nobody deserves to feel so hopeless. Having the ability to help and not doing it is heartless. I'm a lot of things, but cold isn't on the list.

"Okay, I'm in... the 'reveal' is up in the air." I nod, and he returns it without any more mention of the plan.

Grady reclaims his seat, digging into his food. Parker eyes me, like he's afraid I'm going to get up and run. Maybe I should. But I've come this far.

"Once I'm invested, I don't back down, just be warned," I mumble around a bite of waffle.

Parker's hopeful smile sends tingles down to my toes. "That makes you perfect."

I sure hope I can trust them. My life goals are on the line.

Four

Parker

Dropping Leah off at her cabin was hard to do. An idiot could see that she doesn't trust me. Who could blame her? Twice now, I've let on that I know she's hiding something. Each time, she gets more panicked. At the end of the day, I can't let it get to me. I need to get us free from Henrietta's clutches. What Leah does after the fact is none of my concern.

Even if a small part of me secretly hopes she'll stick around.

Curled up in bed, I pull out my phone and open Grady's conversation thread.

Me:

Home now, how are you feeling?

Hulk:

Honestly? Not great. Do you think she'll stick around?

Me:

I sure hope so. She's got the attitude to make it. I just need to get her in the saddle and see how they move together. I can tell you from watching her dance that she has rhythm. With any luck, Tally does, too.

Hulk:

Yeah. We can only hope. Do you feel bad for using her?

Me:

Are we technically? I feel like I laid it out really well at lunch. It's a mutually beneficial situation, one I didn't even have to tell her about. If I never filled her in, she'd probably think I'm just REALLY dedicated to seeing her succeed. Instead, I chose honesty. There's no harm in that.

Hulk:

I still don't know how this is going to work, but I appreciate you for looking out for me. It really means a lot, given the circumstances.

Me:

You're not to blame for the situation you're in. I wish you'd open up to me some more. But I understand. Just know that I'll never look at you poorly for being "imperfect" as they've led you to believe.

Hulk:

I know, I'm 25 and need to grow up. Heard it plenty.

Me:

You know I didn't mean it like that. I'm sorry for prodding when I know it's a sensitive topic. You're also already stressed about everything. So, forgive me?

Hulk:

I'd never be upset with you for caring.

If only he knew how much I truly care. One day, when we're not shackled here, I hope he'll understand. Until then, I'll bide my time.

Me:

I know, I wish I had a solution now.

Hulk:

I'm not your problem to solve. But thank you for being here anyway. Leah and Tally are good, I can feel it.

Me:

I hope so. See you when you're done at the stables.

Curiosity prevails. The need to know what I'll have to work with itches at the back of my mind. I scroll through every video I can find of our new pink-haired partner and her raven-black steed. There aren't many, but the ones I manage to get my hands on show immense amounts of potential. They move well together. The bond between them is strong. Anyone with the slightest understanding of dressage could tell that they're spectacular. Her positioning is spot-on. They hit the beat with precision. Tally carries herself like a supermodel.

This might actually work.

I think I'm nervous, that's the only way I can describe the jitters, how rapidly my blood is rushing through my veins. Today is the day I start building the foundation for our future. Grady is tacking up the horses now as the girls change into their riding gear. It will be interesting to see their personalities clash.

Bridget sucks. Hard.

Leah is not the type who will put up with her shit. She's short and feisty, with curves as far as the eye can see. I'm going to be in trouble if I get too close. It's... actually problematic. So, I'll keep my distance as much as I can manage, but building a good friendship with her can't hurt. If she knocks Bridget down a peg or two along the way, I'm here for it.

Grady slides the stable doors open. Naturally, Bridget is the first to ride out, the smug expression on her face failing to conceal her uncertainty. She's already leaning too far forward. Sloppy, that's the best word to describe her form. Fortunately, her Dutch Warmblood is from championship lines, so he can compensate enough to keep her upright. Poor Champ—the most pretentious name she could have given him—looks miserable.

He's a beautiful horse, immaculately groomed—thanks to Grady—the fifty-fifty ratio of white to his dark bay base coat is breathtaking. He wants to move with a naturally fluid gait so badly. Too bad Bridget has apparently never ridden a horse before *right* now.

A whinny from behind them echoes through the otherwise empty stable. A strange sense of pride and hope washes over me as Leah and Tally ride out. Straight in the saddle, Leah's form is perfect, confidently guiding her partner around the paddock. Tally's movement is somehow even more majestic in person, which is nearly criminal.

Grady—standing in the shadows of the stable—has his eyes locked on them. His inability to contain the smile on his face is a great sign. If he's awestruck, we're in business.

"Good morning, ladies. Welcome to your first lesson. Today is only an introduction to see where you're both at in terms of skill level. This way, I can better cater your individual classes to your personal needs going forward." My voice booms through the paddock, demanding everyone's attention. "You've got a couple of magnificent horses under you. Let's do them justice and shape you into the riders they deserve."

"I cannot *believe* Mother has me training alongside some... nobody." Bridget wrinkles her nose, side-eying Leah, who couldn't be less affected.

"Leah is special." *Shit.* Shocked faces stare back at me. "W-what I mean is she's a special exception. All of the seasoned trainers refuse to work with her," I sputter, scrubbing my hand over my face.

Bridget fans herself dramatically, wobbling in her seat. "Wow. Tall, handsome, *and* charitable." Pushing her chest out, she doesn't even try to hide her flirting.

I school my features, hoping to keep the peace between them. As obnoxious as she is, I can't lose the paycheck. "I'm also almost ten years your senior," I deadpan. Leah rolls her lips between her teeth to hold in a laugh. "Now, we're going to start with walking. I want to see how you move." I regret the word choice as soon as they leave my mouth.

The prodigal Hart daughter shoots me another flirty look, and my mouth presses into a flat line as I stare at her.

"Your horse is beautiful," Leah speaks up, making an attempt at civility.

Bridget's only response is to turn up her nose.

Leah scowls, nostrils flaring. Her mouth begins to open, but I interject, "Okay, let's get a move on, steady circles around the paddock."

Little Miss Money Bags sways back and forth on Champ. He does his best to make up for her lack of coordination. Any horse with less natural inclination would likely be brought to a halt, or buck her off out of frustration. Her legs are too straight, arms far too high. Imagining how long it'll take to get her posture and positioning correct is giving me a migraine.

Leah, on the other hand, rides like a born natural—breathtaking in her gear like a ray of sunshine breaking up the dread of this place. Grady has braided Tally's mane beautifully. Her jet-black coat shines under the midday sun. Moving as if they should be at a Grand Prix event, they're the embodiment of hope. Mesmerizing, even at a walk.

My thoughts get a bit carried away imagining how Leah will move with a faster gait.

Biting my cheeks, I raise a hand, signaling for them to stop. "That's all for today. I'll see each of you for your scheduled classes tomorrow, starting with Bridget. Have a nice day, ladies." I tip my head and scurry away, putting much-needed distance between us.

Being alone in the same space as either of them is going to be an issue for *very* different reasons.

I return to my cabin to contemplate our situation, this plan, the year ahead, my life and how I got here. A bottle of whiskey paired with some classic rock will get my mind right. It always does. After a few fingers of amber-colored goodness, I decide to visit my new favorite videos... Watching Leah in action is borderline erotic. When I hatched this hair-brained idea, I never accounted for her being such a distraction.

No. Don't do it.

Sighing, I close the video and pull up my contacts. It's been plenty long enough. Grady should be done with his duties for the day. Time to see what he thinks.

Me:

So?

Hulk:

She's good.

Such a Grady response. My face hurts from how hard I grin.

Me:

She's far better than good, even you can see that.

Hulk:

Fine. She definitely has the potential to make it. This idea of yours, this agreement, it's going to work.

Me:

Well, hello, Captain Positivity. What have you done with my Hulk?

Hulk:

You know what I mean. As long as you can get her qualified, she'll make it, regardless of the timeline.

Me:

That's the idea, man. We're getting out of here when this is all said and done. Just hold out.

Hulk:

I've been here "holding out" for years. One more won't be the death of me.

Me:

It better not. Someone's gotta put up with me. :)

Hulk:

Lucky me. :)

My chest tightens. I don't know if he understands how our small interactions like this affect me. I will get us out of here if it's the last thing I do.

A knock at my door kills my slight buzz. My eyes widen when they land on Leah, standing on my front steps in another adorable little dress. She sucks in a breath at the sight of me.

Now abundantly aware that I'm shirtless, I clear my throat. "H-hi. What brings you here?"

"Oh, I just wanted to ask how you felt about me." Her gaze drifts down my bare abs and back up to meet mine.

Keep it cool, dick. Don't even think about it.

"How I... *feel* about you?" Tilting my head, I almost laugh as she gasps.

"N-no. No. Not like that! Oh gosh. I mean, how do you feel about my riding? Er—the way I ride." She clamps her mouth shut. "You know what? Just forget I even asked. I'll leave you alone." Nodding curtly, she attempts to leave.

When I grab her arm, she turns and stares at my hand.

I give her a soft smile. "You want to come in and have a drink? We can talk about it."

"Only if you put a shirt on. You know you're ridiculously hot, right? I don't *want* to sleep with you, but if you look like that—" She waves her hand around, gesturing vaguely at me. "—and give me alcohol, I can't promise anything. Drunk me is a hoe."

"You're an open book, aren't you?" A laugh rushes out of me. "Come on, I'll put a shirt on just for you."

She follows me inside, clicking the door closed, and I can't resist the urge to pick on her. Without a second thought, I gasp and say, "Did I just let a strange woman shut herself in this—suddenly very small feeling—cabin with me?"

Laughing, she playfully shoves my shoulder. "You know who I am now. I had *no* idea who you were at the time. I also didn't mean to *say* that, and you know it!"

"Oh, sorry. I said the inside parts out loud." I flash her an impish grin, strolling into my bedroom.

When I return—now wearing a plain black shirt—she's already settled on the couch, glass of whiskey in hand. Circling the sofa, I sit next to her, pouring myself another drink. As I kick my feet up on the coffee table, she sighs. We're silent for a moment, letting one another enjoy the pressure-free company. I normally only get this with Grady, having her here to share the peace with is... nicer than I expected.

"Hmm," I mutter under my breath.

She turns to face me. "What?"

I appreciate the fact that she's direct and assertive. I'm not used to people giving me their full attention. Yet another trait that makes her perfect... for this agreement, that is.

"Just thinking. You've probably still got some questions. I'm also very aware that our previous conversations were not exactly reassuring to you. But please believe that I do honestly want to see you succeed. You deserve it. Clearly, the work you've put in came from the heart. You and Tally looked phenomenal today."

Her eyes light up. A genuine tear streaks down her cheek. Instinctively, I lean in, wiping it away before I can tell myself it's a horrible idea.

Exhaling a shaky breath, she flashes a warm smile. "You're probably the first professional to tell me I'm not just *lucky*. Thank you. I hope I'm able to prove all the skeptics wrong, and help you with a shining endorsement for your training abilities."

"Well, Hulk—er Grady is convinced you're gonna make it."

"I should probably get his number from you. So I can keep in touch. About Tally, that is."

"Of course. Let me forward it to you." I fire off a quick heads-up message to Grady first so he's not too upset when she inevitably messages him.

We talk technique and structure for a while. The entire time, I'm entranced by her knowledge of the sport and the passion that coats every word. Nobody else has ever sat here and rambled with me about things like this. She's emanating warmth, cheeks rosy from the alcohol. I itch with the urge to pull her against me, feel how her body melds with mine.

But I can't.

Falling for her would complicate everything. So I guess being a friend isn't so bad...

Five

Leah

Waking up here feels wrong. The chaos of morning chores. Our old rooster screaming his heart out at the sun as it breaches the horizon. Goats bleating as they bounce around their pen. Vibrancy and life imbued in every moment, *that* is normal... Morning in this purgatory is lifeless.

Shuffling to the kitchen, I grab my cast-iron skillet and get to work. I'm no Martha Stewart, but I make a pretty mean breakfast. Complementary meals are part of our amenities here, but the food sucks, putting it as nicely as possible. The guys are bound to love this since I believe in *seasoning*. Does cooking for my trainer and stable hand make me a suck-up?

As if I care. Eating alone is boring.

How much does a behemoth eat? Grady definitely put away two servings of chicken and waffles at Carrie's with ease, so that's a decent enough gauge for now. I grew up with some corn-fed brothers, but he towers over them. Hell, NFL linebackers would probably be intimidated by his size. I bet he played in school.

90s country fills the air. Freshly chopped bell peppers sizzle in the pan alongside shredded potatoes. While they crisp, I whisk together about a dozen eggs. Dancing along to the music, I make the executive decision to add one more into my mixing bowl—just in case Grumpy is extra hungry. Into the skillet they go to get nice and scrambled.

A topping of shredded cheddar, a drizzle of my homemade salsa, and man, is she pretty. If these boys have never had a cowboy breakfast, they're in for a treat.

Transferring the meal into a large container, I place it in my picnic basket. Plates, forks, and napkins packed, I chew over the drink options in my fridge. I'm not sure if they're juice or sweet tea fans, but the cardboard carton is infinitely more convenient to transport. Tucking three cups into the basket, I clasp it shut.

My training session isn't until this afternoon, so instead of getting geared up, I slip on one of my absolute favorite dresses. Mint-green with little daisies all over it, the cinched waist hugs my curves. I also adore the short, fluttery sleeves. Hair tied in a side braid, spring in my step, I grab the food on my way out the door.

Sun rays peek through the trees, casting a golden glow over the immaculately mowed fields. As I stroll down the driveway, it dawns on me that I have no idea where to find Grady, but I'm willing to bet Parker does. It's a short walk to his cabin, and based on the stillness of the morning, he's definitely home.

Knuckles hovering a hair from the door, I falter. Patting my hair down to make sure I haven't somehow messed it up on the way over, I shake off the inexplicable nerves, opting to ring the doorbell instead.

Several minutes pass—silent, doubt-inducing. Maybe I'm out of line? Hand flexing at my side, I debate whether to press the little silver button again, but the lock clicks before I get the chance. Every greeting I had practiced vanishes when the door opens.

Shielding his eyes from the morning light, Parker stands in the doorway wearing nothing but a well-fitting pair of boxer-briefs.

"Oh, well, good morning." A crooked grin tugs at his lips—devilish, tempting, *problematic*.

This shouldn't feel so... illicit. But Parker, being almost nude and completely unbothered, is an unexpected development. He put a shirt on when I asked before, but the sex-starved part of me doesn't want him to cover up now. Defined abs, a sharp V line, chiseled thighs, the man is picture-perfect.

Breathe, Leah. You're stronger than this.

His dark hair is mussed from sleep, voice equally rough to match. I swallow hard and keep my eyes above his shoulders, forcing a smile in return while his gaze trails down my body. "I made breakfast." I wiggle my basket. "I didn't know where to find Grady, so I started here. Sorry if I woke you."

He blinks a few times before his face lights up. "You hear that, Hulk?" Twisting, he calls toward the sofa. "Pinkie brought us breakfast."

I follow him inside, ill-prepared for what awaits.

Rustling draws my attention to the couch. The sight almost makes me drop my basket. Grady is also shirtless, wearing low-hanging sweats that leave nothing to the imagination. Where Parker is all defined edges, Grady is bulky—broad shoulders, chest decorated with a scattering of hair. He doesn't have visible abs, but still showcases a V that disappears into his waistband. What's worse is that he's also completely nonchalant about walking around like an underwear model.

Inhaling, I collect myself and start laying out the spread I brought. When they join me at the table, still half asleep, I can't help but smile. This feels oddly *right*. Their eyes skate over the egg skillet, and Grady's stomach rumbles loudly.

Patting him on the shoulder, Parker chuckles. "Same, man. We're some lucky bastards."

Grady nods, lips twitching—the closest thing I'll ever get to genuine appreciation from him. I'll take it.

I pull out the plates and cups, along with my jug of orange juice. "Do y'all want some?" Shit, I sounded very *me* just now. This accent business is tricky.

"You don't have to serve us," Parker responds, rubbing the sleep from his eyes.

"But I want to. This is almost like home, except you're not my brothers."

"I'd sure hope not. If you undress your brothers with your eyes like you do to us, that'd be concerning." He smirks, sending a chill down my spine.

"You're practically naked already!" I squeak out in a poor effort to deflect.

"Hey, you showed up unannounced. What if we were fucking?" He tilts his head, face flat.

Nearly dropping the jug in my hand, I go still, brain misfiring. Have I misunderstood their "friendship"? If so, good for them. But Parker flirts to no end, there's no way I've misread him... Right? Blinking rapidly, words fail to form. That is, until Grady's shoulders shake from silent laughter.

"I got her good, huh?" Parker slaps him on the back, chortling. "He stays over a lot because it's boring here, we don't fuck. But still, you can't just come over and be upset that we're comfortable."

"I-I'm not upset. I just wasn't expecting all of this." I wave my hands around, gesturing to the excessive amounts of bare skin surrounding the table.

Parker leans back in his chair, stretching his arms out. "Well, if it makes you uncomfortable, we can cover up. You did bring us breakfast, after all."

"No, it's alright. I'm sorry if my slutty little eyeballs made you feel weird," I offer, hopeful that my tone is convincing.

"You're adorable." He beams. "Feel free to ogle me any time. Hulk probably isn't used to it, but if he cared, he would have already put a shirt on."

Grady shrugs, brows lifting. There's a sparkle in his eye, which is new and intriguing.

I pinch my brows together. "You're the exact type of guy that the girls back home would throw their panties at."

Head jerking back, he straightens.

Parker nudges him. "Sounds like he should have moved to Mississippi."

"Maybe so," I agree and return to dishing out food.

Instead of digging in the second they have their plates in front of them, they wait patiently for me to claim my seat. Groans of approval accompany their first tastes, even from Grady. My simple breakfast earned one of his rare sounds. My bones vibrate with giddiness in ways I'm not used to. I'm captivated, watching them devour each bite, barely touching my own food. Admiring their appreciation stirs warmth deep inside of me—kinship that has been greatly missed.

I've cooked for plenty of people. Most of the time, it's taken for granted or simply feels like an expectation. This is different. Rewarding.

Grady stops mid-bite, attention falling to my plate. He scowls at the barely-touched scramble, gaze gliding up to my face. He doesn't make a peep, but the question in his eyes is clear.

"I'm fine, just enjoying the show. Glad you like it." My cheeks are warm, definitely too red.

Nodding, he resumes shoveling bite after bite into his mouth.

Parker swallows a large gulp of juice, wiping his face with a napkin. "I was dreading having to deal with Bridget first thing this morning, but this has made my day. That salsa was divine, just enough kick to really get the blood pumping."

"It's homemade." I beam.

"Better be careful, I might try and keep you." He laughs.

Heat travels up my spine. I can't help but giggle in return.

Grady's eyes dart to Parker, then to my reddened cheeks, down to glare at his empty plate.

Interesting.

"Well, I'd better let you two get ready for the day, then. If you need me, I'll be giving Tally her morning snuggles." Gathering the dishes, I wipe them down and pack them up.

"We'll see you this afternoon, thanks for breakfast, Mom," Parker pokes, waving me off as I roll my eyes.

Quick as that, we're back to platonic jokes, which is for the best.

Tally is cranky today. She's snorting at Bridget, who is standing at the threshold of Champ's stall while Grady tacks him up. The prickles climbing my spine tell me she's gawking. I'm sure it's for a combination of reasons. Tally tosses her head up and down as I finish unbraiding her mane. Reaching into the pocket of my dress,

I unwrap a peppermint. She snags it in a heartbeat, immediately forgetting about Bridget.

That is, until she speaks up.

"What is taking so long? Can't you do anything right?" She huffs, pitch elevated, dripping with annoyance.

Surely she's not talking to Grady like that...

I shift in the stall, peeking out the corner of my eye. Too invested in things that don't concern me. Foolish.

She taps her foot, hands planted on her hips. "I've told Mother time and time again that you're useless. If only she would kick you to the curb already. I begged her to assign you to another stable, but for *some* reason, Parker fought to keep you here."

"You know it takes ten to fifteen minutes to properly tack up a horse, right? He's been at it for five. Cut him some slack," I spit.

Damn it, mouth.

This isn't my battle. He doesn't even like me.

Sneering my way, she snips, "Should have known a nobody hussy like you would have a soft spot for the disabled charity case."

Okay, fuck her.

Breathing deep through my nose, I respond, "He's not disabled."

Is he? The lack of conviction in my voice isn't very helpful.

"Oh, you don't know?" she asks with a sharp chuckle. "Who am I kidding. Of course you don't. Grady would rather hide and avoid his problems than face them like a man."

"I don't give a hoot. He does a great job. You're being a bitch for no reason. Maybe if you knew the first thing about horsemanship, you'd understand the importance of properly tacking up your horse," I seethe, face burning.

Bridget gasps with a scandalized expression on her face. "You... you heathen! How dare you speak to me in such a manner!"

"Yeah, yeah, I've heard it all before, you pretentious twat. Go cry to *Mother* about it." I wave her off and return my attention to Tally. Horses can't smirk, but the way she wiggles her upper lip and snorts is close enough. Bridget can eat dirt as far as I care. Nobody deserves to be spoken to like that.

I busy myself with menial tasks to calm my nerves. Grady finishes with Champ and helps Bridget fumble into her saddle, watching her teeter atop Champ as they ride out of the stable.

Maybe I didn't *have* to stick around, but my conscience demanded it—as if Grady needs me to stand up for him. Two hours of downtime await me. Painting will help shake off this tension. But, much to my confusion, Grady blocks my exit. Standing in the doorway to the stall, his expression is unreadable. His chest rises and falls rapidly, eyes darting around as he battles with his thoughts.

I'm burning alive under his intense inspection, unsure what to expect.

When he stalks my way, eyes holding mine prisoner, I stand my ground, ready for his retaliation. Mama didn't raise a wimp, and I don't *think* he'll hurt me... Please let me be right.

Stepping into my space, he dips his chin to look at me, a reminder of exactly how imposing—how impressive—he is. The weight of his presence steals my breath. His gaze dances across my face, filled with uncertain, frenzied emotions. Staring straight through me, he leans closer, bodies nearly pressed together.

Oh, have I misunderstood?

Catching the scent of his cologne, my senses come alive. Through my lashes, the glimmer in his eyes is evident. Nose nearly brushing mine, flaring with each exhale. The tip of his tongue peeks out, wetting his lips, breath fluttering against my skin. I'm almost certain what he's about to do. I won't—I can't—stop him. For a fleeting second, I tingle, imagining his lips on mine.

And then he turns and stomps off.

Six

Parker

Delicious food is the secret to true happiness, or at least tolerating the likes of Bridget Hart. This morning would have been impossible without a belly full of spicy, cheesy cowboy skillet. Now that Leah is in front of me, I can't shake the feeling that something is wrong. The vibrance of her smile is missing. Her groove is off. What could have possibly knocked her off kilter in the past few hours? Maybe I did too much at breakfast?

Should I ask? Will she give an honest answer if I do?

Why does this woman have me so twisted up inside?

Grady stands behind them, watching in the stable doorway. The scowl and tension on his face tell a troublesome story. Whatever has Leah upset is bothering him as well. For now, my curiosity will have to wait. Training is more important than playing therapist.

"Okay, let's work on halts today. I like the way you move, but I need to see you stop," I command.

She goes through the motions—straight in her saddle, arms at a beautiful height—but her heart isn't in it. Tally is a lot of horse and, if left unchecked, will run the show, much like she's doing at the moment. While she *is* halting, it's not fluid.

"Leah, I need your head in the game here. Our first event is in a little over a month. You're good, but I want you to be great."

"Sorry, just a bad day. I'll be better tomorrow," she mumbles, barely loud enough to hear.

Missing a class is a non-option. We have too much work to do. Sitting through this one while she's not mentally invested is also pointless. Something has to give, but I have them continue anyway.

Another half-hearted maneuver seals the deal. We're not going to make any progress like this. There's no point forcing her when she's not in the right place.

"Okay. Double lessons tomorrow, be ready. For now, go on," I concede.

She dismounts without a reply, leading Tally toward the stable.

There's *definitely* a problem. This woman loves riding her horse, there's no way she'd get off sooner than necessary.

She hands the reins to Grady with a blank expression—no acknowledgement of him at all.

Ah.

Whatever her problem is, he's at the heart of it.

Great.

My plan is slowly going up in smoke before my eyes. These two coexist like water and oil. Somehow, I need them to work together, find common ground, not kill our chances before they even begin. Leah may not open up to me, but Grady will. He'll be more relaxed and open to hashing out the details once his duties are done. So for now, I have the excruciating luxury of calling it an early night. Not fucking lame at all.

I make a point of walking through the stables on my way home, stopping at Tally's stall to catch a glimpse of Grady as he works. He's not wasting any time, clearly eager to get the hell out of here.

Good. The sooner he's done, the sooner I can get some damn answers.

The instant I enter my cabin, the cheap polo I'm forced to wear comes off. Kicking back on my couch, random nonsense plays on the TV. What it is doesn't matter, it's something to shatter the depressing silence.

Endless questions rampage through my mind despite my efforts to space out.

Wondering what happened is torture—cruel and endless. After thirty agonizing minutes, I pull my phone out and open Grady's texts. He should be done by now.

Me:

What the hell does that mean?

Hulk:

I don't know.

Jesus, he's hopeless. This is getting me nowhere. Groaning, I pinch the bridge of my nose.

Me:

Explain it to me like I'm two years old.

Hulk:

She… I think she wanted me to kiss her.

What the fuck?

I read his message over and over again. Seven times and it's still the same. Of all the things he could have said…

Me:

DO NOT KISS HER.

Hulk:

I didn't.

That's not the same as saying he doesn't want to. I'll pocket that for now. If he didn't do it then, I have to trust that he won't in the future.

Hulk:

I'll avoid her if I have to. Whatever is going to be best.

Me:

No, you quite literally can't avoid her. Just try to give her some space and don't do whatever it was that made her want to kiss you.

Hulk:

I didn't do anything.

Me:

Well, just distance yourself a little, but stay civil.

Hulk:

Okay. Sorry.

Me:

No. You didn't do anything wrong, okay? I just want to get us out of here.

Hulk:

I know. It'll all be alright.

God, he's so pure. If the only thing I ever accomplish in life is getting him away from this place, I'll die a happy man.

Me:

Wait. Why do you think she was uncomfortable with you kissing her?

What a flurry of words. Hopefully he doesn't pick up on my spiral.

Hulk:

When I almost did it, her body language changed. She got all tense and held her breath. I think she was afraid of me.

Fuck. He was *actually* going to kiss her. What the hell is the right response? Yelling will do more harm than good, so I'm going with educational. Life hasn't given him any experience with this. It's not his fault that he doesn't understand.

Me:

She wasn't afraid, she was probably a little anxious, and I'm sure she was confused. I don't know all of the context, but I do know that you two don't understand each other well enough to be kissing.

Hulk:

I know. It was just a moment of heightened emotions. I almost messed everything up. I'll be more careful.

Me:

You're fine, I promise. Don't stress, okay? She's a gorgeous woman. I don't blame you for wanting to kiss her.

Shit. What the hell am I doing? This is *not* how you talk someone out of falling for someone.

Hulk:

She's beautiful on the inside, too.

His message makes my heart pound, booming in my ears like a bass drum. This conversation is derailed beyond salvation at this point. Instead of peace of mind, his answers have raised more concerns.

Leah is about to be the one with a surprise visitor.

The faint sound of music echoes from inside as I approach her cabin. When I knock rapidly, it stops. She's covered in—what I can only assume to be—flour as she opens the door. Her apron and messy bun do inexplicable things to me.

Grady's right, she's beautiful, and this version of her is my favorite by far—casual, relaxed, domestic.

"What's that look for?" she asks, brows scrunched.

Okay, still grouchy, got it.

"You seemed like you could use a friend," I reply as gently as possible.

"I don't." She moves to close the door, but I notch my foot in the opening.

"Wait. I-I talked to Grady..." Wincing, I prepare for her to freak out.

Instead, her shoulders slump. With a heavy sigh, she ushers me inside. Heading straight to the living room, I sit on the couch and she plops down beside me. For a moment, I think she's going to spill her guts, but I'm met with silence. As if I don't get enough of that with Grady.

Pressing for information she's not ready to give will upset her. Judging by her flat expression, her mind is racing, deciding what information is safe to share with me. With a deep inhale, she lets out an exasperated breath, rubbing her eyes. As she leans back, our gazes connect.

That's it, let me be here for you, too.

She tucks a foot under her knee. "There was... an incident at the stables this morning." Chewing her lip, she exhales a heavy breath through her nose. "Bridget, she... she was saying things to Grady. Terrible things."

My blood boils. Everything starts to make sense. "Like what?" I ask, even though I don't need to. I've heard it all. He has, too, repeatedly.

"She called him disabled and useless. Really nasty stuff. I told her off, but I think it upset him." Her face pulls into a sorrowful scowl, emerald eyes glistening.

"She does that pretty much every day," I confess.

"What?!" Her breath falters.

All of these secrets suck. I'm not a fan at all. Walking on eggshells is not fun. Soon, we need to get everything out in the open before I combust.

"There are things you don't know. Things I won't tell you without Grady's permission. I don't think you upset him. Just know that what you saw today isn't even the half of it. The plan I have—the one that depends on you—is ninety percent for him. He doesn't want your pity, so don't go trying to offer it. But, keep Bridget's deplorable behavior in mind on the days you feel like quitting."

By the way she's sitting—straighter, dialed in—my serious tone has taken her by surprise.

Mouth open slightly, she stares through me so hard her eyes must hurt. "No pressure or anything. I thought I was just here to chase my silly dreams... didn't account for being a half-assed heroine."

"You're not half-assed... in any sense of the word." I waggle my brows, giving her a playful nudge.

Fortunately, it seems to do the trick. She giggles in return, body relaxing. I don't want her to dread training or get in her head because of the stakes. Some day I'll tell her more, but that can't happen until I know we can trust her.

The problem is, she's still keeping secrets of her own. How can we make her trust us, too?

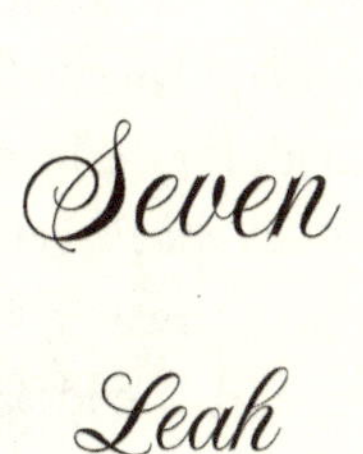

Seven

Leah

So far, this has not gone according to plan. I had thought a friendship with Parker and Grady would work out. Apparently, that's the dumbest idea ever. Aside from our brief interactions before and after training, Grady completely ignores me. The part of my mind that believed he was warming up has finally accepted the fact that it's never going to happen. No matter how sweet I try to be, he stays straight-faced, stoic, bordering on cold.

Parker is indifferent to the whole ordeal, carrying on with training like he's oblivious, but he's clearly not. Maddening, that's what it is. Every part of me is irked by the situation. No more breakfasts, no more lunch dates disguised as "business" meetings. It's like the first couple of days before the altercation never happened. Except we all know they did.

Despite the tension I've been carrying, Parker is satisfied with my progress. I thought I had learned quite a lot before coming here, but he truly is a visionary. I don't know his whole story, but whatever Henrietta saw in him, I see it too. While she may be a frigid old hag, she's smart and business-savvy.

New bonding techniques have Tally molding like putty beneath the saddle. We were best friends before coming here, but she's undoubtedly more attached to me now. I love it. She's much more responsive. I almost miss her attitude and the way she would push back just enough to remind me she's a badass. We've got a lot of work to do, though, so it's for the best.

Today is our rest day. Except Parker gave us homework. No time in the training arena, but we're going for a nice ride on the back trails of the property. I had no idea they existed, but he gave me directions.

When I enter the stables, much to my annoyance, Grady's just... around, coming out of the supply closet. Startled, his face goes tight when he sees me. I offer a soft smile, which he ignores, re-entering the room he *just* left, closing the door behind him.

What is his problem?

Shaking off the frustration, I return my attention to Tally. She nuzzles into me as I scratch behind her ear. As we ride out of the stables, she whinnies, excited for the fresh air. She's spent a lot of time in the stall recently, I'll turn her out in the pastures later tonight so she can graze. If only there were other horses around for her to socialize with. Bridget has deemed her unworthy of mingling with Champ.

Trotting along, we pass by the cabin neighboring mine. The Jeep parked outside sends zips of interest coursing through my body. Some new faces would definitely break up the overbearing sameness. But there's no time to introduce myself. Training comes first. Friends aren't going to win the Olympics for me.

We continue toward the tree-covered path. My eyes widen when we breach the threshold. What lies beyond the perimeter is an entirely different world, fantastical even. The tropical paradise is mesmerizing. Thick foliage lines the gravel trail. Signs mark the path, but don't give any details of where it leads. Lizards and birds skitter about while we disturb their morning. Tally jolts slightly at first, but quickly calms under my soothing pats.

"I know, T, we didn't have all this back home," I murmur, admiring the endless beauty around us. It's inspiring, bringing a sliver of renewed hope.

Growing up, my parents always called me a dreamer. Now they say I'm a foolish girl chasing unrealistic fantasies. Funny how the tone shifts when you can make them a reality. I haven't taken any time in the last couple of years to chew over their judgment.

I know this plan, these aspirations, are harebrained and likely unattainable, but I have the means now to actually *try*. I'm going to give it my all, damn it. If I fail, so be it. I'm no quitter, and don't plan on coming this far to let the likes of Bridget Hart or Grumpy Grady bring me down.

Does it normally take a few years to qualify for the Olympics? Yes. But I believe in our ability to do it in one year. We're going to need every waking moment of training to get there. Taking all of Parker's advice is the first step.

Lost in my musings, I nearly miss the small spring to our left. Halting Tally, I dismount and hitch her to a post. Aside from the gravel and markers, it's almost easy to forget this is a man-made trail. Thankfully, whoever made it thought of the horses that would be traveling through.

I settle onto a large rock sitting on the edge of the spring and kick off my riding boots. Serenity embraces me when I dip my toes into the cool water. Tally, basking in her own bliss, lies down and nickers. She's so lazy when she wants to be, and I'm glad I tacked her up with my everyday saddle. The nice one we use for competitions would need a hefty cleaning, thanks to the dirt and debris under her. Instead, I giggle as she rolls, disregarding the gear on her back.

"I have to sit there!"

Head bobbing, she lets out a lighthearted whinny.

I swear she understands me more than any "friend" I could ask for. People don't *get* me the way she does. While she's a total butt-head to those who don't respect her space, I like to think we're kindred spirits. Her breeder gave me a discount because of her "undesirable temperament" but I saw right through the nips and snorts. When she loves you, she's the most loyal and fun-loving horse there is. She's just picky. A girl's gotta have standards, after all.

Lord knows I've given my time and energy to the wrong people more often than not.

Parker and Grady pop back into my mind. "What do you think about the guys?" I ask Tally.

She bobs her head and blows out a low, easy snort.

"Yeah, they're decent enough," I agree, "I just wish I knew what I did wrong to make Grady hate me."

She grunts, tail flapping.

"He... I thought he was going to kiss me. Can you believe that?" I lie back on the rock, enjoying the coolness through my shirt. "He won't even look at me now. Parker doesn't seem to give a hoot. How am I supposed to help them if he won't give me any reason to care?" Exasperated, I groan and roll to my side, letting my feet dry off.

Tally flops her lip and nods.

"I'm glad you agree." I chuckle, slipping my boots on. "Thanks for the chat, Bestie. We should probably head back. We rode for a good bit. Gotta be close to dinner time."

Once she's on her feet, I do my best to dust off her saddle. I guide her toward the rock I was resting on and use it as a makeshift mounting block. She's *tall.* I'm not about to mount her from the ground if I don't need to. My hip flexors are grateful for the break.

I'm not entirely sure why Parker wanted us to ride this trail, but it served as some much-needed self-reflection time. For that, I'm thankful. Being in nature always brings me comfort. This may be a new environment, but the effects are the same.

When we near our stable, I'm surprised to see Parker in the training corral with Bridget and Champ.

Did he tell me to take the trail ride so I wouldn't know he's giving her extra lessons? Is he backing out on our deal and deciding to work with her after all?

No, he said that wouldn't work.

Trotting through the doorway, I attempt to shake off the simmering betrayal and focus on Tally. Once I have her saddle off, I grab my dandy brush and get to work cleaning her up. A full bath will be necessary, but the bathing station is out back near the corral. I have no interest in being within earshot of the training session.

Traitor. Stupid man thinking with his dick, surely.

I huff to myself as the agitating sound of Bridget's overly forced laughter echoes through the stable.

Great.

The storage room door creaks open. Grady is there, a clearly despondent expression on his face. My eyes meet his for a heartbeat before he stares at the ground.

Awesome.

Maybe I should just re-tack Tally and ride back to the trails. This day sucks otherwise.

"Here," Bridget barks, thrusting Champ's reins toward Grady. He takes them, avoiding eye contact. His timidness is confusing, being a walking brick house and all. "Take care of him, I'm going to lunch with Parkie." She links her arm through Parker's, and I twist my face and scoff. "Oh, I'm sorry, does the nobody have something to say?" she quips, chin raised.

Parker offers a tight-lipped smile to Grady and me, dipping his chin in a way that begs me not to make a scene.

Too bad, I live for humbling pompous bitches. "Oh, no, I have better things to do than give a shit about you." I smile widely, still brushing Tally.

Parker closes his eyes, rolling his lips between his teeth as Bridget gasps.

"You, you'd better care about me! My mother—"

"May own this place, but *you* are nothing more than an entitled brat. Go on, enjoy your lunch with *Parkie,* hope the bonus training sessions will be enough for you to stay in your saddle at our first competition."

Grady doesn't quite stop the snort before it leaves him.

Bridget, slack-jawed, directs a sharp glare his way. Before she even opens her mouth, my hair stands on end. "How dare you! Once Mother hears about this, it's over for both of you. I don't know who you think you are, acting like you're better than me." She pokes him in the chest, and I see red.

Dropping my brush, I'm outside of Tally's stall and between them before I can think—chest puffed, staring into her beady eyes with laser focus. She might be five or six inches taller than me, but I'm no yellow-belly, and I'm not one to turn a blind eye to bullying.

"You'd better keep that bony finger to yourself," I snarl, "let me see you get cross with him *one* more time. I dare you."

"What *is* it with you? Why do you care about him? Oh, oh my, are you two an item?" Her eyes widen to the size of dinner plates.

"No, I just give a shit about people other than myself. Parker—" I shoot my gaze up to him. His silence through all of this is damning, and I am not impressed in the slightest. "—kindly put your bitch on a shorter leash... and get her a muzzle. If she starts a fight, I can't promise it will end well for her."

"Easy, ladies, let's all just take a step back," he speaks up, finally.

"She's the one getting belligerent!" Bridget wails.

"You're the one laying hands on people," I spit. "Grady might be too nice to put you on your ass, but I'm damn sure not."

She gasps, clenching her hand to her chest. Looking over me to Grady, her expression shifts into one of malice. "How cute you've got your little girlfriend to fight your battles for you. Pathetic as ever."

I lunge, but a set of strong arms wrap around me. Kicking, flailing my arms, I try to free myself from Grady's grasp, but it's no use. My blinding rage dampens as I inhale his crisp, clean scent—lemon or grapefruit laced with a woodsy undertone. With my back securely against his firm chest, I relax, still scowling.

"Good gracious, you're a mess." Bridget sneers, latching onto Parker. He doesn't say anything, but the sorrow and apology in his eyes confuse me.

Why is he entertaining her?

Champ, completely unbothered by the near fist fight, has wandered into his stall and is munching away on his hay as if nothing happened.

I huff, realizing that Grady is still holding me, chin resting against the top of my head. His arms have loosened, but his hands have found the curves of my hips. The rightness of being pressed against him makes my heart stutter. Leaning into him, I sigh, letting myself enjoy the moment for as long as I can.

His silence and strength are calming. The rise and fall of his broad chest is almost hypnotic.

"I'm sorry, I know you don't particularly like me, and I'm sure you don't appreciate me always butting in... I just—" I bring my hands to his, lacing our fingers together. Callouses beg for me to drag my thumbs over them. "—I don't care if you hate me, I hate seeing you upset by her unwarranted hostility. You're gentle and kind. You deserve better."

I squeak as he spins me and stares into my eyes. When I move to step back, he pulls me into a hug, lifting me off the ground. His hold is nearly crushing, but I love the pressure, how secure I feel. More of his scent tingles my nose. For a second, I almost wrap my legs around him.

Almost.

Until Tally neighs from her stall

I laugh as he puts me down, giving her an apologetic look. Apparently, that's all it takes for him to remember that he hates me. His features harden. Giving a tense nod, he excuses himself to tend to Champ.

The hug is enough of a victory. I'd better not press my luck. One day at a time.

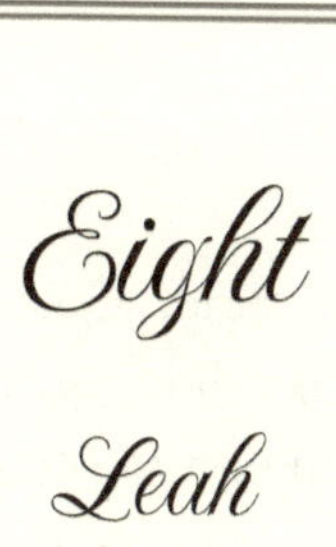

Eight

Leah

Apron tied securely around my waist, I stare into my mixer as the butter and sugar cream together. Everyone loves cookies, so I'm making Granny's chocolate chunk delights as an apology for my outburst earlier. If Parker and Grady don't appreciate them, I have exhausted my best option.

Eggs and dry ingredients join the party in my mixing bowl, just as a knock sounds at my door.

Seriously?

Marching over, unbothered with the mess I'm wearing, I tear it open. "Won't you give me the chance to grovel?" I ask, nearly falling over.

Who the hell are *they*?

"Pardon?" the tall blond asks. His deep blue gaze glimmers as he takes in my cow print ensemble.

"Who would ever make you grovel?" the slightly shorter man to his left asks, red locks poking out from under his black ball cap. Their eyes are almost identical—expressive, full lashes. Gorgeous.

Blondie has his pink shirt tucked into light-wash jeans. The ginger with a dangerous smirk next to him has his gray tee loose, but intentionally so. Black tattered jeans hug his thighs. Men should not look this good.

Words? I have none.

"I'm Warren," the blond says, full lips pulling into an easy smile.

The other man tips his head. "Quincy."

"Uh. Sorry, you're not who I was expecting. I don't make a habit of groveling, so don't get too excited." I place my hand on my hip and lean against the doorframe, grateful that my brain has snapped back to reality. "To what do I owe the pleasure?"

Please be strippers. It's not even my birthday, but golly, I could use some visual stimulation, and they're both *very* adequate.

"We're your new neighbors," Warren answers, expression still casual.

"If we're imposing, we can come back later," Quincy offers, face pulled taut.

Neighbors? New faces, in general, are exciting. They must own the Jeep I saw earlier.

"I love inviting strange men into my home. Get comfy, I'm making cookies." I beam and motion for them to follow me inside.

They don't budge. Surely they think I'm insane. They'd be correct, but at least I'm not boring. Boring people suck.

Okay, this is awkward. Best try and smooth it over. They're the first new people I've seen here, except Grady and Parker... and, unfortunately, Bridget.

"Sorry, bad joke. But I *am* making cookies, and you're more than welcome to come in." I flutter my lashes.

Flirting always works... usually.

Quincy blinks while Warren chuckles, shaking his head as they step inside.

Yup, still got it.

"Wow, this place is lively." Quincy admires the living room, face filled with wonder.

My lips pull into a wide grin, eager to brag a little. "Thanks, I painted them all myself."

"I feel like I know everything I need to about you now." Warren laughs, stopping at my bookshelf to admire Tally's picture. "You own the Friesian?"

"Yup, that's my T. Don't try to pet her. She bites and I will not accept the blame."

"Uh." Quincy, standing next to Warren, scrunches his brows. "We've already introduced ourselves. She poked her head out of her stall and nickered at us to come over."

"She what?!"

"Yeah, the stable hand gave us some peppermints and she just about melted. Then he turned her out." Warren smiles, completely unaware that he could have lost a hand earlier.

"His name is Grady," I grumble, pouring chocolate chunks into the mixer, setting the speed to low.

"Is there a problem?" Quincy asks, leaning on the counter. The veins in his biceps bulge, begging for me to lick them. Why does he have to be a redhead? My kryptonite.

No, Leah, get it together.

"Nope, no problem... So, are you two trying to qualify for the Olympics, too?" I deflect to the best of my ability.

"Ah, no. We just enjoy the sport and want to better ourselves," Warren replies, coming to the kitchen as well. "You want to make the Olympics?" He hoists himself up, plopping on my counter.

What is it with men making themselves at home here? Weirdly enough, I don't really mind. They're close, but it's not intimidating. Loneliness is making me too accommodating. That's got to be it.

"I do, that's my main goal in life. Even if I flop and don't do well, I just want to make it."

"That's inspiring." Quincy leans a little closer.

My skin pebbles, breaths becoming shallow. It's been a while since I've had a man this close to me, aside from Parker and Grady anyway—but that'll never work, we have to maintain healthy work relationships. These two absolutely perfect men, on the other hand? They're creeping into hookup territory.

I can't do that.

But I *want* to.

I wonder if they would be into a threesome?

Oh, right, he complimented me.

"I have dreams, that's all. Everyone does, mine are just a bit wild."

Warren chuckles. "You seem more than a bit wild."

Looking him in the eye is a horrible idea, but I do it anyway. "Wouldn't you like to find out?" I spin away from him to put the dough in the fridge. "So, do you two know each other?"

"We're brothers. Trained together at our last facility. When the opportunity to come here arose, we took it. They were kind enough to offer a discount if we shared a cabin." Warren answers, voice light.

Brothers make sense. Matching eyes, eerily similar sharp jawlines, muscular but with slim waists. The resemblance is strong.

Damn it. Why does this place have to be crawling with men who could double as models?

I untie my apron, hanging it on the magnetic hook on the fridge. "It's almost dinner time, my cookie dough has to chill. Wanna go to the diner in town?"

"Wow, already asking us on a date, huh?" Warren jokes, dropping off the counter.

"Well, I was thinking I could invite Parker and Grady, too, since you're going to be working closely with them." I place my hands on my hips, raising my chin in challenge.

"The more the merrier," Quincy answers with an impish smirk. "Grady was nice enough earlier, but he seems sad."

"You have no idea." I groan. "Bridget treats him like shit. I almost kicked her ass for it earlier. Hence the reason I'm making apology cookies."

"Ah, that explains the groveling." Quincy snickers.

"He hates me. I don't know why, but he does."

"Want to make him jealous? We can pretend to be your boyfriends." Warren raises a brow, glancing at Quincy.

"What? He'd have to *like* me to be jealous. Your plan is flawed."

"He'd have to be blind not to like you," Quincy speaks up, cheeks slightly flushed as he dodges my gaze.

"He's not wrong," Warren agrees. "Maybe he's just awkward and doesn't know how to act around you."

"What is this, high school? I'm *not* going to try and make him jealous." Straight-faced, I shut them down.

Warren pouts, fluttering those damn lashes. "So, no flirting?"

"I don't mind flirting. Hell, you could hit me up for some casual fun. I don't care, sex is great. Where I draw the line is manipulation."

He groans. "Fuck, you're hot."

Quincy lets out a hearty laugh, leaning in for dramatic effect. "He's definitely going to take you up on the sex."

"Don't act like you won't, too," Warren quips. His face softens, gaze drifting over me from head to toe. "In all seriousness, you'd look great between us. Something tells me you'd make us earn it. *That* is fucking irresistible."

"He's not bullshitting," Quincy says, face flushed, posture relaxed, but carrying himself with confidence. The duality is delicious.

I clear my throat, getting my thoughts back on track. Their words have jolted my body awake, exhilarated by their heated promises. I could see myself with them—both of them. My cheeks heat against my will. So much for containing my enthusiasm. "I'm just going to send a quick text to Parker and Grady, and they can meet us at Carrie's. Let me clean up real quick." I excuse myself to the bathroom, letting out a held breath.

Somehow, some way, I'll survive these men.

Warren and Quincy are sitting on either side of me. My stomach aches from the slight pang of guilt, as if I'm cheating on Parker and Grady. There's no reason for it, but rationality has never been my strong suit.

Why can't I accept the fact that nothing will happen between us?

As Warren throws his arm around me, the door opens, and in they walk. When Parker spots us across the room, he does a double-take, eyes flashing wide for a split second. They take seats across from us, faces pulled tight.

Parker squints at the men at my sides. "I thought you invited us to dinner as an apology."

"I... well, I sort of did, but it's more to introduce everyone. This is Warren and Quincy. They're your new trainees." I force a smile, trying to shrug Warren's arm off my shoulder.

"Looks like you're well acquainted already," Parker deadpans.

I've never seen him like this. The shortness of his answers, how tense his shoulders are, icy-blue gaze unnaturally sharp.

"What's good to eat?" Quincy looks at Grady, knowing damn well he can't answer. They met him earlier, he *has* to know.

To his credit, Grady doesn't flinch as he flips a menu open, slides it across the table, and points to the chicken and waffles. Never once breaking eye contact.

Great, this is going fantastic, love it.

"It's funny." Parker flips through his menu with nonchalance. "I was not informed of any new trainees."

Weird...

"Yeah, we don't officially start until next week. Something about Mrs. Hart not wanting to take up your time with the upcoming competition. We're totally tagging along for that, though, gotta cheer on hot stuff here." Warren squeezes me.

My eyes roll painfully fast. I've been called a variety of nicknames, "hot stuff" sure as hell isn't original or appealing. It's becoming abundantly clear to me that these two are nothing more than pretty faces. Your typical douche bags who know they're hot. Undoubtedly used to women falling at their feet. Weeks ago, I'd have gladly joined the ranks, but now the thought is oddly repulsive.

As if he can sense my awkwardness, Grady shifts his attention from Quincy to Warren, gliding to the spot where his hand rests just above my breast, finally landing on my crinkled brow. Tilting his head, a scowl pulls at his lips. I offer a faint smile, hoping to de-escalate his... worry? Anger? Whatever it is, silence has never been so intimidating.

Darlene, as always, steps up to our table with a vibrant grin, bursting the testosterone bubble I've been trapped in. As we place our orders, Quincy and Warren break the unwritten rule and order burgers.

Grady's face shifts to one of disgust. Silly me for thinking he hated my guts. Right now, I'm certain he wants the men at my sides dead—for various reasons. The way he's staring holes through them is terrifying. I don't quite understand his obsession with the chicken and waffles, but they are delicious.

Warren tilts his head and leans forward, finally giving me a chance to relax now that he's not draped over me. "You got a problem with the burgers?"

Parker mirrors Warren's pose, resting his elbows on the table. "He told you guys to get the chicken and waffles."

Grady chews his lips, jaw working as he stares at me.

"Oh shit, I see it now." Quincy titters. "He has it *baaaad* for her, War."

I whip my head toward him so fast I sway in my seat. "You don't know what you're talking about!" I protest too loudly, drawing the attention of people seated around us. Several regulars catch my eye, expressions full of questions. Great, they think I'm crazy. We can never come here again.

"Go on and lie to yourself, but I know the eyes of a man who wants what he can't have," Quincy continues. "Tell me I'm wrong, Grady." He raises his chin, face pulled into a taunting simper.

"That's quite enough from both of you," Parker seethes. "This dinner is over. Grady and I will get our food to go. Good night, Leah."

Parker's face is rigid; meanwhile, there's nothing but pain in Grady's eyes.

Disgust sours my stomach, appetite thoroughly ruined. When Darlene delivers our food, I barely register the conversations filling the diner. Quincy and Warren eat their burgers, chattering on about things I don't care to hear.

Mentally, I'm in a different place, one from long ago.

Small and helpless, curled up on the locker room floor while other girls kicked and spat on me, for no reason other than envy. As one of the first in my grade to hit puberty, I looked like a grown woman at fifteen. Boys spread filthy rumors around our small town, claiming I did things with them that I'd never heard of. Eventually, I embraced it, convinced myself that sex is all I'm good for. Before long, I was labeled the town slut.

I knew nothing of love or loyalty.

And still don't.

Life with no female friends, raised in a house full of boys, and a mother I wasn't close with. Nothing could prepare me for the cruelty of teenage girls. Sure, as a grown woman, I own my sexuality now. But tonight, the way these guys came out and peacocked... I loathe it. Any attraction I felt for them is dead.

Ears hot, shoulders tight, I interrupt whatever conversation they are having, "I told you I don't do manipulation."

"Calm down, Baby," Quincy jokes. "We'll show you a great time, don't worry."

"You've shown me the exact opposite of a great time. Parker and Grady are—"

"Too scared to act on their impulses," Warren interrupts, rolling his eyes.

"You're insane," I fire back. "They're friends, and I'm literally paying their salaries."

"Wow, you're actually stuck in denial. Whatever, go on and keep telling yourself it won't end badly." He stands to let me out of the booth, face blank.

"I hope you choke on your burgers!" Stomping off, I pay my bill at the counter and beeline for my truck, thankful that I drove myself.

So much for my apology. Why is everyone around here so shitty to my guys?

No, they're not mine. I need to stop that.

Nine

Leah

Screw those two. My cabin smells like toasty brown butter and gooey chocolate. Rage baking always soothes the soul. I'm better than the drama they were trying to cause, and I know it. Gone are the days when I seek out male validation. There's nothing a man can do for me that a toy can't, and silicone doesn't come with an ego.

Wiping down the counter, I package up my peace offering and begin the longest, strangest walk of shame ever. What can I say? I'm a glutton for punishment and refuse to let Parker go to sleep angry with me. With any luck, Grady will be there, too. If not, I'll text him and call that good enough.

Hand hovering over the door, counting down from ten, my knees wobble. The doorbell will be better, less harsh. Pressing the button, I shift back and forth on my feet. As the door swings open, Parker's face tightens in a troubling way. His normally cheerful, relaxed expression morphs into something darker.

My mouth moves like lightning. "Before you turn me away, which would be completely valid, please let me explain, and apologize." Lifting the container, I bat my lashes, giving him my best puppy dog eyes.

Sighing, he turns toward the living room. Grady is sitting on the couch, arms crossed over his chest.

"You feeling up to an apology, Hulk?" Parker asks, voice careful, measured.

Grady stands, approaches the doorway, and inspects my surroundings.

"It's just me, I left the douche bags to their burgers and stormed out of the diner. After the scene I made, we may never be allowed back." Chewing my lip, I fight a grimace.

Grady puffs out a laugh, eyes landing on the package in my hand, flitting to my face.

"I made Granny's famous cookies. Supposedly, this recipe is what made Gramps marry her." I beam.

Brows shooting to his hairline, he snatches it with superhuman speed, jerking his head toward the living room.

Parker chuckles. "Well, apologies accepted, I guess."

"No, it can't be that easy, make me earn it." I take a seat on the middle cushion, and they sit on either side of me.

Grady usually keeps a safe distance, opting for the other sofa. Their combined closeness electrifies the blood in my veins, forcing heat up my neck. He opens the container, inhaling the aroma with a sigh. The smallest smile plays at his lips. A deep, gravelly hum rumbles through him with the first taste.

Holy horniness, do not *moan, Leah.*

Parker kicks his feet up on the coffee table, long legs stretched out casually, ankles crossed. He drapes his arm over the back of the couch, fingers brushing against my shoulder absentmindedly. "How exactly would you earn our forgiveness?" His words stop Grady mid-bite, and he gives him a curious look.

Filthy images fill my mind.

"Oh, I was just... I don't know." I shake my head, gathering myself. "I was going to tell you that I told them to get lost because you're my friends and I can't stand the drama. The cookies were honestly my secret weapon." I pass Grady a pitiful pout, chuckling as he shoves another cookie into his mouth, groaning louder.

The sound sparks more explicit thoughts. His enjoyment of something so simple, his blissful expression while savoring it, makes me curious if he sounds like that in the bedroom.

Husky, unfiltered, *raw*.

Squeezing my thighs together, I remind myself that we're nothing more than allies working toward a common goal. Even that is questionable at times. If anything, his tolerance is solely thanks to my cooking.

"Do you enjoy having men act like jackasses for you?" Parker asks with an edge I'm not used to.

"No, they were acting stupid for *them*. Some ego trip, thinking it would work. I'm not that girl anymore. Men showboating for my attention isn't what does it for me."

He twirls my hair around his finger, humming once. "Good answer."

Grady, in a rare display, scoots closer, arms open, eyes much softer than usual.

With a shaky exhale, I lean into him. "I'm sorry for letting them treat you like that. I'll be a better friend. I promise." Tipping my head back, the sight before me is beautiful. Warm and shining, his eyes don't leave mine. I go still in his arms, breath held for fear of ruining this. His jaw ticks, throat bobbing on a swallow. Then, in an instant, he replaces the mask of indifference and slides away from me.

Oh well, I got a second hug, I'm going to cherish it as much as the first.

"Come here," Parker says. His position hasn't changed, so hugging him is a bit awkward. I nearly have to throw myself into his lap to make it work. "You're a beautiful soul," he murmurs, tone warm. "Grady doesn't need you to stick up for him, but it's endearing to see. I also find it very adorable that you care about him enough to threaten to kick Bridget's ass." He titters against me.

"That's right! I was so sidetracked by the jerk squad that I forgot why I actually needed to apologize. But also, what the hell were you doing with her?"

"Oh, yeah, so... Henrietta knows that Bridget is *not* ready for competition, so she's had me triple the training. Bridget, being delusional as hell, thinks I'm using our extra sessions as a front to spend more time with her. I'm one more 'Parkie' away from sticking pens in my ears." He huffs, reaching over me to grab a cookie.

"But Paaarkieee," I whine, doing my best Bridget impersonation.

He stops, cookie in hand, and stares at me. "I'll keep these, and kick you out of here *so* fast," he deadpans, but the smallest bit of humor peeks through. Grady snorts, shoulders shaking. "Keep it up, Hulk, I'll send you back to the stables," he quips.

"The stables?" I blurt out.

"Uh, yeah, just an inside joke. Thanks for these, by the way, they're delicious."

Tingles fill my body when he licks melted chocolate off his fingers.

God, I need to get laid.

"You're welcome. I miss having people to cook for. Sorry for... whatever I did to push you guys away. I swear I'm not some hussy or any of the things Bridget says about me. We have a lot of work to do in a short amount of time. I need us all on the same page."

"Nobody ever said you couldn't cook for us and come hang out. Your food is the best I've had in a long time, Hulk too." Parker squeezes my thigh, nearly pulling a whimper from my lips.

Instead, I flash him a vibrant smile. "Don't threaten me with a good time. I love seeing my people full and happy."

"Your people, huh?"

"Uh, friends? Family? Anyone I care about, really."

He grips my thigh harder, the pressure is nearly enough to make me throw caution to the wind. "You're a good woman, don't let people like Bridget and those two idiots tell you otherwise."

Working to swallow the boulder in my throat, I nod. "I'd better get some rest, I have a lesson in the morning, and my trainer is ruthless." My coy smile earns a genuine chuckle. "Good night, guys." I stand and tip my head toward Grady.

To my surprise, he waves, mouth corners lifting ever so slightly.

Maybe all hope isn't lost.

Morning has always been my favorite time of day. Something about the stillness being broken up by the waking world is energizing. My lesson doesn't start for a couple of hours, and I have every intention of making the best of them.

By that, I mean I'm making breakfast for the guys.

This morning calls for my 90s hits playlist. Since I have time, buttermilk biscuits are on the menu. A little egg and sausage with cheese, and they're about to be the best damn breakfast sandwiches those two have tasted. My brothers love them, and they're picky as hell.

Cutting the dough, I place them on a pan and toss them into the oven, bouncing around to the music. It's very important to eat these fresh, so I get to work cooking the eggs and searing off the sausage patties. By the time they're done, the biscuits have cooled enough for me to handle them.

Wrapping each sandwich in parchment paper, I grab my trusty orange juice—which I know Grady in particular loves—and head out.

The stables are dark, training grounds empty. This place would look abandoned if it weren't for the horses in the pasture. Which reminds me. I peer around the corner of the stable as I pass. Tally is grazing alongside Champ. Apparently, Bridget decided she's worthy of his company now. There are no other horses to be seen in their pasture. So, where are Warren and Quincy's?

Oh well, no time to worry about all that, breakfast is getting cold.

I practically skip to Parker's cabin, basket in hand. Words can't describe how excited I am to watch them enjoy my food again.

A sleep-ruffled shirtless Parker opens the door, one eye still nearly closed. "You really jumped at the opportunity to feed us, huh?" His raspy laugh does something inexplicable to my insides.

Am I falling in love with this man?

Impossible.

He motions for me to enter and I immediately look to the couch, not surprised to find Grady there.

"Does he live here?" The question flies out of my mouth like a racehorse when the gates open.

"Uh, well, sort of. Unofficially. Don't say anything to anyone about it, though, okay?" Parker's face and voice both fill with tension.

"Okay..."

Not odd at all.

They don't sleep together, so they're not secretly dating. There are no real signs that Grady actually lives here, aside from his constant couch surfing. Whatever their reasoning, it's no concern of mine.

I shrug and move to the table, unloading my basket. "Hope you're ready to propose, fellas." My face pulls into a giant grin.

Grady groggily ambles over, drooping into a chair, bare chest on full display.

I count my breaths, focusing on anything but burying my face between his pecs, and hand them their biscuits—two for Grady with extra cheese. They unwrap the golden, fluffy goodness and immediately dig in.

"Fuck," Parker says on a moan. "You made these from scratch?" His eyes widen as I nod, admittedly more sheepish than I expected.

Grady chews his first taste with a blissful smile and hooded eyes. He hums around each bite, finishing half of sandwich number one in seconds. I can't help the small laugh that escapes me.

"So which one of us do you want?" Parker asks.

I nearly drop my biscuit. "Uh. What?"

"You said we'd propose, I'm asking which one of us you want to do it. These are to die for."

"Oh. I'm not the marrying type. Don't worry." Sharp and dry, I laugh, but it's not convincing in the slightest.

Grady slowly tilts his head with scrunched brows.

Okay, they're definitely not buying it.

"What? I'm not the type of girl men marry. Nor am I capable of love. I've only ever been the 'good time'. Then I get tossed aside," I grumble into my orange juice, praying the glass hides my pitiful frown.

"You're not just a good time. You deserve to be an 'until the end of time'. Don't sell yourself short because nobody has bothered to appreciate your efforts. The right man will adore you."

There it is, the clear-cut "not it" buried under fluffy words.

Friends or hookups, that's all I'll ever be.

"Do you understand how many letdowns I've suffered through? Young me wanted something that doesn't exist. Love is a lie." I toss myself back in the chair and groan.

Parker arches a brow. "How many of those guys started as hookups?"

Grady drums his fingers on the table, expression blank, but heavy.

"You don't understand," I say to my lap. "I've never been important to anyone. If it wasn't for my body, I would have nothing to offer."

"You made us a full-on breakfast after knowing us for a day. You've nearly fought Bridget on Grady's behalf twice now. Just yesterday, you organized a dinner to introduce us to new people with the best intentions. It's not your fault they suck. Your heart is huge and beautiful." Parker takes my hand with a warm smile.

A tear trails down my cheek. "It's all a product of my desperation. Always eager to please, up until it gets tiring. Then I crash and people turn their backs on me when I become too much."

Grady scoffs. Storm clouds fill his eyes, head shaking slowly, deliberately.

This is too real, too personal.

"Sorry, didn't mean to bring the mood down. I'm fine, really. Who needs love when you have a horse and a dream?" I force a smile and return to my breakfast.

It's obvious that they don't believe my lies, but neither of them pushes for more. It's funny how part of me wishes they would.

Ten

Leah

My eyes almost roll out of my head when the doorbell rings. Parker is training Bridget right now, so whoever is on the porch isn't him, and I'm not delusional enough to think Grady is paying me a surprise visit.

Paint is splattered all over me. The *one* time I try to enjoy my morning, it's interrupted. Damn it.

My face twists, blood scalding as it races through my veins.

"Before you slam the door, just hear us out," Warren blurts, hands raised in defense. "We're here to apologize."

Lips pulled tight, I quirk a brow.

Warren scrubs a hand down his face. "We acted like total assholes."

"The worst kind of dicks," Quincy adds.

"That's the best you've got?" I fire back. "Typical. Pretty boys never have to work for it, and it shows."

"You didn't let us finish," Warren's face softens. "It's obvious that Grady has eyes for you. Parker, too. We were intimidated and let our dicks do the thinking."

I sigh through my nose. "They don't like me like that, Grady actively avoids me, actually."

Quincy hikes a shoulder. "Believe what you want. We know what it looks like to yearn."

"So, what? You showed up here to beg for a second chance? You realize that I have to work with them, right? Jealousy is gross. You lost at least ten points each by acting like toddlers."

Warren's hands twitch at his side, avoiding my gaze. "We don't expect forgiveness."

Quincy's jaw works, attention glued to the porch. "We just wanted to set the record straight, so you know we're not the colossal assholes we presented as."

I swallow around a lump in my throat. For some unknown, absurd reason, I step to the side, inviting them in. Clearly more rational than I, their eyes widen. For a minute, their silent stares hold me in place.

Eventually, I snap out of it. "Well, I'm not gonna keep letting the bugs in. Come on, I've got drinks and snacks."

Warren's chest deflates with a relieved sigh. Quincy's eyes glimmer, bright as the sky overhead.

Looks like my art time is over. I untie my paint smock, draping it over my easel, keeping my back to them until I'm ready for whatever comes next.

Drinks, that's a good distraction. I'm nothing if not hospitable. It'll also buy me a few more minutes of procrastination. Perfect. Sweet tea in one hand, mismatched glasses in the other, I join them in the living room.

Their eyes are glued to the pitcher, watching intently as I fill the cups.

Warren grabs one, sniffing it.

"Never had sweet tea before?" I tilt my head. "Or are you worried I poisoned it. I'll drink first."

"Never had it." The raw emotion in his face gives me pause.

Quincy, far less skeptical, takes a sip. His eyes flash with surprise at first, filling with glee as the flavors mingle.

Gone are the assholes from yesterday. Somewhere along the way, they've had a change of heart. Then again, this could be part of their scheme, but they're... human right now, albeit a little weird.

Screw it.

Their energy is infectious, and I want to give them the chance to show their intentions. No time like the present. I sit between them, relaxing into the cushion.

Warren, to my left, takes a sip of his tea and groans. "God damn. Bitter and sweet all in one delicious, cold package. This is amazing."

Quincy turns to face me more directly. "Did you make this?"

"Yeah, I always have a jug ready to go. Love the stuff. No matter how bad it is for me." I let out a soft chuckle.

"Listen," Warren mutters, voice ghosting over my shoulder. "We have our reasons for acting the way we did. Not saying it's right, but the version of us you were introduced to, that's not the real us."

Goosebumps line my skin, heart dancing in my chest as Quincy scoots closer. This is bad. But it feels right.

No. I cannot be this drawn to *four* men.

I straighten. "Swear you're not going to be assholes anymore. I don't like hating people, but if you're rude to Grady one more time, or if you give Parker one more nasty look, I'll never talk to either of you again, neighbors or not."

"I swear," Quincy answers immediately. "It fucking sucked seeing how upset you got. I... I don't want to be that guy. You looked so happy and excited going into the diner, and we ruined that." Swallowing hard, his finger brushes against my leg.

"Yeah, it was a big eye-opener. We can tell you a million times that we're decent guys, but it's not going to matter unless we show it. We're prepared to put in the effort." Warren lifts one corner of his mouth, eyes softening.

My nerves stop burning, breath slowing. "Okay. Friends?"

They sigh in unison. "Friends."

Each day here is the same monotonous mess. Sure, I try to find little things to do with the guys when we have time. Food is pretty much the extent of my abilities, since there's nothing else around. Tonight, I'm making dinner. They always appreciate a break from the catered slop this place gives us.

I've had a roast in the slow cooker all day, and the garlic mashed potatoes I just finished whipping up are velvety, creamy perfection.

Day in and day out, for the past month. I've been training, avoiding Bridget as much as possible. Parker does his best to keep Grady civil with me, which is appreciated.

This whole dynamic is exhausting.

Warren and Quincy have stayed true to their word so far, not causing issues. Oddly, they're never training. Not that I particularly look for them. But they do come to keep me company occasionally, and I have noticed them lingering during my sessions.

The fact that their stalls remain empty is another mystery, but I've decided it's not my business.

Meal packed, I head over to Parker's cabin.

He answers the door with an inquisitive glint in his eye, inspecting the bowl in my hands and the padded bag on my shoulder. "To what do I owe the pleasure?"

"I brought dinner, it's not chicken and waffles from Carrie's, but it's still tasty, promise." I grin a bit too wide.

"Oh, you can do more than breakfast and cookies? You're a regular little housewife, huh?" His eyes crinkle as he returns my goofy smile.

"I-uh."

I wouldn't mind being your wife.

"Is that so?" His whole face lights up, voice mirthful.

I groan, shoving the bowl of potatoes into his chest. "You know my thoughts don't stay where they belong."

"Do I ever." He tips his head toward the table with a chuckle. "Keep it up and I might just take you up on the idea."

My cheeks flush, stomach dipping. Outlandish images fill my head. Future us with a couple of babies, the training facility of his dreams. I could make it happen. Easy as pie. If only I had time to get all the gears in motion. Would it be careless of me to start looking at land?

Of course it would. These things take time, and for now we're all content enough to stay here.

My musing is interrupted as Grady shuffles to the table. He stares intently while I unzip the carrier for my slow cooker. As soon as the lid is off, the savory smell permeates the air—beefy, herbaceous, and tangy from the Worcestershire sauce.

"Fuck," Parker groans, bringing over plates and silverware. "I want to do unspeakable things to you."

The way he says it is meant to be in good fun, but my body does not get the memo. I have to squash the desire before it bubbles over and lets my desperation show. Somehow, I've let this man—all four of them, actually—under my skin in ways they shouldn't be.

Schooling my features, I grab a plate. "I just figured we could do with a good home-cooked meal. The measly little scraps they give us here are a joke. And Darlene is going to get sick of seeing us if we keep going to Carrie's three or four times a week." I dart my eyes to Grady for a second, and he lurches his head back. "Oh, come on, you're singlehandedly going to eat all their waffles."

Parker lets out a faint snort. "We've been going just as often for months before you got here."

"Well, I'm here now, and I'm not trying to come on too strong, so I gave it some time before pulling out the big guns. If you think my breakfasts are good, just wait."

I portion out chunks of tender beef, along with carrots and tomatoes that have been stewing in the juices. When mountains of garlic mash join the party, I know I've got them.

Sitting with a bright grin, I wiggle my shoulders. "Dig in, boys."

Hums of approval echo through the room. Appreciation dances on their faces as they devour their meals. As warm as this makes me, there's a strange ache deep in my chest. One that has nothing to do with the men at the table. It makes no sense, but the empty chairs pull at my heartstrings.

Parker notices me staring. Brows arched, he wipes his mouth and asks, "What's wrong?"

"Do you think, one of these days, we can invite Warren and Quincy? I know, I know, but before you say 'no', hear me out. Please?"

Matching tight expressions meet me from across the table, but they don't interrupt.

"Okay," I continue, "I've spent some time with them over the past couple of weeks. They seem decent beyond their original actions. I've been getting to know them, and I… I want to do things like this with them, too." I stare at my untouched food, fidgeting with my fork.

"You've been spending time with them?" The tension in Parker's voice makes my skin prickle.

"Not a lot. But they promised to try, and I promised to give them the chance. I've kept all of you separate because of the situation at the diner, but they swore to do better. So far, they have been." Chills run up my spine, stomach churning.

Parker looks at Grady. They share a silent conversation, but their clenched jaws and brow twitches are *loud*. Every time they do this, my head spins. It makes no sense to me, but they understand perfectly.

Grady gives a final nod, and Parker turns to me. "Let's give it a little more time. I need to tell you something about them, but I can't yet."

"What?! Why?" I wail, skin pebbled. "What is with all the secrets?"

Parker goes still, eyes moving to Grady for the faintest moment. "They're not my secrets to tell, or I already would have."

I want to scream, to jump over this table and smack Grady senseless. But whatever his issue is, the reason for his secrets, it scares him more than my disapproval. Based on the pain in his eyes, he hates himself enough for it. Realistically, I don't know anything about him. I barely know Parker. They feel like friends some days, and total strangers the next.

"I don't like being kept in the dark. You're going to have to tell me eventually, or this will never work." I stand too fast, banging my knee off the table leg. "Son of a gun!" Huffing, I give them a final, frustrated sigh. "I've lost my appetite. I'll pick up my stuff tomorrow. Enjoy your dinner."

"Leah, please," Parker begs, and they both stand to follow me.

I toss a hand back, thankful that they freeze. My nerves can't handle them right now. Something has to give. For once, I'm determined not to let it be me. "I'm going to bed. See you both tomorrow. Forget about my pipe dream." I hobble-stomp out the front door and go straight to my cabin.

We have a week until my first competition. I don't have time to care about any of them. For some reason, I still do.

This is not how I saw my life devolving when I got the "yes" email from Hartbrook.

Stupid secrets.

Stupid men.

Leah

Should it feel wrong sitting here with Warren and Quincy? My cabin feels too empty without *someone* else here, and my mind is full of bullshit feelings. Talking out my frustrations always helps. While I'd rather do it with Parker, that's not an option this time.

"I hate it." My voice breaks as I lean on Quincy.

The two of them are slowly creeping into friendship territory, despite Parker's hatred. I don't know what they ever did to him. Well, aside from the whole diner situation. Still, that was all a misunderstanding. Parker and I can't ever be a thing, so he has no reason to get territorial. Even then, I'm *not* property, I'll sleep with every single one of them if I want, nobody can stop me.

Except me, that's working out so far.

Warren pulls my feet into his lap, massaging my arches. "You're valid for feeling that way, but I'm sure they have their reasons for keeping things from you. Some of us have had hard lives."

"Do you think I haven't?"

"Hey," Quincy speaks up. "He doesn't mean it like that. We all have our issues. The reality of it is that none of us really know each other well. Don't hold it against them."

They're right, which is annoying. Why can't I be angry in peace? Damn these emotionally mature men. Sometimes a girl just wants to scream out her anger and be heard.

Warren's gaze holds steady on my tense expression. He won't say it, but I can tell there's an eagerness to cheer me up behind his stoic persona. Quincy is much more transparent. If they weren't still trying to show me they're different, he'd probably have me under him already.

Not that I would mind one bit.

All this testosterone is wearing me down. It's only a matter of time until one—or two—of them break my restraint. No part of me will feel bad about it when that day comes. Will I still freak out? Oh yeah. It'll be justified. Sleeping with any of them will come with blowback, and I need to be prepared for that.

Until I am, nights like this will have to be enough. And breakfasts with Parker and Grady. Because at the end of the day, I'll forgive them, I always do and probably always will. The pull I feel for them demands it. It's inexplicable.

"They're not bad guys, are they?" I sigh.

Warren squeezes my foot tighter. "No." His response comes out through a clenched jaw.

Chuckling, I reply, "You seem rather upset about that."

"It's because he's jealous," Quincy teases.

"Like you aren't? What I wouldn't give to have you cook for us on the regular." Warren groans.

Oh, he's genuinely upset over missing out. It's strangely endearing.

Quincy pulls me closer. "Yeah, you're right. Fuck them, let us come over for breakfast in the mornings."

I gasp, shoving him playfully. "Maybe I can rotate. One day I'll get you all in the same room."

They both go stiff, faces blanching.

I tilt my head. "What? You wouldn't want that?"

Warren swallows hard. "It would never work... for many reasons."

Fine, guess I can forget about that. Clearly, the tension is mutual.

Great.

"Well, I'm tired. You should probably get some sleep, too." I stand, hugging them both good night.

They smell so delicious, so masculine, it's hard to let them leave. Past Leah would drag them both to bed in a flash. The best way to forget my woes is to be fucked into blissful delirium, after all. Sadly, that's not the answer now. It would only make things more complicated.

The silent pleas on their faces tell me they're onto my deflection. Too bad. I'm over all this drama for the day.

"I promise I'm not upset with you guys. Okay? I just need to breathe."

Quincy pulls me back against his chest. "You're allowed alone time to process everything. Sleep well." He rubs his chin on the top of my head.

My stupid stomach fills with flutters.

Warren straightens my hair, tucking loose strands behind my ear. "Sweet dreams."

Why are they all so adoring when they want to be? How can I get them to *like* each other so I can enjoy all of their attention at once?

Right, as if that would ever happen. For now, I'm taking things one day at a time.

Tomorrow will be better because it can't possibly be worse.

Twelve

Parker

It shouldn't surprise me that Leah has been hanging around with those snakes. Lying bastards. I'm not sure why they're here, but I don't like it. Either Henrietta or Bridget played a part in this, probably both. I can smell the bullshit from here. Every member of the Hart family is a fucking joke.

Well, not *every* member.

I'm honestly a bit shocked, pleasantly so, that she has been stopping by most mornings. Grady is still keeping a good distance, which I understand. It works best for him. She's alluring, and he's inexperienced.

Anyone with eyes can see the way he softens when she's around. Even when she was in Bridget's face, threatening to knock her teeth out, he had stars in his eyes. Such a sweet giant of a man, all it takes is standing up for him, and he's a goner.

It *was* hot as hell, so I can't blame him. It took every ounce of willpower I possess to contain my glee.

Knowing she's been hanging out with *them* must hurt for Grady.

If only he'd let me be more of a comfort.

Unfortunately, we have jobs to do, and Bridget is first on my lesson schedule for the day. I've been unintentionally half-assing her classes for the past couple of weeks. She's atrocious and is barely putting in any effort. So why should I?

You can give someone all of the tools necessary for success, spend painstaking hours teaching them how to use them, and still see them fail because of their own lack of passion. Sure, natural inclination is a factor, but even the sloppiest riders can be decent if they try. Bridget is lazy, entitled, and thinks her name is all she needs to succeed.

Too bad for her that Henrietta wants a worthy heir to the empire.

Too bad for Henrietta that Bridget has no idea how this sport actually works.

There's no way her mother is going to pay off *every* judge. One or two will help raise her scores, but not enough.

Tucking my Hartbrook polo into my waistband, I pomade my hair, making sure my appearance is pristine. Anything less means Bridget will complain, and I don't want to deal with that today. I can only hope she focuses on her training. Competitions will be upon us before we know it.

When I reach the stable, Grady is already getting Champ ready. He's been tacking him up before Bridget shows her face to avoid as much interaction with her as possible.

"Good morning, again." I smile at him. The warm smirk he gives me in return makes me melt a little. "She'll be here any minute, best finish up and hide out." I take Champ's reins from him.

Like a kid hiding from the boogeyman, he swiftly retreats into the supply closet.

Minutes later, Bridget struts into the stable sporting an over-the-top smile—the same one that haunts my nightmares.

"You look so good in that shirt, I love the way it makes your eyes pop," she purrs, running a finger down my chest.

Choking back the bile in my throat, I force a smile. "Let's not waste time. I have back-to-back lessons today."

She pouts, folding her arms. "Aren't you going to help me?"

"You know that's not part of the job. Let me get the steps for you," I grit out, as if we don't do this *every* day. The pathetic questions may differ, but it's all the same. Feigning helplessness in hopes I'll swoop in and rescue her like a false knight.

She scoffs. "It's not cute when men play hard to get. Especially when they're beneath me."

"Good thing I'm not playing then," I grumble.

"I bet you'd help that harlot onto her hell-beast if she asked." She stomps her foot like a child.

"That's the difference, she *doesn't* ask. She's capable of doing things on her own." Shit, I'm getting too worked up. Ducking into the supply closet, I give Grady a sorrowful smile, grabbing the three-tier mounting block on my way out.

"Well, excuse me for wanting my man to be there for me!"

I set the steps on the ground. "Here, these are more helpful than I would be anyway."

Rolling her eyes, she casts me off with a cold shoulder. Good. It doesn't hurt my feelings in the slightest. Maybe she'll actually focus today instead of flashing "fuck me" eyes through our whole session.

I make my way to the training arena, fighting a groan when she awkwardly rides out. My future here depends on her ability to—at the bare minimum—stay in the saddle. Champ can compensate quite a bit for her lack of control, but wobbling around is not a good look. Fortunately, there are several competitions between now and the Olympics, so she'll have the opportunity to improve by then. I can only hope it will be enough.

As she brings Champ to a halt, I almost applaud her for not rocking in her seat.

There may be a chance yet.

Time to get this mess over with so I can watch my star shine.

I'm exhausted, leaning against the fence, fighting a world-class migraine. I perk up at the sound of Tally whinnying. My attention snaps to the stables. The sight of Leah—confident and competent—rejuvenates me. Which is odd since I'm nearly breathless as she trots my way.

"Are you okay?" Leah asks, bringing Tally to a flawless halt.

I push off the fence. "I am now, thank you for not sucking."

"She can't still be *that* bad with all the extra sessions… can she?"

"You wouldn't think so, but Jesus, I've trained children with more coordination. I'm fairly sure she's gotten worse somehow."

She snorts—the cutest fucking sound ever. What makes it even better is the fact that she owns it. No bashful blushing or apologizing for being her genuine self.

Her adorable, beautiful, playful self.

Training, Parker, she's here for training. Do your damn job and stop fantasizing.

"You're beautiful," I say, immediately coughing as her eyes widen. "I-I mean your form, you're doing beautifully."

Judging by the glimmer in her eye, she's not fooled by my bullshit.

"What are we covering today?" she asks, giving me a free pass to get back on track.

"Well, you're in good shape. I mainly want to take you through the routine we've been prepping." I pull out my trusty Bluetooth speaker, preparing her pop medley. "Go ahead and get in position."

She lines Tally up with their starting marker, nodding when ready. Her shoulders are relaxed, form perfect, showing no signs of apprehension. As the first note sounds, she flawlessly moves Tally into their starting trot. They bounce along to the beat of "Crazy" by Britney Spears, seamlessly transitioning into a beautiful diagonal.

On the far side of the stable, Warren and Quincy are watching. My skin always itches at the sight. Something is off with them, for sure. Shade obscures their faces, making it impossible to read their intentions. They're always *around* but never close. It's unnerving.

Am I annoyed that Leah seems to have patched things up with them? Oh, yeah. But, she's a grown woman, and assures me that they're just being friendly.

I don't know many "friends" who make it their daily task to watch your every move, but who am I?

I bring my attention back to the spectacle before me, admiring their smooth shift into a collected canter. They glide effortlessly into a working gait in preparation for a flying change. Tally swaps leads on beat and snorts, letting a small bit of her personality shine through.

Grady watches from the stable entrance, face filled with admiration. I smile at him, and he returns it without hesitation.

Hopefully, I'll see more of them in the near future. Witnessing the grace of Leah and Tally always does the trick, even if he won't let her see that.

They work through the rest of the routine, and my heart skips a beat. The reality of our agreement settles in. She can do this, and when she does, we'll likely never see her again.

The final note of her medley sounds as they finish their last maneuver. I applaud them with less enthusiasm than they deserve, which earns me an adorable head tilt.

Damn it if my face doesn't pull into a sappy smile.

I pat Tally on the neck. "That was nearly flawless."

"Yeah, our piaffe felt a little too tense."

"You'll get it, I know you will. Then we have a month to perfect the next routine. Gonna have to tighten your canter pirouettes. I let you get by with an easy routine for this competition since it's the first one."

"Yes, sir," she jokes, and my heart stutters so hard I almost collapse.

Grady's boots kick up dust as he crosses the paddock.

Leah's face fills with curiosity. "Were you watching, too?"

He nods, giving her two thumbs up.

"Do you even know anything about dressage? Or are you just trying to be a good friend?" she asks with a small titter.

If she had any idea...

He rears his head back with a faint scowl.

"What? Just because you're a stable hand doesn't mean you know how scoring works."

I shoot him a questioning look. His eyes tell me not to say too much, so I opt for *just enough* instead. "Grady grew up around the sport. You'd be surprised how much he knows."

"Interesting, wouldn't you want to be a trainer instead of a stable hand?" There's no way she misses the glaringly obvious anguish on his face.

"It's a touchy subject," I offer as he grits his teeth.

"Because he can't talk?" she presses.

Going straight for the kill, I suppose.

Red-faced, brows pulled close together, it's hard to tell if he's angry or embarrassed. He hasn't stormed off, so I'm going with the latter. Not that I've known him to storm off.

I step next to him and place my hand on his shoulder. "Talking is a pretty big part of the job," I explain as if it isn't obvious. "If our arrangement works out, he'll be a routine planner, and I'll find a way for him to train as well."

Eyes sparkling, he turns to me, a soft smile pulling at his lips.

She drops off Tally's back, grinning at him. "Well then, I'd better hold up my end of the deal. Gotta get you away from the likes of Bridget. I know you don't like me, but that doesn't mean I'm not going to help you."

Their height difference is almost humorous. He's got at least a foot on her. His attention shifts down, brows furrowed. She holds his gaze, unblinking. Silence fills the air as their stare-off remains unbroken, but the twitch of his hands gives enough away. This is going to end badly.

"Who wants to go grab food? I need a refuel before round two with Bridget tonight," I ask, breaking up the tension.

"Ew, you're going to run yourself ragged trying to train the bitch out of her," Leah grumbles.

Grady lets out a laugh, chest shaking.

"You're something else, Star." I immediately bite my tongue for letting the name slip.

"Star?" Her eyes glimmer.

"Sorry, I only call you that in my head."

She bounces and hugs me. "It's cute, unique. I love it."

As she melts into my arms, I watch Grady over her shoulder. His face gives nothing away as he stares. I'm fairly certain he's admiring how round her ass looks in these riding pants.

"Way better than Pinkie." She laughs, pulling away. "Are you hungry too, Grady? Or are you going to make me keep him company by myself?"

Slightly flushed from *definitely* checking her out, he shrugs with a nod.

Looks like it's the three of us again, just the way I like it. I let my attention wander to the spot where Warren and Quincy were watching. They're gone now, which is a relief. I don't like their random appearances one bit, and definitely want to avoid any other train wrecks at Carrie's. It would also be incredibly unfortunate if word got back to Henrietta about the way we keep flirting with Leah.

We turn Tally out in the pasture, then go our separate ways to change, regrouping at my car. Our drive is fairly quiet, the easy companionship is enough.

We're escorted to our booth as soon as we arrive. I take the window seat, Grady sits next to me, and Leah claims the far side for herself.

As we wait for our food, I decide it's now or never. "Hulk," I start, voice shaking slightly. He considers me, single brow raised. "We... uh. We should tell her about the thing we discussed." I fiddle with my silverware, afraid of the emotions in his eyes.

"What thing?" Leah asks, tone tentative but curious.

She's not stupid. My horrid poker face has clued her in.

Grady blows out a heavy sigh, tapping his fingers on the tabletop. His jaw clenches and relaxes rhythmically as he contemplates his next move. To Leah's credit, she doesn't say anything. While she waits patiently, all I can do is hold my breath.

Several minutes of heavy silence pass.

I almost say something, but Grady beats me to it. "I...c-c-c." Biting his cheek, he draws a shaky breath in through his nose, closing his eyes to avoid Leah's awestruck expression. "I c-c-can t-talk."

"Wow," she breathes out, blinking slowly. "Your voice is so nice." Her smile is so warm it could melt steel.

Clearly unaccustomed to the compliment, he jolts.

She's not wrong. No amount of stuttering could hide the rough timbre of his voice. Deep and gravelly. It may be due to the general lack of use, but either way, it clearly affects her the same as it does me.

"Th-th-th—" He pauses, swallowing his nerves. "—Thanks."

"Don't mention it," she replies, without a trace of judgment.

"See? I told you she wouldn't think less of you."

"Wait, you thought I'd make fun of you because of a little stutter? That's no biggie at all! One of my brothers has a stutter, too. His isn't bad, it mainly shows up when he's nervous, but still, it's nothing. I wouldn't even need to warn my mama about it."

"R-r-really?" He sits up straighter, shoulders relaxing.

"Yeah, if you don't feel comfortable talking, though I've gotten pretty used to reading you... Not that you've given me a lot to go by." She chuckles.

Appreciation shines in his eyes. A small part of his long-lost self-worth comes back to life. Our food arrives on cue, giving him a free out to end the conversation. Together, we enjoy our chicken and waffles in peaceful, familiar silence.

I had no doubt that she would treat him the same, but he has been terrified of her finding out. After the last altercation with Bridget, I pushed him to get the gall to tell her before Bridget did. Thankfully, he listened, and now we're that much closer to transparency.

Secret one, shared.

Now to get them on board with the rest.

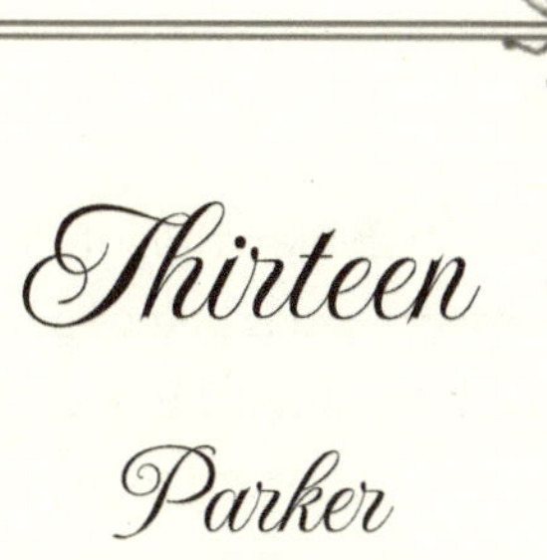

Thirteen

Parker

We're all at the stable, packing up to hit the road. Tomorrow morning will come fast. I'd like to be at the hotel early. Fortunately, Leah and Grady share my penchant for punctuality.

Bridget? Not so much.

Haven't seen her, but we've taken it upon ourselves to pack her things as well. How she and Champ get there is none of my concern. We all have to transport ourselves. But at least she can't say we left her totally high and dry.

Grady comes out of the supply closet with a bag in hand, filled with his change of clothes and toiletries.

Leah quirks a brow at him and he avoids her questioning look. When his eyes land on mine, I give him a "you can't hide forever" glare. His shoulders drop, and he walks out the door to toss his things in my trunk.

"He's especially grumpy today," Leah grumbles, taking careful inventory of her gear.

"He's still adjusting to you knowing."

"That he can talk? It's really nothing. Haven't pressured him to say anything to me since."

"Yeah, but it's still terrifying for him. There's... more to it than just his stutter. The things he's endured because of it. Someday he'll tell you more." I smile, hoping my words ease a bit of her tension.

She frowns, and an adorable wrinkle forms between her brows. "Doubtful, every step forward is followed by two steps back."

Foolishly, I reach out, smoothing the little crease with my thumb. Her skin is soft and warm under my touch. Those gorgeous, large green eyes nearly cross as she stares up at me. For the first time, I'm able to see her truth—something vulnerable hiding beneath the surface, carefully concealed by the bright colors and spunkiness.

My pulse picks up as her breath falters, cheeks staining a perfect shade of red to make her freckles pop.

Fuck.

I swallow and withdraw my hand, kicking myself for touching her. We both felt the electricity, I know we did.

"Sorry, I just..." Just what? For the first time in my life, I'm at a loss for words.

"It's okay," she whispers, as if she can't trust her own voice.

Grady chooses that moment to come back inside, huffing as Bridget nips at his heels. Leah goes still next to me, eyes zeroed in on her.

"Oh, Parkie, did you get my things ready for me?" Bridget bats her lashes.

"All three of us did, actually. Though it was mainly Grady," I answer, voice a little too sharp.

"Well, did you supervise to make sure he did it correctly?" she asks with a scoff.

"Are you seriously stupid? Genuine question," Leah spits.

"Excu—"

"No. First of all, *you* should have done it your damn self if you're that concerned. But we all know you wouldn't have the foggiest idea of what to bring or how to pack your gear properly. Hell, do you even know *where* we're going?" Leah seethes, giving her no chance to utter a word.

God, she's sexy when she stands up to Bridget... who is extremely red in the face.

"Mother will hear of this!"

"Yeah, yeah, Princess. Go on, same old threat I've heard before." Leah rolls her eyes, turning away.

The disbelief and gratitude on Grady's face speak volumes. He's not used to anyone having his back. The fact that Leah does it, even though she thinks he hates her, is fucking criminally attractive. Good people with equally good hearts are so few and far between in this world.

I'm starting to think she may be worth risking everything for. Judging by the way Grady's attention stays on her, he's having the same epiphany.

While she finishes loading her bag with the last of Tally's brushes and soaps, Grady takes it from her with the smallest trace of a smile. From him, it may as well be a full-fledged grin.

We've got a few hours of drive time ahead of us before we reach Ocala. This event will set the pace for the coming months. If she can knock this one out of the park, we've got all we need to fast-track her Olympic qualification. A few routines we can rotate between, with enough high skill transitions, and she's a shoo-in.

I only hope my extra hours with Bridget have been enough to make her mother believe I'm worth keeping around. This has to work out. Leaving Grady here is not an option, and he damn sure can't leave if I can't afford to support us.

My legs are cramped from the drive, but we've made it. Grady and I are waiting at the boarding stable for Leah to arrive. Hairs raise on the back of my neck, my skin tingles. There's no way she shouldn't already be here, she left thirty minutes before us.

I pull out my phone and call her.

"Hey," she answers after two rings.

My stomach nearly jumps out of my throat as the dread settling in it dissipates. "Hey, we made it already. I was sort of worried you'd gotten lost or something."

"No, just... okay, I did get lost for a teeny, tiny second. Missed an exit and had to re-route. GPS says I'll be there in five."

I chuckle into the phone. "Do I need to make Grady ride with you from now on to navigate?"

She grunts. "See you in a minute."

When the line goes dead, I let out a laugh. "She got lost, so I told her I'd lend her my navigator." I flash Grady a smirk.

"N-n-no th-thanks." The twinkle of humor in his eyes doesn't go unnoticed.

"I bet she's a riot on road trips. Just imagine the playlist, her singing and dancing as she drives. Probably not the safest, but damn would it be a blast!" I beam. He raises his brows and shakes his head, expression full of mock terror. "You love her quirkiness just as much as I do, don't try to downplay it with me."

Blaring country music fills the air as Leah's truck rolls into the drive. Windows down, hair up in a pink mess, she's wearing ridiculously oversized white sunglasses.

As she backs her trailer up to the doors, a stable hand comes to greet us, likely to see what all the racket is about. He's a young kid, maybe sixteen, scrawny with mousy brown hair. Timid.

Our little star hops down from her driver's seat, wearing a baby-blue sundress that clings to her curves in a way that should be illegal.

"Hey there! Leah, from Hartbrook." She wiggles her fingers.

"Tallulah Does the Tango?" His voice cracks.

"Listen, rule number one about my horse, she *loathes* her government name. Call her Tally and feed her peppermints, and you *should* live to talk about it." Somehow, she maintains her bright expression while instilling bone-chilling fear into this poor kid.

"Okaaaay," he says, gulping as she opens the trailer.

Tally, to her credit, backs out with minimal theatrics. She looks better than ever and is definitely ready to crush this show tomorrow.

As we follow the stable hand through the barn, I admire the high-end establishment. Hartbrook is clinical, sensible, nothing too extravagant. This is the exact opposite. Everything is polished. The stalls all have a certain rustic air about them. There are about thirty horses here already. While I'm sure not all of them are competing at the same level as Leah, there are some notable contenders. Several rising stars, other Olympic hopefuls who have been working for the last year or two for this.

As we stop at Tally's designated stall, the stable hand ushers us inside. Leah gives him a peppermint, and his brows knit together, barely visible under his shaggy locks.

"This is really the secret?" His eyes bulge as he reaches out.

Tally sniffs the candy for a second, then grabs it with a nicker, crunching away.

"Told you. You're besties now… just keep the supply on hand." Leah claps him on the shoulder, and he gives her a tense nod.

"The horse next to her was a top contender last year." I point to the large Dutch Warmblood. He's gorgeous, as black as Tally with a small white snip on his nose.

"Yeah, Captain Clancy's Revenge. I know him well. I mean, I don't *know* him, but I'm familiar. The same goes for the Holsteiner over there." She points a few stalls down to a bald-faced bay. "Little Lady Luck. Great horse, her canter transitions are flawless."

So she does follow the sport, noted. Not a surprise, but knowing what I do, it was up in the air.

Grady nods. An impressed smirk tugs at his face.

"Well, we should probably go settle in for the night, yeah?" I jingle my keys.

Leah pats Tally, kissing her nose before we leave.

Our lodging is right down the road from the stable, which is extremely convenient. There isn't a whole lot else going on in this area. We're not *in* the city by any means, so hopefully they at least have a continental breakfast. We're going to need all the energy we can get to survive tomorrow. Of all the things we packed, none of us thought about food—not even a granola bar or some trail mix. One skipped dinner won't kill us, I suppose.

The hotel is smaller than expected, considering the size of the stables. When we walk into the lobby, the frail old lady at the front desk gives us an interesting look—wrinkled eyes doubled in size, lips pursed.

Unease creeps up my spine, slow and stinging.

When she opens her mouth, I have to practice my breathing exercises. "Good evening... uh, I'm afraid there has been a misunderstanding." Her tense smile stabs me in the gut... this isn't happening. "You see, the hotel is very booked due to the event tomorrow, we only have one room left... is that an issue?"

There it is, another cosmic joke.

Shoulders slumping, Leah lets out a dramatic sigh. "I mean, I would love to watch some trash TV and binge eat candy in my underwear, but whatever."

Grady puffs a single laugh through his nose, completely unbothered by this development.

Face pulled tight, I reply, "We have no other choice, aside from sleeping in my car, so we'll make it work."

"Wonderful. I do apologize that your facility manager didn't secure proper accommodations." She hands me a key card. "Room twenty is all yours!"

Rolling our suitcases behind us, the worst sound possible echoes through the long hall.

"Parkieeee." Despite the plush carpet, the blank beige walls act as amplifiers, helping Bridget's voice penetrate my eardrums at a piercing level. "You're supposed to be bunking with meeee, we got the honeymoon suite on the top floor." She speed walks toward us, fake smile on her face as usual.

"I'm with Grady," I deadpan, leaving no room to argue. "One of us can sleep on the couch or something. Leah can have the other bed."

"What is so special about them? Why do you constantly blow me off?!"

"Bridget, it's late. I'm tired from the drive. Can we talk in the morning?" I don't give her time to answer before swiping the keycard at our door and ducking inside.

Out of one nightmare into another.

The room is *small*. Short moss-green carpet, beige walls like the hallway, brown curtains covering the large window. It would be perfect for a couple... seeing as the only furniture is a small table with two wooden chairs, a TV mounted on the wall, and *one* bed. King-size with a cream-colored comforter featuring little blue cornflowers, a handful of pillows and lovely little chocolates.

How quaint.

"You've got to be kidding me," I groan, throwing my head back. "There's not even a couch! Guess we're on the fucking floor tonight, Hulk."

Who knows what secrets this carpet holds... I'd rather not think about it. My car might be a better choice.

Grady shrugs. This isn't the worst place he's ever had to sleep. Still, the thought is beyond frustrating. They host events three times a year here. How is there not more places to stay in the area? Dozens of teams come at a time. Where do they normally keep all these people?

Probably at the nicer places nearby, the ones Hartbrook would never pay for.

Leah places her hands on her hips. "Don't be dramatic, we're adults. We're friends. We can share the damn bed."

Heart in my throat, I tilt my head. "Share? You'd be comfortable with that?"

"I'm not a teenager. I'll sleep on one side, Grady can take the other, since he likely won't want to sleep near me, and you can be the buffer in the middle. First, we need showers." She marches off to the bathroom.

I stand here, staring at Grady, and we have a wordless conversation, agreeing that the bed sounds far better than the floor.

This is fine.

Sleeping between the two people I can't have won't go wrong at all.

Fourteen

Leah

What time is it? I don't even remember falling asleep. The last I knew, we were sitting in bed, watching *Seabiscuit*, snacking on vending machine goodies.

Faint murmurs catch my attention, the rise and fall against my cheek is unsettling.

Am I between them? Snuggling?!

Parker's voice is coming from behind me... which can only mean one thing—the bare chest I'm lying against isn't his. Not that cuddling up with him would be all that much better, but at least he doesn't actively despise me.

Should I move?

Part of me doesn't want to. Even if Grady hates me, he's allowing me to use him as a pillow. I'm not entirely sure how I got in this position, but I have zero complaints. He's warm and smells good—like hotel soap and his usual citrus. No matter how bad my hand itches to acclimate itself with his abdomen, I have to resist. He's obviously awake. Parker isn't talking to himself. If I move, he'll undoubtedly push me away.

"Just relax. She won't bite... unless you want her to, in which case I'm sure she'll oblige," Parker says, voice low.

When the arm underneath me moves and his hand comes to rest on the curve of my hip, my breath catches. Fortunately, I recover quickly, so they're none the wiser.

Parker shifts behind me, clicking the TV on.

Acting like I'm asleep, I give in to my impulses, trailing my hand up Grady's bare torso, resting between his pecs. He shudders under my touch, chest rumbling with the gravely sound that escapes him.

Burning alive, I squeeze my thighs together, almost blowing my cover.

"She looks so perfect curled up against you. I'm almost jealous," Parker mutters with a softness that turns my heart to mush.

Fantasies race through my mind—him scooting in close, hand ghosting up my side as Grady kisses me. Damn, it's been so long since I've been touched. I need to get a grip.

"You enjoying yourself, Hulk?"

"Mhm," Grady grunts, hips jerking the faintest amount.

I haven't heard his voice much, but it sounds different right now—deeper, huskier. If I didn't know better, I'd think he sounds aroused.

Surely I'm wrong.

Or am I?

Curiosity killed the cat, as they say. This might end badly, but I can't help it. I lightly drag my fingertips through his chest hair, tracing tiny circles. He audibly gulps, breaths faltering. The hand on my hip gently squeezes, prompting me to open my eyes. His heart thumps erratically against my ear as our gazes lock.

Neither of us makes an immediate attempt to separate, which is both confusing and reassuring. Another subtle shift of his hips draws my attention downward. Through the thin hotel blankets, the unmistakable outline of his erection stands out.

Parker chuckles, but I don't spare him a glance. When I return my focus to Grady's face, a vibrant blush has stained his cheeks. His chest hair tingles under my fingers while I continue to caress his heated skin.

For however long this lasts, I'll allow myself to revel in his reaction to my touch.

Practically trembling, he licks his lips, eyes drifting to my mouth. Peering up at him through my lashes, I finally understand his avoidance all these weeks. How could I have been so blind?

"Would you like to kiss me?"

His attention darts behind me, eyes filled with eagerness and a silent request.

"He's wanted to for a while," Parker answers, sliding closer—hot breath dancing on my shoulder as he curls around me. "So have I. The question is, whether you'll let us."

"Both of you?" My pulse quickens, nipples pebbling at the thought.

This is a dream, it has to be. I've finally lost it.

"It's not a dream, we talked about it while you were asleep," Parker murmurs, fingers trailing up my side.

There's no time to hate my mouth for letting the thoughts slip. Not that I could form a coherent sentence right now if I tried.

Parker's lips meet the back of my neck for a fleeting moment before he continues, "Grady hasn't kissed anyone before. He's nervous to mess it up, but it's okay. If you'll be patient, I'll coach him through it."

This shouldn't happen. Part of me is drawn to them, but the rest can't get past Warren and Quincy. How will they react to this?

My racing thoughts stop at the anticipation in Grady's soft, warm eyes—filled with uncertainty that I'm sure mine reflect.

Repercussions are a problem for future Leah.

Tipping my face toward his, I nod in silent consent. His lips part a sliver as he slowly closes the gap between us. The instant his warm mouth meets mine, sparks erupt inside me. Gently, tentatively, he moves, as if he's afraid to be too much.

"Give her a little more. She wants it," Parker commands, nose brushing against my neck.

Grady does just that, leaning further into me, letting a faint groan roll free.

"Fuck, you're a natural. Open up for him, Star." Parker's lips ghost over my ear as he whispers directions.

I do as he says, and Grady slips his tongue into my mouth like he's waited an eternity to taste me. His free hand moves instinctively to my side, trailing along my ribs. The feather-soft touch tickles, and I squirm, accidentally pressing against Parker's extremely hard cock. Gasping at the feel of him against me, I pull my mouth from Grady's and turn my head. In an instant, Parker hungrily stakes a claim on my lips.

Where Grady's kiss was soft and timid, Parker is all practiced confidence. Moaning as he pulls my ass against him, my body comes alive. Heat builds in my core, wetness pools between my thighs. When he releases his hold and turns me back toward Grady, the air feels ten times heavier.

This little room may as well be a shoebox.

Biting his lip, Grady's eyes are locked on my chest.

"Would you like to play with them?" Parker asks.

Grady nods with unbridled enthusiasm, pupils blown wide.

Parker's hands move to my waist, slipping under the hem of my tank top. "Can we take this off?"

I should say no, stopping this before we go too far. There's no coming back from the path we're barreling down. Instead, I make the horrible decision to prop myself up on my elbow and nod.

Together, they pull my shirt up, sliding it over my head. Grady rolls onto his side, cupping my breasts in his large, warm hands. When he kneads firmly, I arch into Parker with a moan so needy I should be ashamed. But there's no space for shame between us. This is what we've all been keeping bottled up, and the cork is about to blow.

"Just like that. Look at how good you're making her feel. Go ahead, suck on one." Parker thrusts against my ass as Grady pulls one of my hardened nipples into his mouth.

They're everywhere at once, and I'm floating on the edge of madness. Parker nibbles at my neck as Grady worships my chest, grinding against the thigh I've tucked between his legs. He's solid, powerful, and captivating as he works.

"Please," I mewl.

"You want me to show him how to make you come?" Parker growls low and breathy, fingers trailing to the waistband of my shorts.

"Yes, I need it."

"Well, Hulk. Hope you're ready to finish what you've started. Come here, Star." Parker rolls me onto my back, spreading me out like a sacrifice. "Mind if we all get naked?" A lazy grin pulls at his face.

"Please," I beg, too far gone to care about the consequences. Giving in feels too right.

Grady stands, shedding his sweats without hesitation. All of his trepidation has faded, and rightfully so. I'd be confident as hell with a cock as nice as his. Thick and heavy, a large vein runs along the underside. He's already dripping precum, eager for his own release. He kneels between my legs, attention directed to Parker, face filled with questions.

"Take her shorts and panties off, nice and slow. Enjoy the moment." Parker lazily strokes himself next to us. He's a bit longer than Grady but not quite as thick, still one of the nicest cocks I've had the fortune of seeing. He bites his lip when he catches me looking, working more slowly with heat in his eyes.

Grady slides his hands up my thighs, demanding my undivided attention. His grip tightens when he reaches my hips. Trembling, he slips his fingers into my waistband, watching intently as he guides my bottoms lower and lower.

Each new inch of my body is met with wonder. He takes his time, as directed, chest rising and falling more rapidly with each passing second. He won't last at this rate. The thought only amplifies how much I ache for him. Once I'm fully exposed, he leans back, taking in the sight of me dripping wet and ready.

"You want a taste?" Parker asks, voice rich like velvet.

I flush. "H-he doesn't have to if he doesn't want. A lot of guys don't."

Parker looks between us. "There will be no selfish lovers here. Understood?" When Grady nods, I nearly fall apart. "Good. Now, go on. Her clit is at the top, that's where the magic is, everything else is just fun for you."

Resting on his elbows, Grady starts slow, movements unsure. Parker shifts to get a better view, and offer support. As Grady slides his tongue over my aching clit, I squirm, whimpering with need.

My reaction is enough to encourage his boldness. Exploring more, he buries his face against me and sucks, squeezing my thighs as I grind into him, seeking delicious friction. A low groan rolls out of him as he licks from my entrance back to the top, beard hairs adding a ruggedness I never knew I needed.

"That's right, fuck she's gonna come so hard for you. Go on and slip a finger inside, get a feel for how she'll squeeze your cock," Parker grits out, breathing frenzied at the sight.

Grady pulls away for a second, swallowing harshly.

Needy and desperate, my hips move, attempting to follow.

He slides a thick finger through my wetness, gasping as it slips inside. As he leans in to trace my clit with his tongue, the added pressure is the final straw. In seconds, I shatter into a million pieces, clenching around his finger while he moans against me.

The mixture of pride and awe on his face when he leans back on his knees is infinitely sexy. Panting, I lay limp, captivated by his reaction.

I nearly burst a second time when Parker takes Grady's hand, sucking his finger clean, then leans in close. "Can I taste her on your lips?" he pleads, barely audible.

Grady's cock twitches. Without a second of hesitation, he nods.

My mouth goes dry when Parker grabs him by the back of the neck and pulls him into a passionate, all-consuming kiss—one that has clearly been on the forefront of his mind for quite some time. The attraction they share for one another isn't hard to see. This is obviously the first time they've acted on it. How lucky am I to bear witness?

Watching them like this, I'm instantly aroused again, dying to be in the middle.

When they part, lips swollen and chests heaving, Parker gives me a devilish grin. "You ever had two cocks at once?"

I'm done for.

"Yes. But not two as big as yours," I answer honestly. "But I do love a challenge."

"You heard our girl. Go on and bury that glorious cock of yours inside of her, and I'll work out the details of getting mine in there too."

Our girl.

I like the way that sounds, even if it can never truly be. Falling apart on both of them is going to ruin me for other men… as long as I can take them. Fortunately, I'm no stranger to creative positioning. I already know exactly how I want this to work.

"Lie down, I'll ride you. Parker can fuck me from behind." I guide Grady onto his back, straddling him as he relaxes. "This is your first time, and you're already doing better than most of the men I've been with." I smile down at him.

He returns it, genuine and bright.

Taking his cock in my hand, I stroke a couple of times. He throbs against my palm, holding his breath as I line him up. Leaning in, I kiss him softly, taking the first few inches with ease. He gasps as I slide lower, nearly swallowing all of him before lifting back up.

Looking into his wonder-filled eyes, my chest tightens. He's been waiting for this, for me, for us. The pure, blissful disbelief on his face as I bottom out will live in my fantasies forever. If this is the only time he lets me this close, I need to commit it to memory.

His hands grip my hips as he releases a shaky breath. I roll my body a few times, adjusting to his size. I don't know how, or if I'll be able to take Parker, too. But judging by how painfully hard he looks, I'll have to figure it out, and fast.

"You're doing so well," I praise, leaning in to kiss Grady with everything I have. Our tongues find a comfortable rhythm, working in a slow, beautiful dance.

His hands explore the curves of my ass while I leisurely ride him, getting lost in the sounds of his enjoyment. Every grunt, each whispered "oh", groans that border on animalistic, he's everything I've dreamed about, and then some.

"Fuck I'm going to come before I get the chance to feel you at this rate," Parker hisses as the mattress shifts. He settles behind me, caressing my lower back—a silent request that I sit still. My body obeys, quivering with anticipation of being stretched to a new limit.

"Just breathe, Gorgeous, we'll take our time," he murmurs, inserting a finger to begin preparing me.

I moan loudly against Grady, digging my nails into his shoulders as Parker works. Methodical and determined, he presses another inside. Grady holds my lips hostage, silencing my whimpers while I climb closer to the brink of feral insanity.

Once Parker's able to fit a third finger, he groans, satisfied with my progress. When the head of his cock lines up, I hold my breath.

He eases inside, agonizingly slow. The stretch is exquisitely painful, sending thrills through me. Keen for *more,* I press back, taking both of them deeper. The pure euphoria on Grady's face makes me snap. He's already in heaven, and I want to see him break.

Moaning, I beg for everything they've got as my body adjusts to the intrusion.

Parker finally bottoms out, leaning down to kiss my back, lying against me until I'm sandwiched between them. It's strangely romantic, endearing even. He runs his fingers through Grady's hair. "You ready to feel our girl come for us?" he asks, voice strained.

Grady responds by thrusting slowly, biting down on my shoulder.

As Parker matches his rhythm, the only thing I can manage are moans and incoherent praise. Parker pulls back while Grady slams into me, alternating with perfect synchronicity. They fuck me together like it's always meant to be done this way. There's no end or beginning, just a perfectly coordinated dance while they build me up until I careen over the edge, screaming into Grady's chest as I break, overwhelmed in the best way.

Four greedy hands caress my trembling body. Grady is the first to come after me, filling me with waves of warmth. The sensation of his orgasm creates a shockwave of ecstasy, and Parker follows not far behind.

Full of them, I manage a faint giggle while they pant around me. "That was the best sex of my life... and I've had a lot of sex." I sigh, breathless, barely conscious.

"I concur." Parker titters. "Hulk, how was losing your virginity in a threesome? I'm jealous I didn't get to do it the same way."

A soft puff of breath rushes out of Grady. The sated smile on his face is the only answer needed.

I don't quite hide my shock when he mumbles, "G-g-g-good." Flushing as he struggles to get the word out.

Following Parker's advice, I school my features and don't make a huge deal about him talking. Instead, I lean down and nudge the tip of his nose with mine.

Parker kisses my shoulder as he pulls out. "I'll be right back." He slips into the bathroom, leaving me tangled up with Grady. I take full advantage of our size difference, curling into him. Chin nuzzling against me, his beard tickles the top of my head.

Parker returns with damp cloths and helps me maneuver off of Grady. Without missing a beat, he gets to work cleaning us both up. The warmth in his eyes as he carefully wipes the evidence away is unmistakable. This might not have been his first time, but it means something all the same.

If Grady has an issue with Parker touching him, he doesn't make it known. I'm not sure he could if he wanted to. We're boneless heaps, clinging to reality with the last drops of energy in our bodies.

Satisfied with the job he's done, Parker kisses each of us on the cheek and stands. "This has been an eventful twenty-four hours. We should sleep. Tomorrow we need to have a good sit-down and figure out our next move." He smiles softly and takes the cloths to the bathroom.

The weight of what just happened hits me all at once. My heart is full, but my stomach is in knots.

Fifteen

Parker

Leah is freaking out. It's written all over her face—the crinkle between her brows, mouth in a straight line as she gets ready for the arena. Silently, brooding in ways I never do, I watch as she finishes adjusting her riding jacket and steps out the door, without so much as a word uttered in our direction.

"Fuck, this is bad." I rake my fingers through my hair, cataloging the change in Grady's demeanor. This man has never, in the months I've known him, looked so at peace. Great sex with a firecracker of a woman will soothe even the most troubled soul.

I sure hope he'll stop being so cold toward her now, even though it *is* my fault that he has been in the first place. Still, it was all to avoid *this.* At the end of the day, it doesn't matter. The lines were growing blurrier by the day. Now they've damn near dissolved.

All of my carefully laid plans went out the window the instant I saw Grady's face in the low light of our room—eyes glittering as he looked down at her, body visibly relaxed despite his clear awkwardness from being so close to her. The amazement on his face as she took every spectacular inch he had to give.

He'll definitely remember it forever. Being here while he experienced the love of a woman for the first time, sharing that moment with him, is something that I'll certainly never forget.

Stop daydreaming and get going.

Grady is already dressed, wearing a nicely fitted button-down and black jeans. This cleaned-up look is unfair. I can't help but gawk. His face heats as he catches me.

Interesting.

He kissed me without a thought in the moment, but until now, I could only assume it was just that—acceptable because Leah was involved. Now? I can't help but walk toward him, still in nothing but my boxer-briefs. He doesn't move, not even a twitch of uncertainty. When we're chest-to-chest, I tip my head up to look him in the eye, silently challenging his conviction.

With an audible gulp, his attention falls to my mouth.

Fuck.

"Did you like kissing me?" I keep my voice soft as I lean into him.

He nods, dragging his tongue along his lower lip. I follow the movement, breathless, aching.

Punctuality be damned, this is happening. "Do you want to do it again?"

Our gazes meet for a mere second before our mouths connect. He's timid, but the pressure is delicious. Slowly, we feel each other out, testing how much we each want this—how much is okay. Only, I know what is comfortable for me, but he won't give it without guidance.

As I open my mouth, he finds his confidence, tongue slipping between my lips, exactly as I'd hoped. We groan together, his gravelly voice rumbling in his throat. My fingers trail a blazing path over the soft fabric of his shirt, descending to his waistband to feel out his reaction. Kissing is one thing, but I don't want to scare him off if he's not ready for more. The faint jerk of his hips and a nibble on my lower lip are all the confirmation I need.

This man will be my undoing.

Moving both hands to his zipper, I free him from his jeans. Frenzied lust blazes in his eyes as I drop to my knees. When I take him into my mouth, his legs nearly buckle. Fortunately, we're against a wall so he can steady himself. Something in the way he laces his fingers through my hair breaks me.

I want nothing more than to savor this, revel in how warm he is, cherish the sounds and groans as I drag my tongue along his shaft. But at the moment, we're not afforded the luxury.

With a free hand, I work myself steadily, building toward my own orgasm as I help him get to the peak. When he's close, growing harder than ever, he tries to push me off. If he thinks I'm not going to swallow everything he has to give me, he's wrong. I shake my head and double down, forcing him into the back of my throat. With a few shallow thrusts, he groans and lets go, pulling me closer.

That's right, give me everything.

Trembling from the intensity, I moan around him, coating my fist and stomach with my cum. When I pull back, he's wearing a sated expression, veiled by a hint of surprise.

"Fucking delicious." I wipe my mouth with a smirk, stepping into the bathroom to turn the shower on. "Let me clean up, then we'll watch our girl kill this event. Shall we?"

"O-okay," he responds, eyes hooded.

"What? Did I not do a good enough job? Do you want to fuck me while I shower?" I ask with a slight chuckle.

He bites his lips and exhales. "Wh-wh—" Swallowing his nerves, he grabs his phone.

I say nothing and get mine off the nightstand while the water heats. His text comes immediately.

Hulk:

What is this? What if she doesn't want us?

He scans my face for a second, troubled gaze dancing across my skin.

"We don't need to worry about that right now. After the event, we'll talk about everything. And I do mean *everything*. You need to tell her the truth, and she needs to tell us the truth. What has happened between us can't continue if there are still secrets. Nothing should have happened while there still are. But that's neither here nor there. I don't know about you, but I want *this*." I motion between the two of us. "And that includes Leah."

"M-me too," he confirms.

With those two words, the deal is sealed.

I gently press my lips to his cheek. "Let's just hope she does, too. Now, I really do need to shower, and fast. We're going to be late."

He watches me step under the spray and I make sure the glass doesn't fog up so he can enjoy the show. We exchange playful, heated looks, and my body tingles under his observation. This feels so right, so natural. Everything I've ever wanted is coming to life, and it only took one shitty hotel room to make it happen.

Who would have guessed?

The crowd is massive. Which makes sense, this is the first eligible Grand Prix show of the year. Everyone wants to get an early start in hopes of expediting their qualifications. Our seats are close enough to see without issue, one small perk of being Bridget's trainer. The first few competitors run their routines well. Generally speaking, their scores are decent, ranging in the mid-seventies. The front-runner is sitting and a staggering eighty-two point nine-one percent.

And then Bridget is announced.

My stomach nearly hits the floor as she wobbles slightly upon entering the arena. To her credit, she has enough awareness to correct her posture and let Champ move more fluidly than I've ever seen. Still, it's not great. If she were any other rider, she would likely be disqualified. Pedigree and pocket lining can only get you so far. Acid churns in my gut as she sloppily maneuvers through the routine—slightly off-beat, missing cues more often than not. Grady shakes his head as she fudges a basic transition before the final piaffe.

As the music comes to a stop, she beams an overly confident smile at the single local judge.

Great, that's her buffer.

Statistically, one judge can only do so much. Shockingly, her final score is a fifty-one point two-five percent. Not enough to count toward her qualification, but better than I expected. She scowls at the panel, huffing as she leaves the arena.

"That was only a mild train wreck. I can't wait to get my ass handed to me by Henrietta," I whisper to Grady.

He takes my hand, squeezing gently. It's a welcome reminder that I'm not alone in my struggles. I'm so lost in the companionable silence that I nearly miss the announcer introducing Leah and Tally.

The first notes start as they enter the arena. Fierce determination is plastered on Leah's face. Tally bobs her head, showing off as she likes to do.

"I'll be damned. They're fucking *ready* for this," I say on a breath.

"Perfect," Grady agrees, without a trace of his stutter to be heard.

I squeeze his hand harder, holding the air in my lungs hostage as they march out the routine. The crowd is equally enamored, bearing witness to such a spectacle at the hands of an unknown team. Pride inflates my chest further each time Tally's hooves land in perfect rhythm. They're so in sync it's unreal, feeding off of one another to drift almost weightlessly from marker to marker.

As the orchestral rendition of her 90s medley ends, Leah contains her emotions—face impassive as she nods to the judges. The only one who matters today is the man from Italy. All the rest are American. She needs two scores of at least sixty-seven percent from two international judges to qualify. If he gives her that today—and after such a clean run, he'd better—she's halfway there, at least on that aspect.

As the final scores pop up, I watch her chest rise, filling with air as she gasps.

"Eighty-one point five-two percent, Hulk! Holy shit! She's a fucking rock star!" I wrap my arm around him and clap him on the back. "That's the second-highest score of the day so far!"

He smiles wide, eyes crinkling at the corners.

This is going to work.

My palms itch, eager for the moment we get to congratulate her. She's got to be on cloud nine. I can't wait to kiss her. The last few pairs run their routines, and the finals are in for the whole show. Leah and Tally take third overall, only bested by last year's World Cup champions and one other well-known pair.

Grady and I shove our way through the dispersing crowd to find her at the stables. She's in the stall, rubbing Tally down as we arrive. I nearly crush her with a bear hug from behind, and Grady immediately gets to work taking her place as she squeals.

"You did so fucking amazing, Star. God, it was a beautiful sight," I mumble against her hair.

She chuckles and swats at me. "Put me down. I'm too heavy, you'll hurt yourself."

Grady turns to her with a single brow arched, arms folded as his gaze rakes over her body.

"What? You can't lie. You've seen me naked now. There's more than a few extra pounds hiding back here." She slaps herself on the ass, laughing a bit too loudly.

"It's just more for us to grab onto. Besides, you're not heavy. Hell, Hulk could probably lift you with one arm," I tease.

She huffs, smile falling into a frown. "We all know last night shouldn't have happened." Her attention darts to the ground.

Grady's jaw works, biting back the sting of her words. I meet his eyes over her head and send him a silent message. Asking him to hold on, to not give up on this. She's as confused and conflicted as we are.

"Let's get Tally taken care of, and then the three of us will go back to the hotel, order a ridiculous amount of junk food, and talk."

She curls her lower lip between her teeth. After a moment, she meets my gaze. "Talk about?"

"Us, our plan... our future. Don't freak out about it, okay? You did great today and deserve to celebrate. I only hope the things we discuss tonight will boost your morale. For now, let's take care of the *real* star." I nudge her, and she flashes a bright smile at Tally.

Grady already has her fairly situated. The last few bits of her mane are still neatly braided, so we work together to undo them and comb out the long black curls. A few peppermints later, and she's as content as possible.

Back to the hotel. For better or worse.

Sixteen

Leah

Parker walks in the door with armfuls of takeout bags, plastic nearly bursting at the seams with a variety of Chinese food. I love a good celebratory feast, but the looming 'talk' has soured my stomach. Still, I portion out a plate of fried rice, vegetable dumplings, and delicious-smelling sesame chicken.

When we're all settled into our spots on the bed, Parker clears his throat, wasting no time getting down to business. Normally, his discipline and structure are appreciated, but at the moment, I wish he would take a minute to breathe and forget about the task at hand.

Despite how well I do under pressure in competition, *this* type of pressure is my personal Hell. I don't like *talking*, not when there's uncertainty hidden under the surface, thinly concealed until the words start coming out.

Sitting stiff as a board at the foot of the bed, I prod a chunk of chicken with a chopstick. Grady is leaning against the headboard, more frazzled than expected. Whatever this conversation is, it's going to be big for him, too. Crazy as it may sound, his nerves help to calm mine. Parker is the only one who doesn't appear particularly bothered, but there's still a hint of worry on his stupidly handsome face. One that says he's not sure how this will go, but the outcome matters a lot to him.

"Well," I speak up, shattering the silence.

With a heavy exhale, Parker looks between us. "Listen, I'll air my laundry out first, then Grady will go... or well, I'll explain for him. Then it's your turn. We know you're not who you claim to be, but we're not entirely sure how you got here. For now, let's get to our parts."

Sweat beads on my brow, a vice clamps around my throat. Sure, he's told me—and dropped plenty of hints—that they know something is fishy about me. Up to this point, I've just brushed it off, decided they were toying with me, and had no *real* idea. But his tone, the tension in his shoulders as he sits across from me, he knows. God, he *actually* knows.

How am I going to play this? Can I really trust them? What if they plan on using me to get ahead and then leave me high and dry?

Life is full of shitty people. I'd like to think they're not among them, but they did sleep with me while knowing the truth...

No, don't think like that. They deserve a chance to talk, to prove they're not assholes looking for an easy lay.

Sitting up straight, I raise my chin. "Well," I repeat.

Grady looks at Parker, warm eyes clouded by a distant emotion, and nods. His jaw works side to side as Parker begins, "As you know, I have a plan, and that plan involves you."

I nod, face expressionless.

"Well, the plan was... never to be *here*." He motions between the three of us. "I, uh." Swallowing harshly, he takes Grady's hand and squeezes. "I have had feelings for Grady for months. I-I'm bisexual, and honestly didn't imagine my future with anyone other than him. But, along the way, I realized that maybe a piece of the puzzle has been missing."

"So... You two have been in a relationship this whole time? Is that why Grady hates me?" I twist my face.

"No, he doesn't hate you. There was a time in the barn, the first time you stood up to Bridget, when he almost kissed you." Parker's gaze bounces between us, and Grady's eyes lock onto mine.

I inhale a sharp breath. "So I wasn't imagining it?"

"No, and when he told me about it... I... I got jealous. Okay? Months of secret pining almost slipped out of my grasp, as if I had any right to stop him from kissing you. But I was also worried that you two would start something that had no business happening. Not until Grady was ready to tell you his story. The two of us, until you, were never more than friends." Parker shifts awkwardly, like a man on trial.

"So, you've never kissed or anything before last night?"

Grady shakes his head, shoulders shrugging as if he isn't quite sure why. The thought almost makes me giggle.

"We never talked about the mutual attraction. Grady is also very sheltered. I didn't want to overwhelm him. Which brings us to part two of our confessions." Parker pats Grady on the thigh, eyes soft as he asks, "Would you like to tell her?"

With a pained expression, Grady closes his eyes and inhales through his nose before directing his full attention to me. "M-m-my last n-n-n-n—" Leaning his head back against the headboard, he blows out a frustrated breath.

"You don't have to tell me, Parker can do it."

He shakes his head. "My l-last n-n-n-name i-i-i-is" Clenching the blankets in his fists, he forces out, "Hart."

Everything stops—time, my heart, the world stands still. I don't know what I expected to cross his lips, but "Hart" was nowhere near the top of the list.

The vice around my throat tightens as my muscles try their hardest to move, aching to take me away from this train wreck. The rest of me is too stunned to think. Am I angry? Confused? Absolutely flabbergasted? Pinpointing a specific emotion is impossible as everything unravels around me.

"Hart," I whisper, more of a question than a statement.

"Yes, but please let us explain." Parker starts to reach for me, then second-guesses himself.

"*Please* do!" I fire back, having settled on outrage as my emotion of choice. "What is this? Some sick game? Get the nobody to fall for Henrietta's son *and* upcoming star trainer so she can milk me for more?! There was never a real plan to escape Hartbrook at all, was there? You just needed me to trust you while I secured your futures!" I flail my arms, knocking my plate to the floor. Rice and dumplings scatter, and for once, I don't give a shit about the mess. I'm wrapped up in a far bigger one at the moment.

Grady leans forward, placing his hand on my foot, eyes crinkled and mouth slightly open. A stray tear trails down his cheek before disappearing into his beard. Somehow, the sight calms a bit of my furious rage. Like the minuscule little droplet could douse a blazing inferno.

"Did it feel good, getting all of that out?" Parker asks, voice timid.

"Yes, actually. Just enough to give you the chance to explain. But this had *better* be good." I pull my foot out from under Grady's touch and stand. Hugging myself, I pray that my knees hold through whatever I'm about to learn.

"It's true, Grady *is* Henrietta's son." Parker takes a second, giving me a chance to process and retort. Met with silence, he continues, "The whole family treats him like shit. That's why they make him live in the stables, which is why he secretly stays with me."

"*Live* in the stables?! I knew the supply closet was like, a hide-out or something, but—"

"That's his home," Parker says, tone laced with clear resentment. "Until I was hired, he slept in that fucking shoebox every day, nobody even fucking checked on him, except to bring him food."

"Why? Why would they do such a thing?"

"He's not *perfect* like the rest of them. Years of speech therapy, a lifetime of bullying at the hands of his own flesh and blood. When he turned eighteen, they finally gave up on him. He was exiled, sent to tend to the unused cabins and land, far away from the actual training facilities. He has no real-life experience, no assets, no identity beyond the property and the local town. I-I just want to get him out so he can *live,* damn it!" Voice breaking, Parker rakes his fingers through his hair.

Grady rubs his back, doing the only thing he can think of to help calm him.

Slowly, I sink back onto the bed, closer to them than before. "So... your plan—"

"Was never actually about me or my training goals." He sniffles, wiping his face. "They have us all in the unused part of Hartbrook for a reason. We're nothing, all three of us. They don't give a shit what happens. I was hired on the cheap for Bridget to fawn over. They plan on giving me credit for training whoever does well this year, falsifying my capabilities so my credentials look good on paper."

"But you're a great trainer, they wouldn't have to lie if they'd just let you *actually* train! What about Warren and Quincy?"

Parker scoffs. "You mean the fucking Hart cousins?"

My heart plummets to the ground. "What?"

"Th-they're my aunt's s-s-sons," Grady confirms, throwing my world further off its axis.

My palms get dewy, stomach tumbling inside of me. So many secrets, and for what? Hartbrook is apparently built on lies.

"What the hell is going on around here?!" I shriek.

"They probably heard you're hot, and wanted to try and hook up with you. I should have said something before, but I didn't know how, not without having this whole conversation before we were ready. They're sticking around, which is weird. Time will tell what they're really up to."

"Gross, just my type." I sneer, scrunching my brows together. "They did come on strong, which usually works to be fair. I enjoy sex, and I like attractive men. Can you blame a girl?" I shrug, turning to Grady. "So then that's why last night was your first... everything?" This poor man. How could anyone be so cruel?

Flushing, he nods. Parker chuckles softly, kissing his cheek. The sight does something to me, something I think I like.

"I'm sorry that we didn't tell you all of this sooner. We should have never slept with you before." Parker's eyes scan my face, surely searching for any traces of remaining anger.

"I understand, truthfully. It's not like any of us could have predicted this situation. Grady didn't want me to know until he could trust me, I can't fault him for that." I gently place my hand on his knee, insides warming as his eyes soften. "You've been treated so badly by everyone, you learned to protect yourself by keeping people at arm's length, but that ends today, okay?"

Gaze dancing across my face, Grady's chest heaves, working to contain a storm of emotions. Brows knitting together, he turns to Parker, who nods with a faint smile. As he shifts his focus back to me, he leans forward and frames my face with his huge, strong hands.

When he tentatively brings our mouths together, I fall into him. His lips part, silently requesting more. He brushes the calloused tips of his thumbs over my cheeks, comforting in a way only he could pull off. I relax into his touch, fully at his mercy, opening for him. His tongue slowly explores my own, and I'm gone, flying, never coming down.

Whatever he wants in this moment, he can have.

This gentle, tortured soul could crush my skull in his palms, and I'd smile as he did it. Thinking about him growing up unloved and lonely—locked away for being anything less than perfect—destroys me. The years of hate he's endured can't be undone, but I'll be damned if he spends another waking moment without knowing compassion and acceptance.

My own problems can wait. I'll process this new reality after the shock wears off. Right now, all that matters is Grady.

"Fuck." Parker groans, the sound dangerously close to a moan. "Okay, okay. We're going to get carried away."

Grady pulls his lips from mine. His blissful expression fills my heart with flutters. Knowing I'm one of the only people to make him feel any sense of peace fills me with infinite pride.

"Do you have any more questions... or anger you need to let out?" Parker pins me with a tense look.

I lower my head and sigh. "No, and I guess it's my turn now, huh?" I mumble to my lap.

"It would be nice to know who we're allying ourselves with."

"Is that all we're doing?" I snap.

"Uh, well." Parker rubs the back of his neck, looking at Grady—still flushed with a soft smile pulling at his kiss-stung lips. "How about we get everything out in the open first, then we'll worry about what this is."

"Guess I can't argue with that logic," I agree. "So then, to save time, tell me what you *do* know, and I'll fill in the gaps."

"We know you're not some pedigreed rider, so does Henrietta. You also didn't go to the World Cup last year... I mean, that *was* a pretty far-fetched lie, after all." He chuckles.

"Hey! People told me she doesn't actually follow the sport anymore. I thought the Photoshop would sell it," I argue my case, though it's obviously a lost cause.

"Riiiight. Grady and I had a good laugh over it the day you got here." He simpers.

"You assholes!" I half-joke, heat creeping up my neck. "Anyway, forget that, okay? Continue."

"Aside from that, we don't know a whole lot. We researched you when Henrietta first told me I had an actual trainee. It was apparent from the beginning that you have *some* training and a natural affinity. But what I *really* want to know is how some unheard-of rider bought her way into Hartbrook. Sure, the old bag is greedy, but Jesus, the zeros on that check must have been longer than a phone number." His eyes widen, brows lifted to his hairline.

Grady, having finally returned to the real world, mirrors his expression.

"I… agreed to pay triple," I admit, so quiet it's barely audible.

"Triple!" Parker jolts. "That's—" He pauses for a moment, calculating. "Leah, that's almost two hundred and fifty *thousand* dollars for the year!"

The two of them go stark white, frozen in place as the weight of my truth settles around us.

"Are you a bank robber or something? Holy shit. How?" Parker continues to ramble, voice trembling. "Are you a fucking con artist? Was it an inheritance or something? Please tell me that money is legal."

Grady squeezes Parker's thigh, helping rein in his spiraling thoughts.

Even mid-freakout, he never tries to leave, doesn't storm off. They need this, and need to know I want this, too. Fear of betrayal be damned, my mind is already made up, I'm going to change our lives. For now, we need Hartbrook, but once this is all said and done, I'm going wherever they go.

All I have to do is tell the truth.

All I have to do is let them in.

All I have to do is trust them not to hurt me.

Seventeen

Parker

Leah might pass out before she speaks. As if we didn't just divulge our deepest secrets. Somehow, in her mind, hers is bigger, scarier, more monumental. Judging by how pale and clammy she is, her worries may be warranted. One thing's for certain, whatever she says, I'm in this. Unless there's a deadly ancient family curse or something. Hell, at that point, I'll accept my fate if it means we all get to die happy.

Shit, maybe I'm getting ahead of myself. Maybe she's about to wreck us.

I inhale, holding for a second before I let out the heaviest breath of my life. Waiting for her to finish psyching herself up is torture.

"Y-you can t-tell us," Grady says with a tenderness that makes my heart ache.

She pulls that beautifully kissable lower lip between her teeth and sighs. "I-It's not that I don't think I can. I just have... history."

"Why?" He takes her hand.

Fuck, he's got it just as bad as I do. The way his brows are pulled together, the fact that he's *talking*. If she hurts him, I don't know if he'll survive. Her eyes glimmer as they meet Grady's, drifting to me.

I offer the most tender smile I can muster. "Whatever it is, we're here. Even if it means a life on the run." My half-hearted chuckle falls flat.

She shakes her head. "It's nothing dangerous or anything like that. It's just... scary for me." Her chest deflates as she lets out a hefty sigh. "I... I won the lottery back home in Mississippi."

I blink rapidly, lips pursed. "That's it? No bank robbing, no mafia, no life or death family curses?"

"What?!"

"Oh, we were just expecting something bad. That's all. A lottery is nothing. Unless you have a gambling addiction or something? Do you need support to stay straight?" Damn it, I'm rambling, but there has to be a catch for her to be so terrified of us finding out.

"No," she shuts down my absurd line of questioning. "It's just terrifying, okay? I've been a multi-millionaire in private for three years now. Aside from buying Tally and getting some training, I mainly helped my family financially—paying off houses and vehicles, buying new clothes, the simple stuff. I'm not a flashy person and don't want to attract that type of man. The ones I have been with since, well, they've all changed their tune as soon as they found out about my money. I-I don't want that with you. Either of you." Voice somber, eyes pooling with waiting tears, she sniffles and looks between us.

Fuck. If she cries, I'll join her.

I clear my throat, fingers fidgeting in the blankets. "Nothing will change, I promise. Well, Grady will stop avoiding you, but that's about it. We're not here for your money, no matter how much there is. We both had figured out you were definitely *not* poor, but that has nothing to do with our attraction to you. You're more than your money." I take her hand and look into her damp eyes.

As her chin wobbles, my heart breaks. Someone hurt her, and she doesn't need to explain that to me. When reluctant tears begin to fall, Grady surprises both of us by pulling her into his lap. She straddles him, sobbing freely into his shoulder.

"I've been so afraid to fall for either of you. I-I didn't know anything about you, and then l-last night happened, and it was... special. I shouldn't h-have." Her body shakes as she lets out all of her troubles.

Unable to resist, I slide next to them, rubbing her back. "*You're* special, we're lucky to share your air. Grady has been avoiding you because he wants nothing more than what you're giving him right now. The same goes for me, but I haven't had the opportunity to distance myself from you. I've been so fucking miserable having you *right there* within arm's reach every day. And your fucking cooking has not helped."

Sobs slowing, she rests her cheek on Grady's shoulder, nose red and puffy. As I brush tear-soaked hair out of her eyes, the hum that leaves her settles in my chest like a brick. Such a shame, this woman takes care of everyone else, but I'm getting the impression nobody ever looks out for her.

That changes now.

Giving her an easy smile, I continue, "Don't get me wrong, I'm not complaining about the amazing food or spending time with you, but it makes me want that every day. Every goddamned day, Leah. All of it. You, me, Grady, it just feels right. So *fucking* right. Your crooked little smile, the way your nose crinkles when you're being sassy, how you bounce on your toes when you're excited. You're the brightest part of this whole fucking place. If you spent every last dime you had to be here and were homeless, I'd smuggle you into my cabin, too." Words keep rushing out of my mouth as she stares, breathless and shaken.

Oh no, I've scared her off for sure.

"P-Parker." Her teeth chatter as she fights to calm herself.

Grady readjusts, kissing her reddened cheek. "Y-you're s-so much m-m-more than m-m-m-money. Perfect."

She shrugs, wiping her face. "I'm not perfect. I'm just me."

"Same th-thing." A softness never before seen fills his face.

My hand glides down her arm. "Don't you see how spectacular you are? This little spitfire of a woman, standing up to Bridget Hart on behalf of a man who avoids you. And now? He's literally said more words to you than I've ever heard. So, don't think for a second that you mean nothing. It's been crazy for the last several weeks, and I know that's not a long time, but when you meet the right people, your souls recognize each other." I softly press my lips to hers, tasting the saltiness of her tears and the rightness of us.

Grady is there as I pull away, claiming a tender kiss for himself, driving home the fact that she's not alone. We're not her past, but damn sure want to be her future.

Once they part, I take his jaw in my hand, bringing our mouths together. It's chaste, but the message is clear, and by the look on Leah's face, she understands. This is about *us* as a whole. Not me and her, nor her and Grady, or us without her. No. We're all or nothing.

The lingering questions hiding under her micro-expressions have been answered. With that, she relaxes, stretching out across our laps. Sighing, content, she nuzzles into Grady's chest. My fingers find her calves, kneading tender knots.

"How long do we have this hotel room? I don't want to go back to that stuffy cabin any time soon." She hisses as I massage a particularly tense spot.

"We have until tomorrow morning to check out. In the meantime, we can enjoy all this food." I pick up my long-forgotten plate, swirling cold lo mein around my fork.

"Oh, I forgot!" She shoots up and practically leaps off the bed. "I made a huge mess, oh gosh." Scooping rice and chicken off the floor, she wipes frantically with a napkin. "Do you think they're going to charge us for carpet cleaning?"

She's so frazzled, it's unironically the most adorable thing I've ever witnessed. Grady is holding back a smirk next to me, clearly equally entertained.

"They won't even notice, it's nothing a vacuum won't take care of. Come back to bed," I plead, with a hint of humor slipping through.

She throws the food away, slipping into the bathroom to wash her hands. The five-minute break was apparently sobering. Standing next to the bed, she swallows hard.

Smoke nearly billows out of her ears while she processes her situation, *our* situation. "Have you two been this hot all along? You're just *sitting there* like some sort of statuesque Gods. So unfair. I have belly rolls, and my thighs eat shorts for a living."

Grady's gaze falls to said thighs, eyes flaring with appreciation. A small lift of his brows says more than words ever could.

With a smirk, I motion for her to sit. "Do you think we give a shit about your tummy rolls?" I ask as she crawls between us.

"Well, no, I guess not."

"You've never once acted insecure around either of us. Why now?" I get her settled, head in my lap, and Grady lays her legs across his.

"Well, gee, I don't know. Until last night, I didn't think either of you wanted to fuck me," she fires back, voice elevated but not overtly angry. Deflection at its finest.

Grady titters, trailing his hand up to her hip. "Sassy."

"I'm just processing. Are we literally doing this?" She scrunches her brows, looking up at me.

"That's the plan. If you're not on board, speak now." I run my fingers through her hair while Grady's fingertips glide down the outside of her thigh.

"I... of course I am."

"You sure about that?" I ask, tilting my head.

"Yes. But what does that look like? I mean, are you two going to be a thing, too?"

"Well, I did give Grady head this morning after you left."

She gasps, face filled with giddy shock. "That's so hot! I can't believe I missed it! I've always wanted boyfriends who are boyfriends. It's the dream."

"Well, that's settled then, but there are some other things we need to talk about. Ground rules, if you will. We can't go parading around Hartbrook putting our business on display. It would not end well." I look to Grady and try to hide my sadness.

His whole life, forced to hide his imperfections, and now that he has something exciting and positive, he has to hide that, too.

"If news gets back to Henrietta, she'll probably lock Grady away somewhere, or kick you out. The same goes for Bridget. She still needs to think I'm *hers* to fawn all over. And then there's the cousins... They're lingering. I don't trust it."

Leah stiffens. "You're not going to humor Bridget's obsession, are you? Why can't you tell her to eat shit?"

My words clearly hit a nerve, but she needs to hear them. They both do.

"It's not that simple. I only have a job there because Bridget wants me. Henrietta doesn't give a shit about me, or my progressive training styles."

"Which are freaking genius, by the way," she speaks up with a half-smile. "Did you *see* us out there today? I couldn't have done it if not for you."

Grady nods in agreement, hands moving to her calves.

"God, that feels good. You have bear paws, and they're like heating pads." She lets a soft moan out, one of pure bliss.

"Back on track." I scratch gently at her scalp. She closes her eyes and hums. "For the time being, until we're in a position to get out of Hartbrook, we have to be discreet. One slip-up, and everything comes crashing down. And we can't just pack up and leave, there's nowhere for us to go."

"What could she possibly do to keep Grady away? She's not a warden, he's not her prisoner."

"No, but without her financial support, he's screwed. And neither of us could help, or we'd also be tossed out. It's a shitty situation all around, but if we're careful and patient, it'll all be worth it once you qualify. Then we can worry about where we settle."

"Qu-qualify?" Grady asks, the meaning behind his question abundantly clear.

The disappointment in his face, how much it's going to hurt him to keep this secret, screams through his silence. Who could blame him? It's a long time to be with someone and not actually be able to express it, at least not in public. I've had secret girlfriends in the past. They never last more than a month or two because it *is* hard. But this one? I want to last forever, so if six to twelve months of secrecy is the cost, so be it.

"We can still get together at my cabin, and we can still go on lunch dates at Carrie's, we just have to be discreet. No affection in the open, keep the 'fuck me' eyes under lock and key, it's not that hard. A lot of our alone time is in private anyway, and Carrie's is a hole-in-the-wall. We sit at the far booth anyway. It won't be much different than before." Even as I say the words, I know they're bullshit.

It's not the same, it'll never be that way again, especially for the smitten man at my side. His face doesn't lie, he's head over heels for both of us. His free hand has found its way around my back, and he pulls me close. Leah shifts slightly as I lean, and before I know it, Grady has pulled my mouth to his.

We share a soft, but possessive kiss, tongues tangling as his chest rumbles—the message unmistakable. He doesn't care about discretion, he wants to be free, which simply cannot happen right now. There's no time to find a place for all of us to go *and* see Leah's Olympic qualification through. No amount of money could make a brand new facility appear overnight.

We separate and I'm breathless, leaning my cheek against his shoulder.

"I'm not sure the cousins are that bad." Leah chews her lip, ruining my basking. "They're hiding something, though. That much I agree with."

I scoff. "We'll see. As long as they keep their mouths shut."

"They did apologize. It seems to be genuine, all things considered. I don't think they're an immediate threat."

Grady shrugs like he is unbothered, and I suppose that is enough for me.

I lean back into the pillows and sigh. “Fine, but we should still keep our distance. I know you’ve enjoyed hanging out with them, and I’m not going to be a dick and tell you to stop. Just, please be careful going forward.”

“Okay,” she says around a yawn, repositioning to curl against Grady.

This is doomed to fail, probably sooner rather than later. But in the meantime, my heart is full.

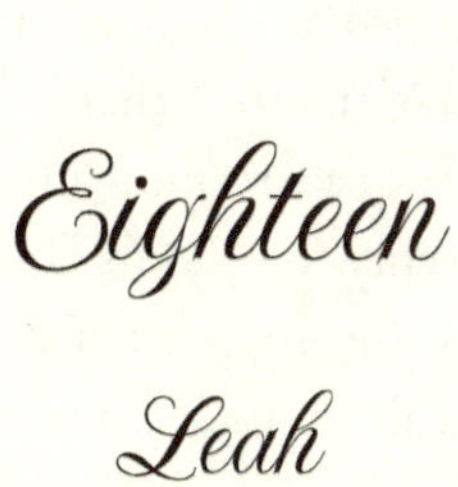

Eighteen

Leah

Pulling up to our—apparently private—part of Hartbrook feels tainted. It's been a ghost town here because we're all just written off in one way or another. I'm used to being a misfit, but the way Parker's eyes glaze over when he talks about it is heartbreaking. Grady is seemingly indifferent, but given his history, seclusion is probably a vacation for him.

They've been living with this the whole time. How sad. No wonder they both appreciate my breakfasts and random check-ins. It makes me want to dig deeper with Warren and Quincy, but Parker's warnings are valid. If they're related to Henrietta, they're probably shady… I'm going to have to play it off when I see them.

I won't risk losing this.

Weeks of hot-and-cold interactions, Grady nearly running away from me any chance he gets, yearning looks betraying his rigid body language. These feelings have been anxiously waiting to break free. I chose to ignore every sign, convinced myself it was all in my head. Now that I have it, I'll do everything in my power to protect it.

The instant we stepped foot in that hotel room, I knew *something* would happen. Man, am I thankful the outcome was a steamy threesome and not a screaming match.

Even now, over twenty-four hours later, my body aches, but I want to do it again. I'm not sure if it's because they're the only men I've been around, aside from the cousins, or because they're somehow different. But sleeping with Parker and Grady was world-altering, and I need more.

Grady's gentle, wonder-filled expression flashes into my mind. The way his eyes widened ever so slightly as I took him was beautiful. No man has ever made me feel like a gift the way he did in that moment. I want him to treat me like a cherished possession over and over again.

Parker—calm, commanding, and reassuring the whole time. Maybe I'm just conditioned to listen to him, but I love his direction and steady praise. Nobody has taken charge in the bedroom like he does. It's hot as Hell.

Okay, Leah, it was just sex. Don't get clingy.

Sure, we talked about making this "official" and laid out ground rules. But it's still terrifying.

They work together to show me true euphoria one time, and I'm hooked. Pathetic. They can't just *do* this; put me under their spell. I have *free will,* dammit. I need to think this through. I can't give in like this. I won't.

Until Grady opens the door of my truck and extends a hand to me, until I take it, and let him help me out as if I *need* it. Wrapping his Neanderthal-sized arm around my waist, he doesn't hesitate to pull me against his chest, staring into my eyes.

Shit.

Pull away.

Nope, can't do that.

Not when his gaze falls to my mouth, begging to steal a kiss.

Not when my stomach flips at the vibrant adoration on Parker's face.

Oh, I'm in trouble. I've never been good at denying myself the things I enjoy. And boy, do I *thoroughly* enjoy the way Grady's breath hitches as I step up onto my toes and press my lips to his—like he doesn't believe I still want him. Fingers gripping my waist, he leans down and deepens our connection, chest vibrating as his lungs struggle for air.

Parker chuckles next to us. "You can breathe. She couldn't escape your grasp if she wanted to. But you wouldn't try anyway, would you, Star?"

Nipping at Grady's lower lip as we part, I pant, struggling to find my own supply of oxygen. "I'm not going anywhere."

Well, shit.

Parker could do casual, I'm sure of it. But the grizzly bear with stars in his eyes, smiling down at me? Hell no.

I'm not a monster. How could I ever break this already shattered soul?

This is bad. I'm not good at relationships. Sure, at the surface level, I could be. Spending time with people, taking care of loved ones, and enjoying snuggles at the end of a long day are all things that make for a great relationship and bring me immense joy.

But the deep, ugly truth is that I'm temporary. Something about me loses its appeal after a while. So, I usually enjoy a good time while it lasts, then sever the ties before things get serious.

It protects me.

But this risk? It might just be worth everything.

"Give him a little more, then come here," Parker says in soft command.

Even if I wanted to protest, my body wouldn't listen. Apparently, eager eyes and plump, waiting lips are all the motivation needed for it to betray me. With absolutely no input from my brain, I'm melting into Grady's lips once again, humming as his hands travel slowly down my sides. His actions are less uncertain with each kiss, and I'm living for it.

Parker takes him firmly by the hair, staring hungrily into his eyes. Like topaz and diamond, they twinkle and reflect sparks at one another.

"My turn, but first, you're mine." He gives Grady a quick, heated kiss, growling softly against his lips. Before they get carried away, he turns to me. "He's going to get Tally settled, we're going to get these vehicles unloaded, and then—" His lips claim mine, searing hot. I nearly moan as he grips my jaw. "—we're going to meet in my cabin. There are conversations we need to have, and things we all need to consider."

Lady boner gone, vanished without a trace.

Grady adjusts himself and nods, placing a soft kiss on each of our cheeks before unlatching the trailer. Tally whinnies, excited to be free of her temporary prison.

Parker lets out a faint laugh, shaking his head. "She'll never change, silly girl."

A tender smile pulls at my lips. "Never. I wouldn't want her to."

"Same here. She's a great horse," he murmurs, leaning in until his words are whispers against my skin.

"I guess I know how to pick em," I tease as best as I can with my knees threatening to give out.

"Hmm. Do you now?" His voice drops, velvety and rich.

"I'd like to think so." I swallow hard as he wraps his hand around my throat with gentle pressure and pins me against the side of my truck, lips crashing together.

In total contrast to his words, this kiss is demanding, hungry, filled with a searing want for more. More than sex, more than us, more than just a fling. He presses against me, and I gasp, met with untamed heat in his eyes as I pull back. Scanning my face, he takes in every freckle as my cheeks flush red-hot.

I've never felt so exposed, so vulnerable, so seen all at once. The way his pupils dilate, how the tension he carries in his jaw loosens. Whatever he finds in my expression gives him the exact information he's looking for. His grip on my throat remains steady, and he revels in *me*. Like I'm the answer to questions he didn't know he had.

Blinking away his trance, he softly clears his throat and releases me. "We, uh. We need to get unpacked. Meet at my cabin in thirty." With a final chaste kiss, he nods and gets in his car, leaving me with all sorts of whiplash.

Grady walks by, leading a very excited Tally. She bobs her head and nickers softly as they approach the pasture gate. My girl loves a good turnout, and after the score we strutted away with yesterday, she's earned it.

"I'll close the trailer up and see you at the cabin," I announce.

He nods with an easy grin, no trace of awkwardness anywhere to be found.

Traitorous stomach flutters return every time he does that. After so long seeing nothing but scowls from him, the tiny dimples hiding behind his beard, and the slightly jagged tooth on his top left side, are endearing and infinitely attractive. It also helps that he smells good. Surprisingly so for someone who literally lives in the stables.

Well, I guess he lives with Parker and only pretends to live in the stables. Either way, his citrusy clean scent is intoxicating.

Parker smells expensive—amber, vanilla, a hint of oak. I'm no stranger to men's cologne, and it's definitely not any of the cheap ones my brothers wear. He's damn near edible.

I really am monumentally screwed.

I drag myself through the front door of my cabin, leaning against it as I step inside. Two days away, and it still doesn't feel like coming home. My things are here, but it's empty, quiet, unnaturally devoid of the chaos I'm used to.

Tears sting my eyes, fighting to break free, but I won't let them. It's ironic, before coming here, I would hardly ever cry. For babies and surprises, maybe, but I prefer to fight or fuck out my emotions. Sure, it's self-destructive, but so are drugs, so it could always be worse. Now I'm constantly fighting emotions that I've ignored until now, things I've never allowed myself to feel. It's scary, in an oddly exciting way.

I roll my suitcase to the bedroom. Unceremoniously plopping it onto the bed, I pull the zipper and it springs open from the amount of clothes inside.

Why did I pack like I was never coming back?

Maybe because part of me was hoping I wouldn't.

Is it a bit melodramatic to secretly wish for failure? Maybe, but what's a girl to do? This place seriously sucks, and I feel trapped. Would it be unreasonable to leave and give up? Ugh, of course it is. I'm not a quitter. In no world do I have plans of returning home, tail tucked, to give my family the gratification of being right. Hell no.

Staying is infinitely more appealing with the new development, but it's also far more terrifying. So much more is on the line now. I don't truthfully know what *I* want, but I have approximately fifteen minutes to figure it out.

No pressure or anything.

Normally, I'd take my time to make a major decision, laying out a careful breakdown of pros and cons. But I won't be afforded that opportunity. This could get very ugly, and I may break a heart or two—maybe even my own. The thought of keeping two men interested beyond the honeymoon phase terrifies me, and I don't *get* scared. Confidence is my middle name, at least it should be.

The fact that I'm this worked up is unsettling. If I could ghost them, it wouldn't be so bad. But ghosting them means also abandoning my dreams and taking this opportunity for granted. I may not like Hartbrook, but I need it. There's nowhere else I can go, I've tried. Now I have two extra bodies to accommodate.

Stupid. Just plain idiotic.

I've come too far, done too much, *proven* myself deserving of this. No way in hell I throw out the chance to make something of myself.

God, why didn't I sleep in my truck instead of sharing that bed?

Because part of you secretly wanted it.

Groaning loudly, I stomp from my bedroom to the bathroom to take a quick shower. There's no time to blow-dry my hair or bother with vanity, so some grungy sweats and a tank top are what they'll get. Maybe it'll turn them off, and they'll realize I'm actually a huge mess under the fun exterior. It just might show them that I'm not the type of girl men settle down with, sparing me the stress of making this work.

But I *want* it to work.

I think.

I braid my hair, give myself a "you got this" nod in the mirror, and head for the front door. Only, I stop by the kitchen on my way out. A brand-new package of chocolate chip cookies stares back at me. Everyone loves a snack, right? Surely a little baked goodness will help lessen any blows tonight.

The early evening feels almost eerie as I approach the all-too-familiar cabin. A lump the size of Texas is indefinitely stuck in my throat.

What I wouldn't do for more time to figure myself out. Staying here is my only option. Quitting is off the table, that much I have decided in the past several minutes. What comes of this talk will determine how awkward my stay will be.

I can do this. And if they want to, I can put in the effort to make it work. They're good guys. Relationships don't have to be intimidating. Just gotta...

As I reach up to knock, the door swings open. What I'm met with steals my breath.

Well, shit, I wasn't prepared for *this*.

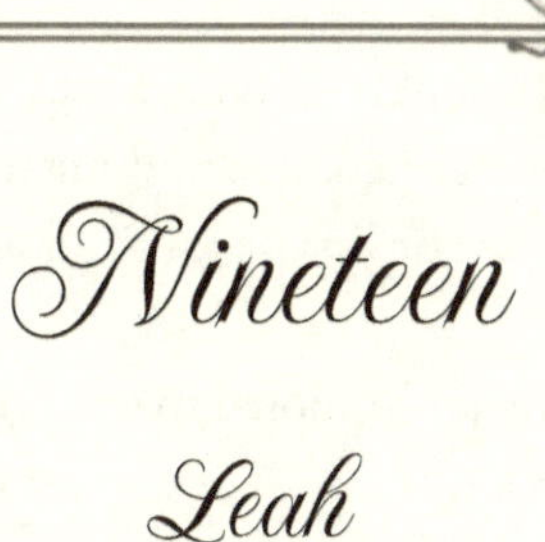

Nineteen

Leah

Unfair. It's heinous how attractive all of the bare *man* skin in front of me is. I have no doubt that Parker put Grady up to this. Somehow, some way, he read me like a book. All of my efforts to hide the reservations and doubt didn't fool him for a second, he merely played along.

They're not going to let me back out.

Slowly, greedily, my visual exploration leads me south, over the planes and valleys of their bodies. Matching loose-fitting sweats serve one clear purpose—to remind me exactly what I'd be walking away from. All of my rebuttals vanish.

Based on their matching smirks, they know it.

Assholes.

This "talk" is supposed to be productive. How am I going to focus on anything other than their bodies?

"Oh, I see you got the sweatpants memo," Parker jokes, as if he's oblivious to the quaking in my soul.

He's not. The shithead can't help himself.

Why must beautiful men be so infuriating?

"Y-yup," I manage to respond after being reduced to sounds just beyond squawks.

"Come on in, if you're ready, that is." They step apart and wait, as if I have anywhere else to go.

Of course I do. I could—should—tuck tail and run. My "no fucks given" appearance has done nothing to deter them. There's not a trace of disgust or disapproval on either of their smug, handsome faces.

Damn it, they're not supposed to want me like this.

I practically scream at myself as my feet move. Each step feels like a mile as I follow them inside, straight to Parker's couch. The same one we've shared several conversations on, but this time the air feels too heavy. Parker drops next to me, casual as ever. Instead of sitting on the other couch like normal, Grady takes the spot to my left, opposite Parker. Intentions clear as the sky is blue.

Enveloped in *them,* my heart skips every few beats, bouncing around erratically in my chest.

"Well?" I sit up straight, question coming out more defensive than intended.

"Well…?" Parker says to my right with a playfully smug inflection.

"You're the ones who want to talk." I raise a brow in challenge. "So, tell me. What's the goal here? Because I've had hookups and fuck buddies. None of them ever required a 'talk' or divulging my deepest secrets." Folding my arms, I look between them and have to do a double-take. They're each fighting a smile.

"What?!" I whine. "I'm serious. This feels like I've been called into the principal's office. I haaaaaaated school. Please just lay it out for me." Tossing myself back into the cushion, I groan, welcoming whatever happens next.

If it breaks my heart, I'll survive.

I hope.

"Leah." Parker places a hand on my thigh. I fight the urge to squeeze them together. "We want you. And I do mean *you,* not just your body. It's a fucking fantastic bonus, but your heart, your passion, that's what we're both drawn to. I'm sorry if our conversation in the hotel wasn't reassuring enough. We were all sort of winging it. But I could tell you still haven't accepted this. We're prepared to say, or do, whatever it takes."

I look at Grady, who nods with a shy smile. His hands are folded tightly in his lap as if he's afraid to touch me.

Shifting my focus back to Parker, I ask, "What about five years from now? When it's the same shit every day, when I've made breakfast every morning. Sure, maybe it's a *different* breakfast, but it's still the same repetitive day." I turn to Grady and continue, "What happens when we leave here and get into the real world, and you realize how absolutely *boring* I am? I do three things: sleep, eat, and ride." I pointedly count on my fingers. "Every. Day. Are you seriously telling me you'll want that forever?"

"I l-love th-th-ose things." By the look of surprise in Grady's eyes, his hand moving to my cheek was *not* planned. Warm and comforting, my nerves settle a fraction from his contact.

"I also only do two of those three things, just substitute riding with training," Parker murmurs close behind me, having apparently leaned in while Grady's touch had me in a chokehold.

"I-I don't know how to let you in. I'm not a good girlfriend. Trust me, I've tried."

The brush of Parker's nose against my ear sends tingles down my spine. "You've been great to us, and didn't even have the title. Those losers who saw you as a paycheck don't speak to your worth."

"I was just being me. I wasn't trying t—" My words die, fizzling out into the atmosphere as Parker's lips press against my neck. Grady, still cupping my cheek, claims a quick, timid kiss.

I want to protest, to tell them they're making a mistake.

That *I'm* a mistake.

But damn if their combined attention doesn't make for a solid argument.

"You're right," Parker says against my burning skin, leaving goosebumps where his breath lands. "You weren't trying because you don't have to. You're enough." Another press of his warm mouth makes my eyelids flutter.

"It's t-true." Grady nods and leans back in. Only, instead of my lips, his kiss lands intentionally on the tip of my nose, sparking an eruption of butterflies in the depths of my stomach.

His tenderness is effortlessly romantic. I don't think he fully grasps how much I love the little things he does. Maybe it's because he grew up surrounded by old money, where they have to put on a front to keep up appearances. But the small acts of affection and chivalry come naturally to him. It's a welcome newness for me. Such simple gestures make a world of difference.

Parker, on the other hand, is walking sexual tension, but not in the surface-level way I'm used to. Sure, he knows all the right spots and how to hit them with precision. But he's not rushing things. Nothing he does is to "get it over with" or make me feel like he cares while putting in minimal effort. There's genuine intent woven into his every move.

They're not using me.

No, I've seen how much passion and dedication both of these men have. It rivals my own. Between them like this, I genuinely feel like I matter beyond their pleasure. This is going to take some getting used to.

"This is just scary," I admit, voice straining around the confession.

"I understand. We didn't exactly ease you into this. Hell, it's a lot for Grady, too. But he's mainly excited by the chance to be loved. Right?" Parker looks around me.

Grady nods slowly, hand leaving my cheek to blaze a trail down my arm. Lacing our fingers together, he brings my palm up to rest on his bare chest. Under the weight of *everything,* I focus on the steady thump under my palm. "Yours," he says, lifting my hand to kiss it.

My panties damn near disintegrate.

"If you don't want us, we'll still have each other, but this—" Parker waves a finger around. "—is a dream come true. One I personally will never stop trying to maintain." A press of his lips to my bare shoulder, and I forget why I had reservations in the first place.

Silly me, so focused on my own doubts. They could quite literally be happy without my involvement. I'm here because it's what they want. *I'm* what they want—not a convenient lay, or an easy release. I'm a choice, conscious and intentional.

My muscles uncoil. Relief floods my aching body. Releasing a heavy sigh, I inhale deep and steady—the first unburdened breath since I walked in the door. "God, I've wanted you both since the day I got here." I clamp my lips shut, cursing my mouth for forming syllables. "That was another inside thought escaping. Ignore me."

"Nope." Parker nods to Grady and their arms slip under me.

I squeal as they work to settle me in Grady's lap. "Mine." He squeezes my hip, gaze drifting to Parker.

Their eyes lock, buzzing with obvious desire.

"Oh god, please kiss." More uncontrollable thoughts escape my mouth, voice breathy.

Parker's tongue trails across his lower lip. "Seems our girl knows what she likes." He runs his hand down Grady's bicep, leaning dangerously close. "Shall we give her what she wants?"

I'm increasingly aware of the rock-hard erection prodding me as Grady nods, lips already parted.

My heart pounds in my throat as every nerve comes to life. Before I know it, they're devouring one another, tongues delving deeply into each other's mouths, hands exploring bare skin. Their shared moans alone could almost get me off.

Grady's hips jerk, growing increasingly needy. My pussy throbs from the pressure, with a desperate need to feel them. It would be so easy to grind against him and come undone right now. But not yet.

I slide off Grady's lap without completely disturbing them. Still, they break their kiss and reposition. Grady leans back against the plush cushion. I drop to my knees before him, taking in his flushed appearance and lust-blown pupils. Parker shifts, kneeling beside me with a conspiratorial glint in his eye.

Oh, it's on.

I bite my lip, fighting the giddy grin attempting to consume my face. Together, we grab our respective sides of Grady's waistband, pulling his sweats down. Flaring nostrils and a heaving chest tell us that he's realized what's about to happen.

Parker locks gazes with me as he trails his tongue slowly up the side of Grady's shaft, moaning as he reaches the tip. I mirror his action eagerly, savoring the salty bead of precum waiting for me.

Our mouths meet, and we take a moment to consume one another with the faint taste of our man lingering between us.

"F-f—" Grady tries to speak, but gives up as Parker takes all of him at once, rumbling around his length.

Grady thrusts into his throat, gripping the cushions with a white-knuckle hold. The instant Parker pulls back, I happily take his place, gagging slightly on the sheer size of him.

Instinct kicks in and Grady's hand flies to the back of my head. He pulls my hair with delicious pressure, drawing a moan from my throat. The vibration makes him gasp, driving into me until my eyes roll back.

"Fuck, look what you do to him," Parker grits out. Through my tears, I watch as he slowly strokes his cock, hissing as he squeezes. "God keep fucking her face. Don't hold back. She wants it, don't you?"

I nod as much as I can, and Grady indulges, giving me a more solid thrust, pushing me to the limit. I dig my nails into the tree trunks he calls thighs, clenching my own together, absolutely dripping wet for them.

"Give it to her," Parker commands, pumping himself faster.

With a shuddering exhale, Grady obeys, thoroughly taking his pleasure from me. Each lift of his hips forces him deeper, until I fear there will be irreparable damage.

Good.

This man deserves a bit of reckless abandon for once.

Getting lost in his broken restraint is delicious.

Tears stain my cheeks, vision blurring as he continues to slam into me. Right as I begin to worry I may faint, Parker steps in and releases me from the onslaught I'm savoring.

When I whine in protest, he chuckles, lips pressing against my forehead. "Trust me, as much as I'd love to watch him throat fuck you until you pass out, I don't know if he's ready for that. Besides, I want to watch you ride him, can't do that if you're unconscious." Kissing my swollen lips, he helps me to my feet.

Grady, having regained some semblance of his self-control, helps position me over his glistening cock. "S-sorry," he breathes out, running a thumb along my lower lip. When I suck it into my mouth, he gasps, eyes flaring. Releasing it with a "pop" I lean into him, arching my back.

Parker has grabbed a chair from the kitchen and positioned himself behind me so I'm on full display.

"She was loving every minute, don't apologize for something she enjoys. Now, be a good boy and fill her up." Parker's words send a fierce jolt of arousal through Grady, causing his cock to jump below me. "That's right, you're close to coming, aren't you?" Parker grits out. By the strain of his voice, he's clenching his jaw dangerously hard.

Grady closes his eyes. "Y-yes." Barely a whisper, his breath catches when I brush my nose against his neck.

"Then fill. Her. Up. I want to swallow every drop when you're done."

Holy shit.

My eyes lock with Grady's. "Let's not keep him waiting. He's too pretty to beg."

"O-okay, Sassy." He lifts the corner of his mouth the tiniest amount, eagerness alight in his expression.

As I slowly lower myself, everything becomes crystal clear. By the love-drunk gleam in his eyes, the desperate sounds Parker makes behind me, and how *right* I feel at the center of all this.

This *is* different.

And I'm about to have a *lot* of fun.

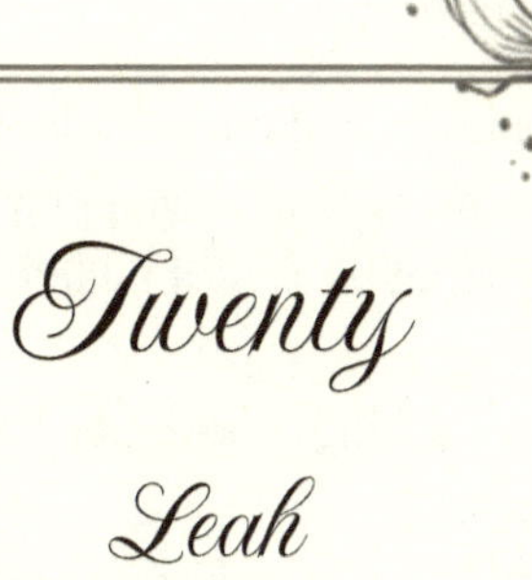

Twenty

Leah

Grady's hands move to my ass, gripping as I adjust. When I lean in to kiss him, he thrusts into me with a hunger like never before.

"Fuck him like you mean it," Parker orders as I roll my hips. "I want to watch him struggle to hold back, only to lose the battle."

God, I want that, too.

The thought of this reserved man falling to pieces because of me has every part of my body screaming. I move my lips to the crook of his neck and bite down, rolling my hips in languid, torturous circles. Moaning as I increase my pace, his grunts grow louder, fingertips digging into my flesh with bruising force.

"Fuck, just like that. Don't fight it, Hulk. You're both so fucking perfect." Frenzied, Parker works himself behind us, trying his best to match my pace.

Grady pulls me down onto him, slamming our pelvises together. I throw my head back, moaning fervently from the blissful friction as my clit rubs against him. Nips at my neck quickly transition to near skin-breaking bites as he begins to unravel.

"God, yes, mark her for everyone to see. She fucking loves it." Parker's voice comes out nearly incoherent as his own climax builds.

"F-f-fuck," Grady moans out as I adjust my angle, giving him exactly what he needs. "Leah," he gasps my name flawlessly, burying his face in my shoulder as he shudders, spilling deep inside of me.

"You're both so fucking good for me," Parker growls out, cum coating his stomach.

"Y-you didn't..." Grady looks up at me and swallows, disappointment dimming his glow.

"Don't," Parker says, suddenly behind me. "We edged you perfectly to give me this. You did exactly what I asked." He lays a hand on my lower back, leaning around to kiss Grady deeply. "You're such a good boy."

Grady's expression softens, shifting to slight confusion as Parker lifts me. "Now, I get to have some real fun and taste both of you together." An impish smirk plays at his lips. Carefully, he spreads me out, settling between my legs.

I've died and gone to heaven.

Without a hint of hesitation, he goes to work, tongue moving expertly as he devours me. Devours *us*. Our combined hungry moans and my desperate whimpers fill the room in an instant. I've never had a man consume me like this—every movement is perfectly practiced, executed with precision.

Grady, half delirious, stares as he recovers, fixated on how eagerly Parker works me over.

A nibble to my clit, and I nearly explode, hips jerking reflexively. But he doesn't relent. Instead, his mouth follows my movements, shifting so he can bury his tongue inside me. He takes me places I've never been with every new flick. I'm not sure how long we're here. The sensations are too intoxicating, borderline unbearable.

Before I know it, he's hard again, gripping himself while he chases my sounds of ecstasy.

Grady drops to his knees at my side, swallowing my moans, hand kneading my breast. In seconds, I'm writhing for them, overcome with the onslaught of sensations. Parker grabs my thighs, holding me in place, growling against me as my walls begin to flutter.

"Break," Grady breathes out a whisper from my lips.

The tension in my core snaps. I free-fall into a nearly endless sea of pleasure. Convulsing, I try to scream for them, but no sound manages to escape.

Parker, breathless and flushed, leans back onto his knees, lines himself up, and plunges inside of me, sending an impossible amount of new thrills through my veins. "So. Fucking. Perfect," he moans out, punctuating each word with a thrust.

I lace my fingers through Grady's hair and kiss him hard. His surprise quickly shifts to frenzied passion, and he loses the last of his control. My tank top, somehow still on, says goodbye to the world as he snaps, tearing it off of me. He clamps his mouth around my oversensitive nipple, nearly rutting into the couch.

"L-let me," I plead between moans, reaching to take him in my hand. His hips move on their own, pumping into my grip as his attention stays on my chest.

"You'd better come in her mouth, or mine. Don't make a mess," Parker orders, slowing his thrusts as he enjoys the show.

"Please come in his mouth." My throat goes dry at the thought. "I need to see it. God, do I need to see it." Borderline pathetic, my request squeaks out around whines.

"Anything for you." Parker smiles down at me and buries himself deep, grinding with precise movements. "Come here so I can make you both melt for me at the same time." He motions for Grady to stand, and he does. No reservation, no second-guessing.

They're breathtaking. Chests glistening from a thin layer of sweat, eyes shining as they exchange adoring looks that have no business in a situation so carnal. Yet, somehow, they fit perfectly.

Is it filthy, hot, raunchy sex? Fuck yeah it is. But the looks they give each other, and me, are proof that this really is more than skin-deep.

Grady gives Parker a chaste kiss, stands tall, and offers his dripping cock like a trophy. He allows Parker a teasing flick of his tongue over the tip before driving into him, hand fisted tightly in his hair. This rough, dominant side of Grady could drive me wild on sight alone. Feeling Parker twitch inside me as he goes feral is just icing on the cake.

Grady thrusts, and Parker does the same. His thumb circles my clit until I see stars, exploding like fireworks in the darkness of my blurring vision. I don't want to close my eyes, but the strength of my orgasm demands it. Hips rolling in time with his strokes, chest nearly bursting as I wail, I collapse.

And then, with a few sharp thrusts, Parker's release fills me as Grady groans, spilling down his throat.

I fear I may actually pass out. They might have fucked me literally senseless.

Blinking, my brows pinch together at the emptiness surrounding me. Are they not here? Holy shit, did I actually black out?

Commotion in the bedroom brings me relief. They didn't go far, thank goodness. Parker is the first to emerge, still nude and flushed. Grady, just behind him, is nearly asleep as he enters the room.

Glad it's not just me.

I smile lazily as they approach. "Hi."

"Welcome back to reality." Parker chuckles. "Let me clean you up, then we can all get some shut-eye." Leaning in, he kisses my forehead, soft and loving despite the things he just did to me.

"Y-you okay?" Grady asks, stepping to my side as Parker wipes me with a damp towel.

"I've never been better. Holy moly. You're both getting a damn good breakfast in the morning... If I can walk." Eyes half open, I do my best not to snort at my own joke.

"I'll c-carry y-you." Grady scoops me up, bridal style, and brings me into the bedroom. "So p-perfect." He kisses my cheek and nestles me in the middle of the king-size mattress.

If he's not the sweetest mountain of a man ever, I don't know who is. How did I get so lucky?

I stretch and reach for him as he slides in next to me. "You two are perfect. I'm just along for the ride."

"Sorry, I was not planning on all of this happening," Parker whispers, curling around me from behind.

With his warmth surrounding me, and my head resting on Grady's chest, I let out a breathy chuckle. "So the dick prints and no shirts were an accident?"

Grady laughs softly, snuggling closer.

"Well, it worked. Be it a little better than intended." Parker trails his fingers up my side. "You're ours, right? Say the word, and we're yours."

"On one condition." They both stiffen, almost unnoticeably, but this close, it's obvious. "You don't nearly paralyze me with your dicks before a show ever again."

Parker kisses my shoulder with a faint titter. "Deal."

Grady, eyes crinkled from his grin, nods in confirmation.

"We'll worry about the logistics and go back over the ground rules in the morning," Parker mumbles half-asleep behind me.

Right, rules. Never been fond of them. This is going to suck. But Grady's peaceful face and Parker's warm breath on the back of my neck are *hopefully* enough motivation.

Hopefully.

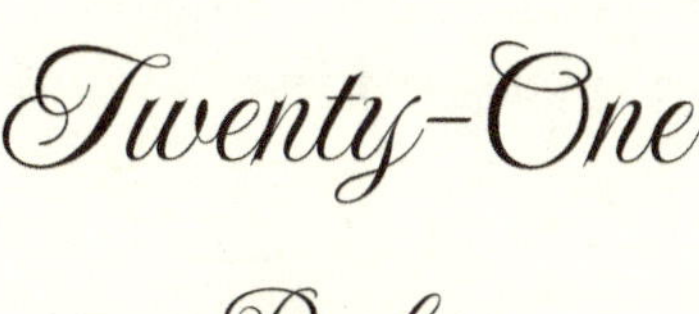

Twenty-One

Parker

The smoky, delicious scent of bacon wafts into the bedroom. A drunken smile pulls at my lips. Grady is next to me, still fast asleep. Scooting closer, I run my fingers through the tangled bedhead he's got going on, and he peels an eye open.

When his senses awaken, the instant that he smells the bacon, his brows rise.

"Breakfast is underway, it seems. Shall we join her in the kitchen?" I place a kiss against his cheek before rolling over.

Pulling on a pair of sweats, Grady strolls to the bathroom to comb out his knots. I opt for warm pajamas, following him to the main room when he's ready.

Her usual music is playing, but barely audible. It sounds like Britney Spears. I don't know, I was never a fan of pop. Still, I'd listen to anything if it means I get to watch her bounce around like this. She's trying to be quiet. It's adorable.

Grady, to my left, is apparently in agreement. For a few minutes, we stand here, admiring the domesticity of it all. This woman is not only the catalyst for our whole relationship, but is easily the glue.

Sure, I have had feelings for Grady as long as I've known him. But I'm a pussy and would have never acted on it without her. I'm not even sure if he's really into guys like I am, or if he's just a man, starved for love and willing to get it wherever he can.

Either way, he's in this, and I won't second-guess him for a minute.

My hand finds his shoulder, lying gently against his bare skin. He turns to me, eyes never losing their warmth. His palm timidly rests on my back. Hesitation I understand all too well. He's just as unsure about me. I've had this man's dick in the back of my throat more than once, and he still doesn't believe that I want him.

Does Leah feel the same? Have I rushed this? God, have I fucked this all up?

I bite back the burning uncertainty. Instead of panicking, I decide here and now to shift course. The sex is amazing, and I will not be stopping, but I need to reassure both of them that this is deeper for me.

Leah has made it clear that she's used to being nothing more than a hookup. She needs to know I'd throw everything away for her in a heartbeat. All she'd have to do is ask. She's gotten under my skin, and I never want her to leave. I could fall asleep counting every freckle on her shoulder for the rest of my life, never tiring of the way she smells like sweet peppermint and promises.

Grady will likely take time. I won't rush him into anything, but I'm going to make damn sure he knows that I want him with the same intensity as Leah.

So, before we fully round the corner, watching her crack another egg into the bowl and shimmy her hips, I lean over and kiss him. Not on the cheek, not in a hungry way, no. I kiss him with more tenderness and sincerity than even I thought possible. His fingers flex against my skin as he hums, eyes fluttering open when I pull away.

Pressing my back to his chest, I remain silent, allowing the moment to settle over us. Strong, steady arms wrap around my torso, holding me closer. When he nuzzles into the crook of my neck, beard tickling as it scratches against the sensitive skin, my heart melts into a gooey mess. I bite my cheeks to contain the grin pulling at my face.

"Mine," he sighs in my ear, voice extra gravelly from sleep.

"Calm down over there, I might get jealous of my boyfriends," Leah says with a giggle.

I expect Grady to pull away, like a kid caught swiping frosting off a cake. But he doesn't. He rests his chin on my shoulder and squeezes. I blush like a pathetic teenager, avoiding her eye contact as she approaches.

"I wanted to make breakfast in bed, you two really over-exerted yourselves last night, plus today is going to be hell." She steps up onto her toes and quickly pecks each of us on the cheek. "Especially for you, Parker. Do you think the old hag is going to be happy with Bridget making a mockery of her name like that?"

I sigh as reality crashes into me. "Is it unreasonable to hope for the rapture to happen before ten? Bed sounds good. Let's rot away and ignore the impending ass chewing I've got coming. Shall we?"

Grady pulls me closer, squeezing with perfect pressure. "Y-you did all you c-c-could."

"He's right, you can train day and night, but she's gotta actually listen. Instead, she gives you googly eyes and tries to get in your pants." Leah's lip curls with contempt, and I hold back a laugh. "What?! It's true!"

"You're adorable when you're jealous," I poke, egging her on.

The tiny flair of her nostrils and crinkle of her brow make my heart skip. Minor, yet effective confirmation that she, too, cares about more than sex.

I think I've actually found my people. Almost thirty years of wandering, thinking nobody would ever love me for me. Yet here they are. The more the merrier.

"How about you two go get comfy? Give me ten minutes, and I'll be in with breakfast, then we can... talk about this situation." Her mock shudder does a poor job of concealing her actual discomfort.

This conversation isn't going to be pleasant, I understand that. While we're all eager to live our lives openly and honestly, that can't happen. There are way too many factors at play. I'm a planner, strategic, always observing.

I guess that's what makes me such a good trainer. I notice all the minute details, what makes things *work*. I've been seeing trends, taking note of things that worry me. I'm absolutely terrified of this conversation, too, but we need to get on the same page before any of us get too invested.

Grady and I sit, backs against the plush gray headboard, waiting for Leah to bring our feast. My appetite is almost nonexistent, but I know once I have that plate of goodness in my possession, it's a done deal. Our girl can cook, and man, can we eat.

It's unfair how much Grady can put down in one sitting, while also having such a brawny, perfect physique. He's the picture of masculinity—broad chest on display, slight belly protruding from sitting—peak male form, as far as I'm concerned. He pulls it off effortlessly. I can't blame Leah for wanting him one bit. I'm just glad she is open to sharing because I don't know I'd survive seeing them together otherwise.

She shuffles through the door, serving tray I didn't know I owned balanced on one hand, a jug of orange juice in the other. I flash her a bright grin, knowing better than to move. Grady, eager to help, starts to get up, until she pins him with a warning stare. "No, no. I'm quite alright, Darlin'," she insists, letting a hint of her true southern drawl slip through the cracks.

Grady's expression shifts, eyes flaring slightly, obviously as enamored as I am.

Plates of scrambled eggs, pancakes, and bacon land in our laps.

She hands me one for herself, climbs into her spot between us, and takes her breakfast from me, laying it in her lap. "Well, we're all here. Do we want to eat first, or talk while we eat?" she asks, turning to Grady. A soft chuckle escapes her when she catches him taking a hearty bite of eggs.

The priceless expression on his face makes me laugh, too. Lips pursed, he looks around the room as if he's not the object of our attention. A shy smile crosses his face as he puts his fork down and swallows.

"It's okay, we can eat first," I say, keeping my voice light.

"I think you're the only one with anything *to* say. So, whenever you're ready, really." She shrugs.

Okay, I guess this is happening then.

"Well," I start, gripping my fork in my fist. "Now that this has had time to simmer, I want to reiterate some essential things. As I said in the hotel, we need to be mindful of our delicate situation." I can't look at them. Their stillness is unnerving. I don't want to see the expressions waiting for me.

Moving my eggs around on the plate, I continue, "Grady may be the family outcast, but he's still a Hart. That means Henrietta has a vested interest in his life. What he does can still tarnish her name, the empire she's built. Being seen fraternizing, not only with a client, but with a *male* trainer as well is a recipe for disaster. She'd whisk him away in an instant." This time, after swallowing the boulder in my throat, I spare them a glance.

Understanding and a hint of sadness fill Grady's face. Leah, much less convinced, speaks up, "So what, you just want us to act like this is nothing?"

"Only in the open, and only until you qualify. After, we can leave here and be free to love each other. Fuck the Harts."

Grady nods in agreement, and it gives me just enough courage to continue.

"We were reckless when we got back yesterday. I felt like repeating the plan was necessary when our emotions were less chaotic... and I need to make sure you're absolutely okay with my need to appeal to Bridget. I can't blow my cover, or they'll assign me somewhere else... we need to be together." I brace myself, having watched her face turn redder with each word.

She has to be biting her tongue so hard it's nearly severed by now.

Instead of an explosive retort, she simply nods.

Skin coated in a cold sweat, I wait for her to say something—anything. But no, this rage, the devastation, is silent. And that is so much worse. She has to understand that this isn't my choice, that I'd never willingly entertain Bridget. But her pain is unmistakable.

We eat slowly, letting the air fill with thick, unbearable tension before I break.

"Leah, I—"

"You what?!" she snaps. "You just expect me to... to sit there and do *what* exactly? Watch as Bridget flirts with you? If I hear *one*

'Parkie', I'll vomit on the spot. And, aaaand, the next time she's shitty to Grady, I'm going to stab her in the eye with a hoof pick." With a final huff, she slumps back into the padding, arms folded as she scowls at her breakfast.

I sputter, not entirely caught off guard by her rage, but surprised by the specifics. Grady moves a hand to her thigh, squeezing in silent comfort. She breathes slowly, blinking away her outrage.

Fix this, damn it. Say something, mouth. "Leah, you're the most determined, focused, and steady woman I've ever met. Don't let her get under your skin. She damn sure doesn't get under mine. Grady is also a big boy." I keep my voice calm, hoping it's enough.

She bites her lip, mischief twinkling in her eye. "Yeah, he is." She raises a fist for me to bump.

Grady swallows his most recent mouthful of food wrong, hammering a fist against his chest as he coughs.

Barking out a laugh, I reach over and tap my knuckles against hers. "That's our girl. We just need to last a few months. Then we can spend the rest of our lives together doing what we love... after we find a new home. But qualifying has to come first."

"Life's too short to stress over a few months. Let's promise to be there for each other in the background, the little moments when we can be. I'm not a patient woman, but I can promise to do my best." Brows pinched, she gives us a curt nod.

Grady, having regained his composure, kisses her cheek. She sinks into him, flushing a beautiful shade of pink.

It amazes me how naturally he's falling into everything. I can't imagine going my whole life knowing nothing but judgment, coldness, and hate. Then one day, it all flips upside down.

Leah is amazing, too. Working so intimately with her has taught me so many amazing things. She's absolutely impatient, but not when it comes to her craft. She'll repeat the same step in her routine a dozen times in a row and never once grumble or complain. Her grit is the biggest turn-on.

I sure hope that Grady can keep his heart-eyes in check, and that she can keep her disdain for Bridget at bay. It's probably a smart idea to hide all of the hoof picks either way.

"Well then. That wasn't horrible. Was it?" I ask.

"I guess not." She sighs, still leaning against Grady. "But I do have something else to talk about."

"Oh?" I quirk a brow.

"Yeah, but we'll save it for later. This has been heavy enough. It's nothing bad, I just want to be transparent. But we don't have time. Henrietta already arranged a meeting, so we gotta hurry to make sure you're there on time." She offers me a weak smile.

"I know... We'll talk later. It'll all be okay."

Grady nods, half-heartedly, but the hopeful light in his eyes is reassuring.

The lack of excitement in the room is still evident. The coming months are going to take forever at this rate. But we're going to make it. If it breaks us, we'll have each other, of that I'm certain.

Twenty-Two

Grady

Tally perks up the second she sees us, trotting over to the gate in search of a peppermint, no doubt. Leah, ever the softie, has one ready for her by the time she comes to a stop. The way her eyes sparkle as Tally takes the little candy from her palm is enchanting.

I hate the fact that this beautiful woman has spent all these weeks thinking I hate her, but I'm so glad she finally knows the truth.

At least, I hope she does. By the way she smiles at me now, she has to. Words are my enemy, so the little touches are hopefully comforting enough.

"You want to go to the stables and eavesdrop on the meeting your bitch mother is going to be holding?" She quirks a brow, nudging me with her elbow.

I hold in a laugh and nod. Of course I want to listen. Not because I care what she has to say. No, I care about the kind-hearted, high-strung man who wears a smile to conceal his worries.

I know my mother, I'm all too familiar with her subtle, festering rage. She's going to eat him alive, and Bridget will happily join her in devouring him. I've had an entire lifetime to learn how to tamp my nerves down and control my reactions—they only make it worse. Imagining her fangs sinking into him has my blood boiling.

This must be what Leah feels when Bridget is... well, Bridget to me.

I hook a lead to Tally's field halter, and we begin the short walk to the stables.

Leah is keeping her face flat, trying to hide her concern, but I can read her. Decades of learning people's intentions through their faces has proven to be a blessing and a curse. Right now, I have to pretend I don't know how upset she is, because I'm also abundantly aware that she's not a fan of being coddled.

In fact, she's quite hardened for such a small woman. I get the sense that her home life had a lot to do with it. She doesn't talk a ton about where she came from, but there are definitely hardships she doesn't share.

And that's okay.

I don't need to know everything about her to want every part of her. The things she does show me are enough.

Mother would surely tell me I'm reckless, naïve, settling for less than a Hart should. If she finds out I'm also bedding my dear little sister's intended husband, well, maybe I could finally get the boot from this nightmare of a family.

I curse myself internally for the thought, knowing full well that she'll never let me out of this hell. Not as long as I pose a threat. Until I'm "perfect" and ready to conform to her rules and expectations, I'll always be just that—the thing that haunts her worst nightmares. A flaw in the family name.

That's what makes my sassy little goddess and secretly sweet bad boy so special. Aside from my cousins, they're the only people I have ever met who *see* me. They never bat an eye or make me feel like a bumbling fool when my mouth won't work. It's freeing and beautiful.

They're beautiful.

And now that they're mine, I'll do anything I can to protect them. Well, anything that won't upset Parker and his rules.

Leah voiced her apprehension yesterday. I should have done the same. She'll work diligently to uphold our promise, so I'll follow suit to the best of my abilities. If nothing else, I respect his determination. I know Bridget, and could never imagine having to be the object of her delusional, self-centered fantasies.

The thought sends chills up my spine, bringing forth a shudder.

"You're stuck in your head over there, huh?" Leah speaks up as we reach Tally's stall.

I sigh, offering a half-shrug in response. If she knew how much chaos was running through my mind, she'd join me, and that would be catastrophic.

"Hey," she murmurs, slinking into the far corner of the stall, finger curling in a silent command.

I freeze in place, glancing over my shoulder.

"They're all in the office. Nobody is going to see."

My body takes control of itself. Carefully latching the door, I close the gap between us in two strides, lips on hers in an instant. Tally, the perfect accomplice, moves to the stall entrance, further blocking the view from outside.

"Grady, wait," Leah whimpers as I trail my mouth to her throat. "I think I heard a car pull up."

Her words extinguish the fire in my veins. Shaking my head, I blow out a frustrated breath. How can I be so careless already? We also don't know how Parker feels about us doing things without him.

Maybe we should have *that* conversation and worry less about what others think.

A pipe dream, I know it is. Keeping up appearances is all we have right now.

Parker is one hundred percent correct, Mother has the money and power to make me disappear. Not in the murderous sense, though I wouldn't put it past her. But she can easily send me away—putting me up in a hovel with no phone or internet. Nothing but a shitty "butler" who would keep me in line until I've "learned my lesson".

She's done it to my cousins on a few occasions. A "time out" as she says. They go dark for a month or so, then come back acting the way she wants, only showing their faces when she instructs. Being raised by her after their parents died has made for a sad life.

Deep down, I wish I could help them. At one point, we were close. Until Mother decided that it was time for us all to "step up".

The way she swooped in and took over everything when Father died still gives me chills. To this day, I'm not convinced that she didn't have him killed just to sit on her figurative throne. I know that's far-fetched. Heart attacks happen, especially when in such a high-stress position. I was barely eleven when he left us, so there was nobody to fight for an investigation. It's a shame.

The stable door opening grabs my attention. Quincy and Warren, faces tense, drag their feet straight into the office.

"I can't believe I almost fucked your cousins," Leah sneers next to me.

I can.

No insult intended to her, but they're attractive and have no problem talking to women. I hate that we're so disconnected now. Part of me still yearns for the brotherly relationship we once had. At least I could live vicariously through them before. The last couple of years have sucked without their stories and kinship.

"Let's move closer so we can try to hear." She tugs on my arm.

We slink out of Tally's stall, tip-toeing toward the solid metal office door. The shrill sound of Mother's voice makes my stomach roll. The benefit of my stable solitude is not having to listen to her squawk on a daily basis anymore. It's actually been months since I've had the displeasure.

For Parker, I'll endure it.

"And... do... have to say..." Her muffled scolds are barely audible through the door. I can almost see the veins bulging in her neck as she chastises Parker for "failing".

We all know Bridget is a bumbling idiot who has no business trying to compete at this level, but Mother needs an heir, and I'm not good enough.

The world beyond Hartbrook doesn't even know I exist.

"And you two!" she screeches—so loud I'm sure it could be heard from outside.

My blood goes cold. She brought my cousins here to yell at them?

Oh no.

"You... distract her... *failures!*" High-pitched, filled with clear malice, the words I can make out have me fighting the urge to vomit... or break the door down.

"Did you hear that?" Leah stares up at me, wide-eyed. "I think... I'm pretty sure she tried to use them to distract me!"

Though she's whispering, it's clearly intended to be an angry scream. "How fucking *rude*. That's low, even for her."

I have no clue how she heard enough to figure all that out, but it's not an impossible idea.

"You, Brat." Seething words filter through the door, clearly speaking to Bridget now. "Try harder." Her command is clear as day, like the threat layered on top.

Bridget says something I can't decipher. She's keeping her voice low and controlled. Probably the smartest thing she's ever done.

The only word of Mother's response that makes it through the barrier is "gone" which stabs me in the chest. Those four letters carry immeasurable weight coming from her.

After a beat of silence, Leah and I retreat to Tally's stall, pretending we just got back from the pasture. I brush her coat while Leah combs her mane, picking out stray leaves.

Mother is the first to exit, paying me no mind as I lean over the door to see the defeat in all four of the others' faces.

Clearly, the meeting did not go well for anyone involved.

What worries me most is Parker. He seems to be in a stupor—eyes glazed over, dragging his feet. He doesn't even acknowledge that Leah and I are standing here, watching with held breath.

When the others finally leave, she rushes to him, framing his face with her hands. "What's wrong? What happened in there?" Her voice wavers as their eyes meet.

Stepping beside them, I squeeze his shoulder. "Carrie's?" I offer, knowing how much he loves it there, anywhere but here, really.

He swallows, damp eyes meeting mine, and nods.

"I'll drive. My truck is right across the road." Leah takes him by the hand, leading him out the door.

Following closely, I climb into the back seat of her truck, sitting behind him. My hands know better than I do, and find his shoulders on their own, kneading at the tension he's holding. Between the massage and the distance we're putting between Hartbrook and us, he slowly relaxes.

With a sigh, he leans back. "Thank you both. I—the things she said. Holy shit."

"We could hear a bit of it. Are you good, Puddin'?" Leah looks over for a split second, pulling off the private drive.

"Puddin'? Hear that, Hulk? We've both got adorable nicknames now." He flashes me a strained smile, his usual "I hope this sells my false happiness" toothy grin. The one I see straight through but never let on. We all wear our masks, who am I to shatter the illusion that his is effective?

"Sorry, old habits. Please ignore me." She curls her lips between her teeth.

"I couldn't ignore you if I tried," Parker effortlessly quips back.

My jaw works for a second. I remind myself to breathe, repeating the word in my head a dozen times before finally mumbling, "S-same."

Years of speech therapy, decades of shame and inferiority, have me genuinely fearful every time I speak. But they never flinch. Even if I get absolutely stuck on a word, they don't rush me or expect me to "spit it out already". Still, I have a small flare of panic every time I think about talking.

And then they prove me wrong.

Leah's cheeks bloom the most beautiful shade of pink, nearly matching her hair. Parker settles into my still-working hands, sighing as I find a particularly knotted spot.

"Keep it up over there. I'm liable to swerve off the road into a strategic clearing," Leah grumbles.

I laugh, loud and genuine, while Parker cackles unexpectedly. "You wanna get fucked in the woods? I'm sure Grady would love to pin you up against a tree and have the time of his life."

My dick twitches at the thought. "O-only if you're the t-t-tree," I manage to work out, cheeks burning.

"Fuck, are you talking dirty to me right now?" Parker fans himself. "I'm a little jealous that you two will have so much alone time. I'm going to be tripling my training efforts over the next couple of months. Fuck her extra for me, I'll be too tired." Despite his flirty words, he can't hide the frustration in his voice.

"There's a whole lot to unpack there, but we're gonna save that for *after* chicken and waffles. Let's go take our usual booth, hide out, and chill for a sec, okay?" Leah puts the truck in park and we all file into the diner.

There aren't many people here, since we've made a midday trip. The cracked pink pleather squeaks as we slide into our booth. This time, we all take one side, with our backs facing the rest of the room. Thanks to my sheer size, I'm on the outside, hanging halfway into the aisle. We're secluded back here, and it's cozy aside from that. Leah is against the wood-paneled wall, and Parker is nestled between us with a light smile on his face.

Darlene stops by with a bright grin, bringing our usual drinks. "Three orders of chicken and waffles for ya, coming right up." She spins on her heel, poodle skirt twirling, and struts away.

Seconds after she leaves, Leah sips her cherry Coke with a curious expression, and Parker squirms strangely next to me.

"Wha—" He chokes on a sharp inhale, biting his lower lip.

His flushed cheeks answer my unasked questions. She's drinking with her left hand. The right one is nowhere to be seen.

Sly little fox.

Looking over my shoulder to make sure nobody else is around, I slip my left hand below the table. She already has his pants undone. Perfect.

When I grip his already-hard cock, Parker's attention flies to me, lips slightly parted. I don't blame him for being shocked as I join her in stroking and teasing him. Until now, he's always been the one to touch me.

"Fuck," he whispers, holding back his moans. "You're both so fucking bad. God, this is hot as hell." His hips move slightly as he throbs in our grips.

Leah trails her fingers over mine, moving her attention to the tip. She focuses on his most sensitive spots while I stroke leisurely, hand sliding lower to grip his balls.

His breaths grow shallow, eyes fluttering as they roll. He's trying to be discreet, but failing. It's maddening in the best way. My cock strains against my jeans as the closer he gets to bursting.

Face reddening, chest heaving, his eyes snap open. "Guys, where am I gonna come?"

Leah looks over at me and I nod, understanding the silent instruction. I slide out of the booth enough to let him move over. Once she has room, she slips under the table and swallows him down, taking the last bit of his restraint with her.

As he squeezes my thigh with his release, I take one final glance around the room, kissing his neck when the coast is clear. A garbled sound squeaks out of him before he can stop it, but he's quick to recover.

Leah rights herself with a smug look on her face. I slide back into the booth as far as I can manage, tittering just loud enough for us to hear.

Parker clears his throat, gathering himself. "You two are filthy, I love it."

Leah pecks him on the cheek, and he gives her a lazy smirk in return. "Figured you could use a mood boost. You were wound all tight."

When he turns my way, his expression shifts, bashful and surprised. "I, uh. You didn't have to—"

Throwing caution to the wind, I kiss him, shutting down his "way out" for me. Just a quick press of our lips, but it sends a message. One he understands completely. His jaw unclenches, and the light in his eyes brightens.

That's right, I wanted to.

He closes his eyes, resting his head against the back of the booth. "Thank you, both of you."

We give in to the silence, allowing him a moment to forget the day, the life we're all stuck with.

When our food arrives, he straightens, swallowing before he begins, "We're fucked."

The way he says it feels certain, finite, terrifying.

What the hell happened in that office?

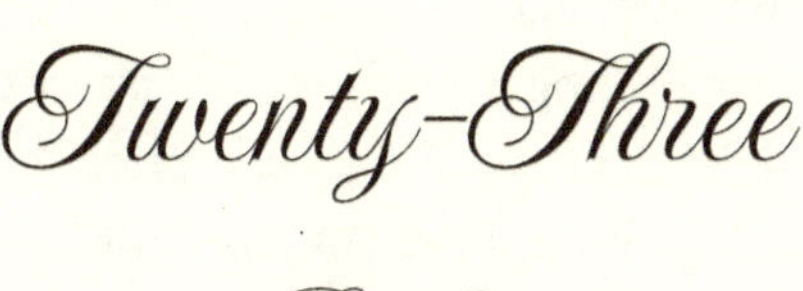

Parker

Leah and Grady's matching expressions scream, "What the fuck did you just say?" and I don't blame them.

"I know," I mumble. "We have to be careful. I'll work overtime for you, Star." I flush as I remember the feel of her mouth around me mere minutes ago.

And Grady… touched me. He actually *touched* me.

I wish they hadn't, because I just ruined their appetites, likely for more than just food.

"Let me get this straight." Leah turns in the booth to face me more directly. "She told you to focus on Bridget, and essentially blow me off?"

"In far more words, yes." I chew my lip, avoiding her fiery gaze.

"And Bridget? The useless, uncoordinated, twat. She just gets handed all of your time?" Her forehead wrinkles as she scowls.

"I'll make time for you." I cup her face in my palm and kiss her with a tenderness even I'm surprised by. When I pull away, I turn to Grady, who is wearing an equally concerned pout. "I'll make time for both of you. Even if it kills me."

He nods, scanning our surroundings, taking the discretion of our relationship very seriously. While I appreciate it, I need him more than air and he needs to know that, outside of Hartbrook, I don't care about appearances.

"Nobody here is going to give a shit." I lean into him.

His hand finds the nape of my neck, playing with the short hair there as our lips meet. Brief but powerful, my kiss gives him the reassurance he needs. The tension in his face is nearly gone as I pull back.

Leah fans her face. "I could watch you do that all day. But for real, you're going to work yourself to death. It's also super messed up that I paid so much, and she's effectively telling you to screw me over."

"Well, yeah, you're nobody to her. Bridget is the next in line to take over. Naturally, she couldn't care less. I just... I need you both to hold tight. We'll get there."

"Promise?" Leah's large green eyes show the slightest amount of doubt.

"With everything I have, I will make this work. For all of us," I confirm, silencing the asshole little voice in the back of my head.

I can do it. It'll be difficult, but we're worth it.

Twenty-Four

Parker

Two months. Three more competitions have come and passed, and Bridget is no closer to qualifying. Sure, she's objectively better than her first mess of a show, but that doesn't mean anything. She can't remember her choreography, and hardly gives a shit when she fails. It's like her mother's words mean nothing to her. But the looming threat of being fired every time she fails is getting to me.

Leah, in stark contrast to Bridget, is a shoo-in for qualifying. She's just got to keep killing the way she has been, then show up and show out at the World Cup, and she's golden.

Even after a few months of witnessing it, I can't breathe when I watch her and Tally command the arena. She's taken it upon herself to practice the harder maneuvers in her downtime, which is often. So her performances are always a welcome surprise.

Henrietta has the cousins watching my every move. They haven't explicitly said so, but I'm no idiot. I can't entirely blame them. They've gotten some harsh warnings, too. I can only imagine what the hell "time out" means. But Henrietta only had to seethe the words in their direction once for those poor bastards to fall in line.

Maybe they aren't to blame as I thought. Either way, after Bridget embarrassed herself a second time, they started lingering more, conveniently "hanging out" during every training session, day or night.

And yes, some of them go into the night.

I'm so sick of dodging Bridget's advances. They're only worse after a late training session.

It's eight pm, and I'm exhausted. Surely, she can see it on my face. Her attempt at seduction is always awkward, like you would expect from a woman who is used to having men fall in her lap. Tonight, Leah and Grady are here to bear witness, standing next to the cousins... which is extremely confusing. But that's not a problem for now.

Both of their faces redden as she practically gropes me through my pants. If my dick gets any softer, it'll melt off my body. I slip out of her grasp and walk away, catching a couple of shit-eating grins from the cousins as I step into the stables.

"Fuck both of you, rats," I spit, far too exhausted for their bullshit on top of all this.

They follow me inside, leaving Leah and Grady at the door.

"Hey, man, we're laughing at her expense, not yours," Quincy explains in a pathetic effort to pity me.

"Yeah, sure." I force out a heavy breath, spine stiffening as Bridget approaches Grady. Her insults haven't stopped, nor has Leah's hatred for them. It's an explosion waiting to happen. One I secretly hope I get to witness.

"You got it bad for her, huh?" Warren asks behind me.

I try to hide my jolt, but their softening expressions tell me it doesn't work. "No, I just admire her morals and work ethic."

"And her ass." Quincy waggles his brows, leaning casually against the wall.

Don't react, that's what they want.

If only my mouth would obey. "You don't get to talk about her like that," I hiss.

"Listen, man, we don't blame you. But it seems our cousin has his eyes set on her, too. You may want to act fast. Sadly, our ship has sailed. And believe me, we tried." Warren sighs—a defeated, love-struck sound that I can relate to.

I hate him for it.

"You're out of your minds."

"No, we just know a good woman when we see her." Quincy pulls his mouth to one side, appearing more genuine than I've ever seen. "We approached her all wrong. But it started as an order from 'dear old Auntie'." He rolls his eyes, making finger quotes.

It's almost... human.

I furrow my brows. "Are you... mocking Henrietta?"

"Come on, it's not like you don't hate her, too. You think we want this shit? We're trained dogs, fully at her beck and call. You think Grady wants to live the way he does? It's diabolical the way she treats everyone except Bitchy Pants over there." Warren tips his head in Bridget's direction. "Getting to know Leah has been the brightest part of our bleak lives."

My world spins, speculation turning into concrete proof. They're one hundred percent victims of Henrietta and I'm a jealous asshole for not seeing it sooner. They've never done anything explicitly horrible to me, or Grady, for that matter. In fact, most of the time they're just sort of... there. Always in the background, doing the bare minimum required to stay out of her warpath.

And then I remember her warning.

"She said you failed, and if you do it again, you're gone. What the fuck does that mean?" I ask in a hushed yell, looking over my shoulder.

"Not here." Warren purses his lips. "We can't. We've already said too much." His eyes dart to a spot in the ceiling, and my blood goes cold.

On a rafter, shrouded by the darkness, is the unmistakable glint of a camera lens. It has to be fairly new. I would have noticed it months ago had it been there before.

Swallowing, I offer a faint, stiff nod. "My cabin, tomorrow morning, seven am." I keep my expression flat, voice low.

Why am I willing to hear them out? Stupid savior complex. That has to be it. It definitely has nothing to do with my tendency to gravitate toward broken men who probably don't want me.

They shift, giving almost inconceivable nods, and leave.

Leah storms out the front door just as Bridget's voice cuts through the room. Something vile directed at Grady, no doubt.

So much happened in the last few minutes, I'm reeling.

Grady can handle Bridget, as hard as it is to leave him. So I strategically wait before strolling out the front door, now that I know we're being watched.

My first stop is Leah's cabin. I knock and wait, no answer. Okay, fine. Let her ignore me like she didn't give me her door code. I enter the digits and the lock chimes, unbolting to let me in. It's quiet, which is impossible for Leah. Where the hell is she? Her bedroom is empty, along with the bathroom.

Okay. She's not here, but her truck is. There's nowhere else for her to go.

It finally clicks. How dumb am I?

I turn off the lights and leave her cabin, locking up behind me. When I get to my place, the door is already open.

Of course this is where she ran to.

A delicious scent hits my nose when I step inside. "It's a bit late to cook," I say as I circle the counter, wrapping my arms around her waist.

"It's just leftover Alfredo. I'm also toasting some redneck garlic bread. You know, good old sandwich bread with butter and garlic powder. I put cheese on it too, real professional like," she explains, voice tense despite the attempted playfulness of her words.

This is what she does. Every time she's upset, she cooks. Even if it's something as simple as reheating leftovers. Caring for people is her love language, and food is at the top of that list. Best believe neither of us complain.

I rest my chin on her shoulder and sigh, feeling her relax under the weight of my embrace. Sadly, it's short-lived because an emotionally drained Grady trudges through the door moments later.

I'm so tired.

Fortunately, he perks up at the garlicky aroma floating on the air. Kissing each of our cheeks, he yawns and claims a seat at the table. Such a simple man, one who has completely taken over my life.

I press my lips to Leah's neck, giving her a swift slap on the ass. Her squeak makes me chortle on my way to Grady. "Was she particularly vile today?" I circle to rub his shoulders.

Groaning under my touch, his head falls back. Exhaustion dulls his gorgeous eyes.

What a night. My next confession is only going to make it worse.

"I... don't want to make you two even more upset after the shit day we had. But, I uh..." The looks they're both giving me make my stomach churn. "I had a conversation with Warren and

Quincy. Something about their dejection made me feel for them. I think I was wrong about them."

"Go on..." Leah offers, voice flat, intentionally holding back.

I know she's still been humoring them for the sake of our future. I'd be lying if I said I'm not irked by it. But it's a necessary evil. Except tonight opened my eyes.

"I don't know what it is, but the way Henrietta talks to them, how they react so viscerally... I don't think they want to be here any more than we do," I explain as best as I can, but the feelings are jumbled. "I know that I have been talking shit about them and complaining that they're always watching. But they showed me something today. There's a camera in the stables now. Telling me about it was a huge leap of faith. I want to trust them. Are you open to it?" I lock eyes with Grady, who is listening intently with a contemplative look on his face.

His jaw works, and he inhales. I can practically hear his mind whirring.

"You can text our group chat if it's too much to say. You know that." I hold my phone up, giving it a wiggle.

He takes his out and rapidly types.

Hulk:

We were raised together. When they were young, about 3 and 5, their parents died in an accident. Mother and Father raised them from then on. She treated them like unwanted children after Father died. Once they got older, she saw them as more people to control. I think they were in their teens when she sent them away the first time. They were never the same after that. But I honestly believe they're fed up with being her puppets. They're not happy. It hurts to see them stuck here, too. But I'm just as powerless as they are to do anything about it.

Leah swallows hard, passing a sorrowful look between us.

The soft spot she has for them is apparent. She has that glint in her eye, the determination to help. She won't say it, I know she won't, so I decide to do it for her. "You're conflicted because you want to give them a chance, but you're hurt by the way they tried to play you."

"It sucks. I feel betrayed and bitter toward them, but I'm also just... confused. I've stayed civil with them, and it's made things complicated."

Something else simmers under the surface, a hint of her desire. There's no room for secrets here, not between us. "Because you're still attracted to them," I state, matter-of-factly.

Grady's attention shifts to the pained expression on her face and tension in her shoulders—the shame she's trying to conceal.

Time ticks by while we give her the chance to chew over her response.

"Yes," she admits, hardly above a whisper. "I—it's not just attraction, okay? We just... We had chemistry before I knew they were your cousins. Before I knew they were using me, or being forced to. The anger I hold for them has made it easy to write them off. But if we forgive them, I-I don't know if I can keep telling myself I don't want them." She fidgets with a loose thread on her shirt, rambling on, "It's so strange to me. I've never been one for relationships or being 'clingy' but you two, and for *some* reason, Warren and Quincy, have all changed that." Her words come out frantic, uncertain.

But Grady and I don't press. She deserves the opportunity to talk it out, to be heard.

Directing my attention to Grady, I ask, "Would you trust them with her if that's what happens? I'm not one to control what anybody does. As long as I'm still included, I don't give a shit. But all of this is brand-new to you. Your feelings matter."

He shrugs. "Th-they're not b-b-bad."

Leah's face twists, as if she were expecting a fallout instead of understanding. She blinks, opening her mouth, only to clamp it shut again.

I raise my brows. "Say what you need to. This isn't a trial. You're allowed feelings and input."

"Di-did you two actually say that I can also date Warren and Quincy if they're on board?" Disbelief thickly coats every word that leaves her mouth.

I chuckle. "Oh, they'll be on board."

She gasps, scandalized, and turns to Grady. "You swear you're okay with it? It won't be weird for you?"

Chewing his lip, his throat bobs, cheeks flushing. He's actively working up the courage to speak, and I know exactly what's coming. With white knuckles, I grip the edge of the table, waiting anxiously to see how this goes. Her reaction to these words will define our future.

"L-Leah." He clears his throat, shaking off his nerves. "I l-l-l-love you."

Her hand flies to her mouth, tears welling in her eyes. Beautiful. We're going to be okay. Those words would have scared her off months ago.

My stomach hits the floor when he turns to me, face warm. "A-and I l-love you."

Fuck.

Leah flies across the room, into his arms to kiss him with such ferocity I can feel it. Numb and shaken to my core, I sit frozen in place. He's never made me feel lesser, always gives me the same energy he gives to her, but I never dreamed he'd say those words to me.

"You swear?" My voice wavers, like a fucking teenager, desperate for validation.

He pulls his lips away from hers. "Y-yes. If they m-make her h-h-happy, g-g-g-good."

I'm squatting next to them in an instant, taking in her still-worried expression. I'm the wild card here, and don't want to be. I run my thumb down her cheek, pressing a soft kiss to her lips, before doing the same to Grady. "I love both of you so fucking much. I mean it when I say that you can date whoever you want, as long as you leave room for me."

A sob breaks free from her. Wiping her nose, she grumbles, "I do *not* cry this much, damn it! But I love the hell out of both of you, too. I swear I won't make a habit of finding new men, I just... something about them speaks to part of me, the same way the two of you do."

"Well then, let's go to bed so we can wake up and either fuck up our plans or have some crazy fivesomes in our future." I snort at my own ridiculousness, but they chuckle anyway.

Through the humor, we all know this is going one of two ways, and no matter which one wins, our lives will be forever changed.

Twenty-Five

Grady

My shirt has never looked so good. Leah tossed it on first thing this morning before scurrying to the kitchen to make breakfast. Her nervousness is strangely calming. She had me quaking in my boots for so long before that hotel room. It's humanizing to see her phased by something.

Her music is a little louder than usual, resonating through the cabin while she dances around. It's Sunday, which means Parker doesn't have any training scheduled, so there's no real pressure to rush. Except Parker apparently told Warren and Quincy to be here at seven am for *some* reason. Sleeping in is a foreign concept to these two.

Honestly, he doesn't know how to slow down. Even now, he's helping her as much as she'll allow. They're worried about nothing. I know my cousins, the *real* versions they keep locked away. Deep down, they're broken, too. Nothing more than bastards in Mother's eyes—inconvenient lives she had to take responsibility for.

Regardless, they're likely as eager to belong somewhere—to feel wanted—as I am. I've found it, and don't mind sharing as long as they agree to the ground rules. They would definitely love the chance to get out of here, out from under *her*. So, if they're not interested in Leah like that, it's okay. They won't betray us, especially since we'll be giving them a ticket to freedom.

I lean against the doorframe, openly ogling Leah. She's working extra hard to make a delicious breakfast. There's a sinfulness in the way my shirt hangs loosely over her curves—barely covering her pink-lace-covered ass—bordering on being too lewd for polite company. Good thing my cousins aren't polite.

They're going to ravage her if she lets them. Parker will probably watch, maybe even join if they're into that.

I'm getting hard imagining the things they'll do together. This relationship is unorthodox by normal standards, but not a damn one of us fits the definition. Nothing that feels this right could possibly be wrong.

I sure hope, mainly for Warren and Quincy's sakes, they're on board with all of this. I do miss them. It's been years since we were what I would call close, but they're always around and have made efforts look out for me, as much as Mother allows anyway.

"You're a pancake machine," Parker says in awe of Leah's prowess with a griddle.

"House full of hungry brothers, remember?" she responds without missing a beat.

"Did your mother not help? You never really talk about it." Parker keeps his tone light, but that doesn't stop her from tensing.

"For a reason. We didn't have much growing up. Ranching doesn't pay super well, and there were five of us kids. Mama and Daddy did what they could, but there wasn't much love in the house. They just weren't those types of parents. We were free labor." She sniffles, adding three more pancakes to the stack.

I can't stand seeing her upset, so I do the only thing I can think of. Padding over, I wrap my arms around her waist, pulling her into a strong hug from behind, savoring her softness.

Parker leans over to kiss her cheek and she hums in my hold. "It's okay, really. I'm obviously in a much better place, mentally and financially. That's an entirely different conversation that I'm *not* getting into right now."

Parker brushes a loose lock of hair behind her ear. "You don't owe us an explanation. I'm sorry for pressing." The doorbell rings and he checks his watch. "Six fifty. I love the punctuality." A bright, genuine grin split this face.

It's hard to believe that he hated them less than twenty-four hours ago.

I should probably release my hold on Leah, in the spirit of easing them into all of this, but their minds are about to be blown either way. Subtlety isn't my strong suit, so I stay put. She's literally wearing my shirt. If that isn't telling, nothing is.

I rest my chin on her shoulder as she finishes the last batch of fluffy, golden flapjacks.

Seconds later, Warren comes into view, mouth falling open. "Oh shit. I fucking *knew* it."

Stepping next to him, Quincy shrugs. "Well, I guess Parker did too, so our advice was for naught, apparently."

By the roughness of their voices and unpolished appearances—messy hair, pajama pants, and ruffled shirts—they apparently rolled out of bed and came straight over.

Good, they're already aiming for comfort.

"Knew what?" Leah tips her head, as if the answer isn't obvious.

Quincy scrunches his face. "That you're fucking Grady?"

"Oh!" She chortles. "Sorry, I kind of forgot it's a whole secret thing."

Why is she acting like this? Is she embarrassed all of a sudden?

"Who wants to tell them?" She tips her head to the side, looking me in the eye.

Oh, I see what she's doing. Sassy, as always. I laugh silently and shake my head, releasing my hold. Warren is already staring *directly* at her hardened nipples. Heat fills his face as he peels his attention away.

They're *so* in.

"Eyes up here, hot stuff." She puts one hand on her hip, wiggling a finger in a circle at her face.

"Fuck, sorry." His blond brows pull together.

"Sh-she's j-j-just p-picking," I say, holding my breath in preparation for insults.

Both of their faces shift the slightest amount—happiness of some sort creeping in. They haven't heard my voice in so long, I should have known they'd be elated.

"As long as you don't kick our asses for looking," Quincy jokes, but it's awkward, letting his genuine worry show.

"She's b-beautiful, right?" I flash a bright smile, willing my mouth to keep working. "Y-you should s-see her b-b-between us."

There it is.

They look at Parker first—eyebrows lifted, lazy smirk, gorgeous eyes sparkling. Then their attention flicks between Leah and me. She's biting back a grin while I pull her into my side.

"B-both of you?!" Warren sputters, brows sky-high. "Actually, I can see it. She seemed totally down for both of us back when we first met her. N-not saying that's a bad thing." He raises his hands in defense.

Quincy offers a tight smile, clearly envious. "Yeah, I mean, good for you guys. It's hard to find genuine connections nowadays. Especially given the circumstances."

"Well, now that the cat is out of the bag, I made a big ole breakfast. Let's sit and talk, shall we?" Leah grabs the platter of pancakes, pecking my cheek as she passes.

I gather the plate of bacon and bowl of grits, following her to the table. Parker trails close behind with the crispy hash browns and fluffy scrambled eggs in hand.

Excitement sparkles in my cousins' eyes. I understand the feelings they're experiencing all too well. This is the first real, home-cooked, made-with-love meal they've ever had. I'm pretty sure Quincy is holding back tears.

Warren, always the braver of the two, like a true big brother, looks at the three of us. His face says everything his mouth can't begin to. Gratitude and adoration shine in his teary gaze. I've never known him to be rendered speechless, but this simple act of kinship and care has done it.

It's settled. He's in, wholeheartedly. They both are.

Leah, radiating compassion, steps between them, juice in hand. Holding back poorly-concealed emotions, they tip their heads toward her. Quincy's chin shakes as he fidgets with his fork.

"Y'all thirsty loves?" she asks, voice gentle as ever.

The way they soften at her tenderness is spectacular. Her ability to know what people need is one of my favorite things about her.

Warren blinks, eyes dancing across her freckled face. Still wrestling with the urge to break down, he nods.

Quincy definitely wipes a tear away but manages to speak, "Y-yes, please. Sorry, this is... nice."

She pours them both a tall glass of orange juice and, having completely dissected their nerves, presses a feather-light kiss to each of their cheeks. Obviously confused, since we haven't even started the conversation, they jolt at the contact.

She doesn't react. To ease their tension, she circles the table to fill Parker's glass and mine, lips meeting our cheeks as well.

Surely they've decided this is a prank by now.

Leah takes her seat between Parker and me, relaxing in her chair.

Parker rubs her back and begins, "So, here's the thing, you two caught me off guard yesterday, and I came home and talked to the beautiful people sitting next to me. We collectively decided on two important things. First off, this—" He motions to the spread around us. "—could be yours every morning, a nice breakfast, good conversation, stolen kisses, and sometimes even a quickie if we have time." He pops a piece of bacon into his mouth, letting the words settle.

"E-excuse you?" Warren stammers, eyes doubled in size.

Quincy, stiff as a board, chokes out, "What he said."

"Leah likes both of you. We see how you watch her when you're surveilling us for Henrietta," Parker spits her name out like it's toxic.

"Sh-she wants y-y-you too," I say since Parker's explanation leaves a lot to be desired.

"Right, but you have to understand that she loves us, we love her, and—" He spares me a glance. I nod with an easy smile. "—Grady and I love each other." Pausing once more, he allows them a minute to process the info-dump.

Quincy stares with intent, mind working. "So... What exactly are you proposing?"

Warren speaks up, "Yeah, I mean, I'm not against sharing, and you're a decent-looking guy, but I'm not about to suck your dick."

"No. I don't expect anything like that. You're both hot as hell, and I won't say no. But it's not a requirement. However, if you want to be with Leah, know that we're part of the deal."

"Well, Grady is family. I know it's been rough, but he's still practically a third brother to us." Quincy's eyes meet mine, filled with longing and silent apologies.

"I d-don't hold it against y-y-you," I say, giving them the most earnest expression I can.

"The things she did to us when we tried to stay close to you were cruel. I'm also sorry for anything shitty I've ever said or done. We're giant pussies who don't deserve this kindness." Quincy works his jaw, face hardening as he fights the memories.

Throat tight, I work to say, "I f-forgive you."

Quincy almost breaks, chest heaving with each forceful exhale.

Warren grips his shoulder, exhaling slowly. "Leah, you've been quiet through all of this. Obviously, we've been interested in you since day one, and fucked it all up out of fear of Henrietta. I'm so sorry for the lies and deceit. The last thing either of us want is to hurt you. Are you sure that you want us, too? We'll understand if you don't," he mutters, body rigid.

"Oh, I hated it when I found out who you were because I definitely felt a spark when we met. Then you were jerks, and it was a *huge* turn-off, but you made up for it by showing up and apologizing. Grady told me about your history and how you are treated, and Parker said he believes that you're actually decent guys. So, if you're serious about this, then yes. But, just so you know, I'm familiar with at least three ways to break a kneecap. So if you cross us, you'll never walk again." Her sweet smile only adds to the seriousness of her threat. She's not being subtle, I wouldn't expect her to.

"Fuck, you're so hot. I'm in." Warren groans and takes a bite of pancake. "I mean, the promise of breakfast would have been enough, honestly." His eyes roll back as he hums around his food.

"I don't know, having a real relationship, instead of settling for sneaky hookups behind Auntie's back, sounds sweet to me." Quincy beams. "Hell, I might actually kiss Parker if that's what it takes."

"No need for all that." Parker laughs. "But, I mean, if the situation arises, I'm not against it. Hell, I'm down with sucking your dick. Leah would enjoy the show." He shrugs, tone deathly serious.

Warren chokes on his food, gaze darting between his brother and the relentless flirt next to me.

Leah sighs dreamily between us, making a laugh rush out of me.

"You're into that?" Quincy's brows shoot straight to the ceiling.

"Yeah, she is." Parker winks, and surprisingly, Quincy raises a shoulder.

"Alright, I can't believe I'm saying this, but enough sex talk. Let's eat. Then we can get to the *real* reason you're here," Leah interrupts the eye-fucking Parker is giving Quincy.

They're going to be trouble. Not that she'll mind. Hell, the thought of Parker fucking them, too, does sound hot... once I get past the fact that we were raised together. But it's not about them, it's about seeing the people I love being loved in return.

My cheeks try to flush, but I wash the images from my mind.

"You're right, Star. We've got all day to... figure out what works for everyone. Food first, business second, then if you're both good, maybe we can help relieve some of that pent-up sexual frustration." Parker shoots a smirk across the table before diving into his—definitely cold—eggs.

It doesn't matter. We all devour our breakfast as if it's fresh off the stove.

Leah worked hard to make it, and every man at this table is beyond appreciative to have someone who cares.

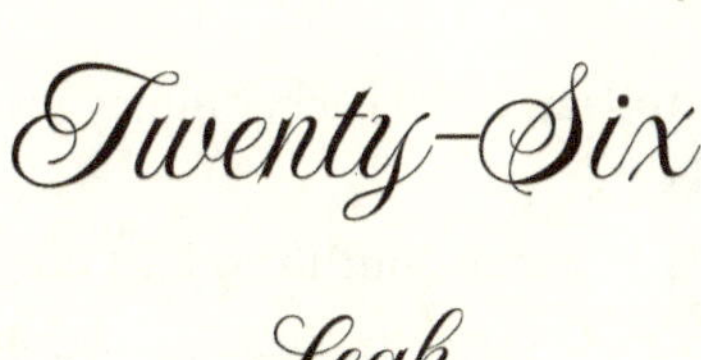

Twenty-Six

Leah

Quincy's jaw is hanging wide-open on the couch across from us. Parker and Grady are at my sides, each holding a hand. We've just finished telling them everything.

Warren is equally speechless, but it's more subtle—shoulders pulled tight, breathing slowed to a crawl.

I only know one way to ease their minds. So I extract myself from the men keeping me in one piece and sit between them. Only, instead of letting awkwardness take over, I grab Warren by the chin, pressing our lips together.

His hand immediately moves to the back of my neck, drawing me closer. He claims me like he's finally coming to his senses, letting the words we've bombarded him with process.

When we separate, his eyes never leave mine, glimmering brighter than ever. "You mean it? Are we really welcome to join you guys? We can get out?" His attention finally drifts from me to the other couch where Parker and Grady sit, smiling softly.

"Of course," I murmur as they nod in agreement.

When I turn to Quincy, he's ready, burning alive with anticipation. I could keep him waiting, make him beg for it, but now isn't the time. So, I let him pull me in, shifting me to straddle him. Our mouths collide with eagerness, bodies seeking one another with a need for connection. Warmth blooms in my core as his hands travel to my ass.

Before we go too far, I pull back, running my fingers through his wavy red locks.

"You're going to change our lives. I... I don't know how to thank you," he whispers, as if he owes me anything more than his presence.

"She loves orgasms," Parker speaks up, voice gravelly.

My first instinct is to scold him for being ridiculous, but I'm not given the chance. My thoughts stop when Quincy quirks a brow, pressing his *very* ready cock against me. "Is that so? Because, for months, we've wanted to hear you break for us."

Well then.

I grind into him, unable to resist the friction. My panties are a pathetic excuse for a barrier, and the thin pajamas he's wearing do nothing to mask his size.

Is this whole family part horse?

"If this is happening... do we need to discuss rules?" Warren asks, squirming next to us.

Based on the bulge he's sporting, he's not completely uncomfortable. It's obvious he wants this as much as I do. Parker and Grady are watching intently with looks that could melt steel, which I'm not surprised by in the slightest.

Parker leisurely strokes Grady through his sweats, unashamed. "We can talk about everything later. Right now, the only thing that matters is making sure our girl gets off. So, if we're all in agreement, please fuck her, Q."

"Oh shit," Warren whispers as his brother slides my panties to the side, fingers grazing my pussy.

Needy, I whimper, lifting myself enough to let him shimmy out of his pants. His forehead falls against my shoulder as I reach between us to grip him.

"Fuck," he growls, rubbing my clit. "I've dreamed of you so many times." Thrusting into my hand, his teeth graze my jaw.

"Warren," I moan, turning my attention to him as Quincy throbs, heavy in my grasp. "Pants off, let me see you too."

He pauses, still uncertain of the situation. His attention shifts across from us. Parker and Grady are fully undressed, rock-hard, stroking themselves slowly.

"You're gonna see a lot of our cocks if you're in this. If not, we'll see you in a couple of hours." Parker tilts his head to the door, making his point clear.

"War," I gasp as Quincy slips his fingers inside of me. "Please? I want you too." I trace the outline of his cock, and his apprehension dissolves at the contact.

"Fuck it." Mind made up, he sheds his pants.

Thick and veiny, he twitches when my fingers wrap around him. My breath catches as I skim over the trail of barbells along the underside of his shaft—four in total.

"Freaky enough for a pierced cock, but too shy to show it off? Shame," Parker prods, breath coming out strained.

"H-hey," Grady speaks up with a warning scowl.

"What? If you're packing like that, be proud. Fuck I can only imagine how they feel." Parker's eyes flutter. "Hulk, will you pierce yours for me?"

"N-no. Fuck W-Warren instead," Grady answers, shaking his head.

Well then, that answers one of my questions.

"No fun." Parker pouts, leaning in to kiss Grady. Their little bickering match dies the instant their lips meet. They stroke each other while their tongues mingle.

"Wow," Quincy breathes out, watching over my shoulder. His fingers have stopped moving, entranced by the show.

"Yeah, they're hot together," I murmur against him, squeezing Warren. "Please fill me up, somebody, anybody, I don't care. You can't just surround me with hot, naked men not let me come for at least one of you."

"If I lie down, you can ride me, and War can take your ass. I love feeling his piercings when we share women like that," Quincy suggests.

I hop off of him so fast the room echoes with chuckles. There's no way I'm going to pass *that* up.

Quincy watches my every move as he shifts onto his back. My panties fall to the floor, and he grips my waist as I line myself up. I'm soaked and ready, but he's thick, rivaling Grady. With the first inch, I know I'm a goner. His flushed cheeks and the stretch alone could make me fall in love. But when he whimpers my name? Deal sealed.

"You're so much better than I imagined. God, we're lucky," he whispers against my lips.

I bottom out, moaning as he immediately thrusts, pressing deeper than I thought possible. "War, please get inside me," I beg, riding his brother with slow, delicious intent.

Nearly a breath later, he's kneeling behind me. "Is this what you want, you filthy, filthy girl?" he growls in my ear and the air in the room shifts.

Maybe it's just the air in my lungs?

I don't know because I'm too fucking feral to understand. But his tone? Oh, it does inexplicable things to me. I clench around Quincy, and he hisses, pinching my nipples through the thin fabric of Grady's shirt.

The next thing I know, the crack of Warren's palm hitting my ass fills the room, echoing off the walls. My eyes water, pussy throbbing from the pain as it turns to pleasure.

Parker and Grady go still, waiting for a reaction I can't give.

"Do you want me to fuck this tight little ass until you break? Tell me." Warren grips my hip, burying a finger to the knuckle.

All I can manage is a needy whine. The sensations flooding my body have stolen my breath.

"Answer him, you won't like the consequences if you don't," Quincy grunts out below me, thrusting steadily.

"P-please," I whimper.

Parker moans from across the room as Warren presses another finger into me, getting me ready for him, for this whole experience.

"Mmmm, fuck. Do you have any idea how many times I've soaked my sheets in cum thinking about this perfect ass?" Warren spits on his cock, lining up.

I go still beneath him, letting my body relax, moaning as he eases in. Inch by inch, he brings me to new, exquisite limits, piercings hitting spots I never knew existed.

Quincy can definitely feel them, too, based on the way his eyes are rolling. Pinned between them, enduring such sweet torture, my needy pleas grow incoherent, maddened by the pleasure.

"Such a cock slut, aren't you? I bet you'd like another one, too." Warren buries himself in me, and my vision blurs. Sensations come to life that make no sense, yet here I am. "Yeah, you do. Make Quincy share that needy little pussy."

"I-I don't know how that would work," I breathe out between my moans as they pump into me.

"But you want it, don't you? Say the word. You can take Parker, too, like a good girl. Let us break you." Warren grits, slamming into me.

"Yes," I cry out, tears welling in my eyes as he wraps my hair around his fist.

Death by dick sounds fantastic.

Warren hisses, yanking my head back. "Of course you do. Fuck you're our perfect little whore. Parker, come here."

With a guttural moan, he obeys, practically crawling across the room—Grady hot on his heels.

Warren pulls out, helping coordinate their positions.

Quincy tilts his hips so Parker can begin stretching me with his fingers. "Oh fuck, I can't wait to feel your cock against mine," he grits out.

"Sounds like someone is a naughty boy," Parker teases, fitting another finger inside.

"Not to rush this, but I'd like to make her scream for us," Warren says with an impatient edge.

Parker, unable to help himself, winks at him. "Yes, Boss."

I see stars when he slides inside, one perfect inch at a time. Once he's fully seated, Quincy lets out a shuddering breath as my body squeezes them tightly together. Blissful tears stream down my face, eyes rolling back

"Look at you," Parker says against my shoulder, thrusting until he's so deep I question my sanity.

Warren groans, shifting until he's practically squatting above me, nearly sitting in Parker's lap. Every nerve in my body lights up when he slowly slides back into my ass. Together, the three of them do things I'd never thought possible.

Through the haze of ecstasy, my gaze lands on Grady. He wipes my tears and bends down, stealing a heated kiss before offering me his cock, completely indifferent to Quincy moaning below me.

He's not demanding, not even expecting me to take it. But the tenderness in his eyes, how gently he strokes my cheek, grounds me in an impossible way. Overcome with sensations, I'm more dick than woman at the moment, so what difference would a fourth make?

I rock back onto the three men currently ravaging me, and open my mouth for him. A chorus of rough groans fills the room as Grady feeds me every delicious inch, agonizingly slow, as if he's afraid to be the one who breaks me. His head rolls back and he moans when I whimper around him, choking and half delusional.

Parker slips his hand around my front, between my body and Quincy's. His fingers find my clit with ease. Slow, intentional circles pull at the tension in my core,

He hisses as I clench tighter. "Fuck, you're so goddamn perfect. Jesus." His breathless praise drives me closer to the edge.

"So spectacular." Quincy watches me sloppily swallow everything Grady has to give. "God, you're such a sight." He grunts, growing harder inside of me, "I fucking love it here."

"This ass," Warren groans out, voice crazed as he drives into me as much as his position will allow. He's the only one actually thrusting at this point. Parker and Quincy are merely along for the ride. "Such a sweet little treat. I can't wait to see you dripping with our cum." He leans back into Parker, reservations vanished.

I scream around Grady when Warren spanks me harder, tightening until they all go still.

Parker flicks my clit one final time as I sit back to fill myself. Mind melting, I shatter into a million pieces, lost in the agonizing euphoria.

Urges take over as they all groan around shaky breaths, spilling into me within seconds.

I collapse against Quincy, delusional and half-asleep. The next thing I know, I wake up with him still inside of me, Grady wiping his release off my lips before kissing me. The others are sitting back, flushed with blissful smiles.

The sound of the shower turning on wakes me next.

When the hell did we come to bed?

I'm... clean. Someone made sure the mess they made of me is untraceable. I peel an eye open, realizing I'm curled up between Warren and, judging by the size, Grady.

"Hey there, Gorgeous." Warren brushes my hair out of my face, kissing my forehead. "Welcome back to your body."

"Oh, is it mine again? You're all done with it?" I joke, nuzzling into his chest.

His chuckle vibrates against my face and—definitely—Grady's hold on me tightens.

"Where are the others?" I ask.

"Bathroom," Grady mumbles against my shoulder.

"Wait." I tilt my head at the muffled moan barely audible over the water. "Are they fooling around?"

"Yup." Warren laughs. "Turns out Parker is a big fan of Quincy's dick and wanted to do more than share it with you. They seem to have similar sexual appetites. Little freaks." His tone is surprisingly light, filled with adoration. This can't be the same man who almost chickened out, I refuse to believe it.

"Oh, thank God, Grady and I were getting exhausted trying to keep that man satisfied." I giggle almost silently.

"Speaking of satisfied, I wasn't too much earlier, right?" Warren leans back to look me in the eye. "I kind of just, I don't know..."

"Rocked my world? Heck yeah, you did. Never really had someone degrade me before. It was hot as hell." I waggle my brows. "But, if orgasms aren't involved, don't you *dare* call me a filthy whore."

"Wouldn't dream of it, Gorgeous." He grabs my jaw and kisses me like he means it, as if nothing else in the world exists. For a moment, it's just us.

Until it's not.

Grady trails his fingers up my side as a gentle reminder that I'm swimming in gorgeous men. He kisses my shoulder, drawing a dreamy sigh from my lips.

"To think I almost ran away from this. I'm the luckiest woman alive."

"Is it you who's lucky?" Quincy asks as he steps into the room, towel hanging low around his waist. The abs on this man are criminal. I can't help but stare as he dries his hair and tosses a lazy smile our way.

"Well, I don't know anymore. You look like a kid who just got all his birthday wishes granted." I laugh, straight from the belly.

"Sex with a literal goddess, and a steamy blowjob in the shower from one of the kinkiest men I've ever met, all after a killer breakfast? You bet your ass I'm a happy little man hoe." Still damp, he plops down on the bed next to Grady. "You know how to pick em, G. Thanks for sharing." He slaps him on the shoulder, grinning brightly.

Parker, flushed and relaxed, saunters into the room a moment later and circles the bed to the empty space behind Warren. "You gonna bite me if I lie next to you, Boss?"

"You'd like that," Warren grumbles. "Sorry to disappoint, but you have three other willing bodies. I'm not a fourth."

"Hey, sorry. Don't mean to push buttons. I'll dial it back if I make you uncomfortable. I want this to work for everyone's sake." Parker slips fresh sweats on and stands awkwardly at the edge of the bed.

Warren sighs. "Just get in the damn bed, Pretty Boy. I didn't say you can't hold me, but if your dick gets hard, one of them is dealing with it." He jerks his head toward us, and Grady snickers.

"Oh, his dick will be poking you in the ass before you know it." I chuckle. "The man has no refractory period. It's insane."

"I'm pretty sure it already is," Warren says as Parker wraps around him, clinging like a baby koala.

"Shh, just let me hold you. It'll go down eventually."

Quincy lets out a boisterous laugh and I snort at the shock on Warren's face. "If we ever share a bed again, someone else gets the horny Velcro. It's between my cheeks," he announces, but makes no effort to move.

"At least he's wearing pants. He tucks it between mine in the nude," I say with a coy smile.

"Pretty sure that's where I draw the line. This is already close to the limit," he grumbles, eyes narrowed.

"It's a nice cock, just appreciate it, man," Quincy says on a yawn.

He's not wrong, they're all gifted to the point I almost feel selfish for hogging them. Not that I am, they could easily find someone else after we leave here. But for now, I'm basking in it.

Parker snores softly behind Warren and tenderness settles into his expression. He shifts subtly, pressing closer into his chest.

"See, he's just like a puppy. He gets excited, tries to hump things, and then falls asleep when he's comfy." I kiss Warren softly and he puffs out a laugh through his nose.

"He is pretty adorable," Quincy agrees.

"He's... tolerable," Warren grumbles.

"He's o-ours," Grady murmurs half-asleep behind me.

That he is.

And they're all mine.

Twenty-Seven

Parker

For the past week, Warren and Quincy have come over every morning for breakfast. That is, if they didn't spend the night. Leah is glowing, bouncing around in her underwear while she cooks her famous biscuit sandwiches. She's genuinely happy, and that warms my insides in ways I can't explain.

Singing off-key to an old Shania Twain song, she's oblivious to our matching smitten smiles. We're all fucking goners for the infectious pink-haired bad ass woman we're fortunate enough to call ours.

Quincy's phone chimes, demanding all of our attention. While he reads, his ears redden, jaw ticking. Leah pauses the music, eyes glued to him.

"Shit," he grits out. "The old bag wants to see us later, War."

Warren swallows hard in the chair next to him. "She'll want her weekly update, asking for any intel we can give her. What do we say?" Nostrils flaring, he looks at me, then Leah, and finally Grady before continuing, "We aren't going to betray you, if that's what you think. Even before all this, we never gave her any incriminating information."

"Nobody thinks you did." Leah moves to his side. "If you had, she would know about Parker giving me lessons outside of regular hours, you two watched every one. But she has no clue because you aren't as conniving as she likes to think. You're good men at heart, which is why you're here, and you'll be coming with us." Her lips press against his temple.

He wraps his arms around her waist, face burrowing into her hair. "Thank you for that. I still worry you think we're lying." His muffled words come out strained.

"Same here, to be fair. But I care way too much about all of you, and I'm honestly ecstatic to have a friendship with Grady again," Quincy adds, voice light, but there's a meaningful tone buried in it.

Grady nods in agreement, grinning vibrantly at his cousins. He's been talking more around them, but still shies away, which will probably always be the case. What matters is that they let him be comfortable. That was my biggest concern going into this. I don't want him to backtrack and shut down again. Leah loves this happier, more outgoing version that has bloomed over the past few months. I do, too.

It's obvious that she worries about me, as well. And she's justified in that. I'm running on empty, and we still have months to go before the World Cup. Once that comes to pass, we can relax and prepare for the Olympics, because she *will* make it, even if it kills me.

Bridget is clearly not going to qualify. She hasn't come close in a single show. Her progress is nonexistent. The unfortunate truth is that my time here will be cut short because of it. I'm supposed to be her golden ticket, the surefire way to skyrocket her to fame and help her live up to the expectations that come with the Hart name.

Truthfully, no amount of dedication or revolutionary new techniques will help. I'd have better luck training a fish to walk.

"Hey," Leah's soft voice wraps around me like a warm hug. She sits in my lap, eyes melting into mine. "Your face will get stuck like this if you keep scowling so hard." She smooths the line between my brows and lays her palm against my cheek. "I love you, and whatever thoughts you've got zipping through that beautiful mind of yours, they're wrong."

"You're wrong," I whisper, crumbling under the pressure of everything.

"Well, tell me about it, tell *us* about it." Sullen expressions on all three of the other guys' faces give me pause. I know Grady loves me, Quincy likes the way I make him feel, and Warren... has moments when I think he finds me funny. Maybe.

I'm an asshole. A monumental, blind, asshole. Quincy clearly wants to hold me, desperate to be a source of comfort in the same way Leah is. And Warren, while he's not going to kiss me or anything of the sort, there is genuine concern in his eyes. Still, I don't know if they feel for *me,* or if they want me happy for Leah's sake.

Talk to them, you stubborn ass.

I sigh, resting my forehead against Leah's shoulder. "I'm just afraid of failing and losing all of this."

"You're not going to," Quincy speaks up. "Look how amazing Leah has done. Fuck Bridget and this place." He sneers, gritting his teeth as his deep-seated loathing threatens to grow beyond his control.

"He's right, she's a mockery of our name. Hell, Q and I ride better than her, so Henrietta has never let us anywhere near a lesson, for fear of us showing her up." Warren addresses Grady,

"You ride a hell of a lot better, always have. Shame she demoted you to stable boy when she couldn't 'fix' you." His face tightens.

It's strange to think about how bothered he is by everything. Just a week ago, I assumed these two were sleazy jerks, only trying to steal my girl. Even if she saw through their façade, I was hard-headed and wouldn't listen.

Now, I'm pretty sure I'm catching feelings for them, too. Which is terrible. Quincy is one thing, but Warren has made it abundantly clear that he's not interested.

At my silence and conflicted expression, Grady stands with determination in his eyes, chest puffed out. "Couches," he orders. When nobody moves, he grunts. "All of y-y-you."

Fuck, shy Grady is lovable. But bossy Grady? My bones are jelly.

The others blink, processing his newfound assertiveness.

"Guess breakfast is going to wait," Leah says, climbing off me, extending her hand.

I take it, and the four of us follow Grady to the living room.

He motions to the large couch, looking me in the eye with determination. "Sit."

Why the hell is this so hot?

I hold my breath and obey, taking the middle spot. He pulls the cushions off the other sofa and places them on the floor at my feet.

"Sit." He points to his cousins.

I nearly erupt as they listen without question.

Leah takes the seat at my left, Grady sits to my right. I expect a moment of silence or... something. Anything other than Grady grabbing my jaw and kissing me silly as everyone else watches. There's no restraint, no modesty in the way he consumes me. His beard scratches against my chin, teeth pulling my lip. Seconds, that's all it lasts for, but I don't need anything longer. I wouldn't survive it.

When he pulls away, a needy whine leaves me, chasing more of his sudden dominance. He pins everyone with stern looks and inhales. "T-tell him."

I let out a humorless laugh. "What is this a fucking truth circle? Who gets the talking stick first?"

The giant man next to me grumbles roughly, and my heart flutters. Whatever has come over him can stay, it's delicious. Maybe I can get him to tie me up. I'm sure we have spare lead ropes somewhere.

"Q," Grady grunts out.

Quincy blows out a harsh breath and runs his hand through his silky hair. "Okay, no pressure or anything." He lets out a nervous chuckle.

Leah squeezes my knee and interrupts, "He already knows how we feel. But Grady and I can see how unsure he is about the two of you. This whole relationship we've barreled into is a lot to handle, more so for Parker than anyone. Sure, I have a lot going on, but I'm not getting jerked around and berated every day by Bridget. He's stressed and naturally wants to find comfort in his people. But, and correct me if I'm way off base—" She looks me in the eyes briefly. "—he's having conflicted feelings about whether you're also *his* people or if you're just here for me."

Warren scoffs, pulling all of our attention his way.

Grady tenses next to me. For a moment, I'm certain he'd willingly fight this man if it comes to that. "Q first," he barks out instead.

"I... I'm not just here for Leah. What the fuck?" Quincy's voice is elevated, but not with anger. A slight frown, pinched brows; he's hurt. "How can I show you that, while I do enjoy my time with Leah, I also want *you* with the same intensity? Tell me how to build that trust, because honestly, you're my first... Boyfriend? The first guy I've done anything with, actually. I've never acted on it before. Being queer in this family isn't allowed, so I ignored the lingering attraction, forced myself to feel self-hatred for being yet *another* imperfect Hart instead. You're worth breaking through all of the barriers I built. I'm sorry if I've been giving you mixed signals all week. I'm just figuring this out as I go, and didn't know if this was just sex for you. Part of me thought I was just kind of *here*, so you fucked me too." He chews his lip, chin shaking.

The pain in his voice stings in ways I can't describe. I want to kick my own ass for being selfish. "I thought the same about you," I admit, throat closing.

"I don't want to just sleep with you, Parker." My name comes out of his lips with a strangled sound. "I-I want *you.* All of you. Every time they touch you lovingly in passing, every playful kiss while you're tucked away out of surveillance, the nauseatingly cute smiles and glances. I want to curl up with you while we talk about the day, lay your head in my lap while you fall asleep on the couch because you're out there killing yourself to stay useful to Henrietta." Tears stream down his cheeks, increasing with each barbed word, hands shaking under the weight of his confession.

"Come here," I choke out, opening my arms.

He moves lightning-fast, to straddle me, slotting his lips over mine. As I taste him—hunger, salty tears, desperation to fit into this relationship—my heart twists.

I'm usually the one who takes time to communicate everything. I don't like "what if"'s and hate leaving people in a state of uncertainty. But I've been so focused on my own shit show that I've taken this fragile, confused man and left him in the dark to fend for himself.

"I'm so sorry," I murmur against his lips. "I never considered that you were going through all of this self-revelation alone. Please give me all of your affection, I'm a whore for it." I bark out a short laugh. "Don't hold back. You'll *never* be too much for me."

"I second all of that," Leah agrees.

"Sorry. I didn't mean to make this about me." He pinches his brows together, blinking back lingering tears.

"You didn't, this is about *us,* your feelings are valid and helped open my eyes to how much of an asshole I've been." I wipe his damp cheeks.

"You're under more pressure than all of us," Warren cuts in, voice surprisingly soft as he watches me comfort his brother. "I think you've earned the right to be overwhelmed and a little distant."

He stands and looks at Grady, who—despite the surprise on his face—moves so he can sit next to me.

"I... I'm not into guys." He keeps his attention glued to his lap, hand resting lightly against my thigh.

"I know." Chest tight, I blow out a shaky breath. "I don't expect you to do anything you're uncomfortable with. I just... I want to know that you at least view me as a good friend, a partner in all of this, that you care about me to some degree. You're related to the others, and Leah is easy to fall in love with, I know. So, I guess I just need validation. As fucking dumb as that sounds."

His shoulders rise as he inhales, chest deflating quickly with the sharp breath he forces out. "Parker, I let you spoon me... in the nude, because you don't like to sleep with clothes. Your dick has been between my ass cheeks more times than any 'friend' would be allowed. I know what your 'o' face looks like and have watched my brother and cousin tag-team you. You're like my freaky, platonic boyfriend." A devilish half-smirk pulls at his lips. "I would burn this shithole to the ground for you."

When his eyes melt into mine, I let out a sputtering laugh. "You've honestly gone above and beyond in the realm of acceptance. I just. I want to fucking kiss you and snuggle you so bad sometimes. And that's not fair to you, I know, but since we're all word vomiting, I want to throw it out there. I don't know how to navigate wanting you when I know you don't want me. But it's my shit to fig—"

I'm floating, brain misfiring as he slams his lips to mine. Leah gasps, and Quincy jolts in my lap, surely fucking flabbergasted. It doesn't last long, but he's not as awkward about it as I'd have thought. When he pulls back, my wide eyes scan his face for answers to questions I can't even form.

He licks his lips, offering a faint nod. "Kissing is fine, it does nothing for me, but I'm not repulsed by it. Same thing with snuggles. Okay? I might even let you suck my dick sometime. Just know that it would be one-sided, and I don't know if I'll ever actually fuck you. But kissing? I'm good with that, if it's what you need."

I hear his words, but my brain is still trying to figure out what the fuck just happened.

Grady steps behind us, threading his fingers through my hair, wrenching my head back. As he claims my mouth, Quincy's lips land on my exposed throat and I whimper. He's still straddling me and definitely feels how hard I am, as if my involuntary whimpers aren't enough indication.

"You're important to all of us," Leah says, making her way to Warren. "And you." She crawls into his lap. "Thank you for being open-minded. I know this has been a lot to process, but you're doing so well."

Warren takes my hand. "I want this to work. I'm not disgusted by the idea of loving you in a slightly less than straight way, but I just..." He shakes his head, warring with his thoughts.

"Hey, honestly, even light physical affection is more than I could ask for. Don't ever feel pressured to do anything on my behalf again. One simple kiss could be all we ever share, and that's fine. It means the world that you are willing to try. But I can't expect you to be something you're not."

"It really isn't uncomfortable. Honestly, you're a good big spoon. The boners are just the cost of feeling secure and loved." He chuckles. "But I'll let the others handle them for you."

"Deal," Quincy says, almost too fast.

"Speaking of..." Leah bites her lip. "There's been a whole lot of hot man-on-man action, and I would *really* like to go deal with my lady boner."

Grady is the first to move, tossing her over his shoulder in a fluid motion. When he slaps her ass, she squeals, giddy and squirming in his grasp. Apparently eager as the rest of us, he unceremoniously tosses her onto the bed, pants falling to the ground while he stalks toward her.

There's a primal energy about him that's fucking delicious. We've awoken the beast in this man.

Eyes sparkling, Leah sheds her shirt. "So glad we talked this out, because the four of you have ruined me for anyone else."

She could never understand how true the same is for me. Based on the adoring glances we all exchange, everyone in the room agrees.

We're not perfect, but today we learned that each of us loves one another regardless. That's all I've ever wanted in life. Having my wildest dreams come true four times over is unthinkable.

Twenty-Eight

Leah

Competition jitters never bother me like this. Maybe I'm choking under the pressure of having four secret boyfriends rooting for me in the audience? Nah, I don't choke. Especially not when Tally is this excited.

Her energy is powerful, nearly vibrating under the saddle. She's ready to show off, and admittedly, I'm eager to do the same. It hits different knowing that the people closest to Henrietta are all watching, rooting for *me*, not Bridget.

Money and power mean nothing when you're an evil bitch.

Tally snorts, already revved up. Another medley of 90s boy bands, remixed with classical vibes, booms through the arena, our signature at this point. Everything else fades away as my mind zeroes in on our task.

Beat by beat, I guide Tally with precision, her hooves landing in the sand with purpose. She's putting all of her energy into this show, hitting every cue flawlessly.

That's my girl.

I believe that she genuinely understands what's at stake and has put just as much of her heart into our mission. The instant I met this horse, I knew she was special, and every single training session and show has reinforced that belief.

With practiced guidance, I move her through each transition with razor-sharp accuracy. My body settles, finally catching up with my mind—concerns fading with every passing second. Our routine isn't long, but the skills are far more difficult than any of our past shows.

Nearing the end, I swallow the last of my doubts. This is simply another day, and we're going to hit this canter pirouette with no issues. It's our first time doing one in an actual show, definitely a main cause of my unexpected nerves. We've done it flawlessly the last five times in training, but it's a tricky move. Anything could go wrong.

No.

Stop thinking about it. You know what you're doing.

We move from our half-pass trot to the far side of the arena, smoothly shifting to a collected canter. I count the beats and hold my breath. Parker has to be quaking as hard as I am. I want to look at them, see the faces of my men before I do this, but I can't. There's no time to get hung up and let myself—all of us —down.

This competition is my key to the World Cup. If we score well today, we're in and can focus on preparing for that—pure practice, and choreographing a kick-ass routine that will showcase how strong we are.

This pirouette is the cherry on top of our performance. Parker is right, we've played it fairly safe up to this point, putting just enough into these shows to earn decent scores—anything to keep me on the comfortable side of confident.

But this is for *us.*

We approach the marker, heart stuck in my throat. It's like the world is speeding by and standing still all at once.

Tally follows my lead, nearly weightless as she pivots. If horses had toes, she'd be spinning on them like a world-class ballerina. Three hundred and sixty degrees of buttery smooth movement, then her front feet come down, and we've done it.

I gather my composition and spare a glance at the guys. Parker wipes a tear, tossing his head back. Grady sits up straighter, wearing a small, proud smile. Warren and Quincy are biting back giant grins, practically bouncing in the bleachers.

That's right, boys, we're getting out of here.

The last few movements in our routine are a breeze. Before I know it, we're awaiting scoring, which is always nerve-racking, but this time it's heavy, crushing. No matter how clean I *think* our routine was, I still prepare for the worst. Even if the pirouette and piaffe felt flawless.

When the scoreboard shows an eighty-three point five-two percent, I nearly fall out of my saddle. God, I wish I could run and jump into Parker's arms and let them all smother me with joyous kisses, celebrating right here in front of the world.

Instead, I remain as stoic as possible.

Patting Tally on the neck, I beam as we ride steadily out of the arena. Guiding Tally to her stall, I dismount, celebratory peppermint in hand.

"We're going all the way. T. You, me, and all four of our boys." I lean my forehead against hers and sigh while she crunches away. "This is going to work. We're so close." Months of treading lightly, sneaking around, training in secret, are all finally proving to be worth it. I can't wait to have this hardship pay off and finally have time to find the perfect chunk of land for us.

I busy myself untacking Tally, taking my time to show a little extra love along the way. Massaging her withers always earns a soft grunt of appreciation. This time is no different. I can't help but reflect on where I was months ago—the judgment in my parents' voices as I told them I was leaving. How quickly my brothers took their side and told me I was being foolish.

I hope they choke on my success.

It's not like I didn't do anything for them with my winnings. I paid off the house, bought them all new cars, and gave each of them hefty amounts of money to spend as they pleased.

But chasing my dreams is "impractical". Making a name for myself is "unfeasible".

According to them, anyway.

Today is the first time I'm able to convince myself that they're absolutely wrong. I never thought I'd see a score anywhere near eighty percent at this level. Most hopefuls will only dream of it, yet we've been doing it consistently. I thought for sure that today would be our downfall. The pressure almost got the better of me. But we rode clean. We deserve it.

The World Cup had better be ready for us. And then, the Olympics are in our sights. I'm a freight train with no brakes now, confidence in overdrive. Nothing is stopping me from achieving this, saving my men from their shitty situations, and throwing my success in my *entire* family's face.

My name has been whispered on the wind in the dressage space ever since our debut. After today, it'll be all people talk about. Nobody else has scored above an eighty at this entire show. The thought is a lot to process.

I went to Hartbrook fully aware that it's unheard of for a nobody to show up, prove themselves, and earn their place as a frontrunner to represent their country in less than a year. The tryouts are usually an extensive process, but damn if we're not showcasing our abilities every time we strut into an arena.

Even if we don't make it, I'm proud of how far we've already come.

Either way, I have a plan and want to surprise the guys, but I need to focus my energy on the World Cup. My scheming can wait until after.

My face is broken. The too-wide grin splitting it won't leave.

We decided to drive an hour away for my celebration dinner. Nobody in this town has a clue who we are, which means our affection doesn't need to be secretive.

"I'm so proud of you." Parker takes my hand as we sit in the booth at this surprisingly fancy diner. I sprung for the best we could find in this little Alabama town.

"I'd be nothing if it wasn't for you." I look around the table, getting lost in their loving smiles and soft faces. "All of you."

Quincy's ears redden, tucking his chin to his chest. "You were so spectacular out there. I'm unworthy of sharing your air."

I roll my eyes with a scoff. "Like hell you are. I just hope Henrietta doesn't get on you too badly. After today, she has to be suspicious that Parker is still training me."

Warren raises a hand dismissively. "You let us worry about her. Parker, I'm sorry, but Bridget is going to be extra unpleasant when we get back, especially after her horrid score today."

"She missed half of her transitions, that's one hundred percent her fault!" Parker huffs, scowling at the table.

Grady watches our exchange, more joy than anything shining in his eyes. Nothing is bringing this man down from the cloud he's on.

"Buonasera, I'm Adriano. What can I get you started with?" Our waiter appears out of nowhere.

My jolt doesn't go unnoticed. Though Grady says nothing, his hand finds my leg under the table with a gentle squeeze, simple and comforting, exactly what I need.

"Oh, uh." Staring blankly at him, my words get lost in the ether.

Parker chuckles. "One order of the family-style lasagna, please."

"Ah, a splendid choice. Will we be pairing it with a bottle of wine?" Adriano asks.

"Yes, you finest Chianti," Warren replies effortlessly.

His wine knowledge shouldn't be so impressive. Surely he has to know these things. But my stomach fills with flutters all the same.

Nodding, Adriano taps at the tablet in his hand, disappearing as quickly as he showed up.

"You g-good?" Grady arches a brow.

"Yeah. It's silly, but I'm still worried we'll be discovered." I offer a tight, apologetic smile.

"Are you ashamed of us?" Warren asks, direct as ever in the way I love and hate.

It's not a malicious question. He wouldn't ask if he wasn't genuinely concerned.

It still stings.

"I'll never be ashamed of any of you. I just don't want to get found out before we have plans in motion."

"Gorgeous, the plan has been in motion. You slammed a brick down on the gas pedal today," he replies, reaching across the table to take my hand. Our fingers lace together, and he rubs my knuckles with his thumb.

"But, my worry is—"

"Me," Parker cuts in, voice tense. "Bridget won't make it to the World Cup, Henrietta can't buy her way in. She won't qualify, no matter how hard I try to get her in shape. This has been my worry all along." His face falls.

Quincy speaks up, "So what? She's twenty-one. She can go to the next summer Olympics. It's not like Champ will be decrepit by then. Renegotiate your contract. Tell the old lady that you can get her there by then, even though we won't be around." The steadiness in his argument catches me off guard.

"Why did we never think of that?" I tilt my head. "None of us ever considered simply convincing Henrietta that she can make it next time, and just needs to improve. It's a great idea, Q."

"I l-love you all," Grady announces, a spark of realization burning in his gaze.

It's as if he's only now letting it sink in that his life is about to change, that breaking free of this prison he's been in is possible. I lean over and kiss his cheek, giggling when he melts against my lips, large hand squeezing my thigh.

"We're so close. Just a little longer. We got it in the bag." I give him a shoulder bump.

If I play this smart, call the right people, and get the right information without being too obvious, I might get us out of here before the World Cup.

Our happiness is in my hands now. Failure isn't an option.

Twenty-Nine

Parker

Two weeks of radio silence from Henrietta. Every day feels like doomsday. I'm still training Bridget, even though we all know she's not making the World Cup and has a zero percent chance of going anywhere near the Olympics. Why has there been no ass-chewing? Who knows.

Quincy and Warren are convinced that Henrietta is plotting our collective downfall. They still report to her, and apparently, the last couple of times since Alabama have been strange. What would normally be concise,. formal meetings with weekly task lists have been replaced by awkward interrogations. She definitely knows I'm going behind her back, so I should probably be more careful.

We all should.

I've found two more cameras in the stables, tucked into corners for better viewing angles. I wouldn't be surprised if she's got one somewhere in the storage room. Just because we can't see it, doesn't mean she's not watching, listening, gathering more ammo for her attack.

"You're worrying again." Quincy wraps his arms around me from behind while I wash our dinner dishes. His lips find my neck and, for a fleeting second, the static fades.

Our dynamic has blossomed into a beautiful thing. Sure, we all have varying personalities, but our mutual love leaves no room for argument.

"You two are gross," Warren walks into the kitchen, grimacing with a mirthful glint in his eye.

He presses his lips against my cheek as he passes by. I still blush every time he does that. He's far more affectionate than I was prepared for. It's a very welcome surprise.

"Bring your asses to the couch, it's movie night, and I'm not getting stuck next to Grady again. He's a furnace." He grabs a bowl of popcorn, jerking his head toward the couch.

I titter. "Why do you think Leah loves curling up on his lap?"

Quincy flashes a magazine-worthy grin. "I'll sit next to him, that way I can kiss her the whole time."

"How considerate." I roll my eyes, grabbing a bowl of kettle corn for myself.

Leah is—exactly as predicted—in Grady's lap. They're stealing small kisses and fawning over each other. Love looks amazing on them, on all of us. As Quincy settles next to them, she leans over and kisses him softly.

"Get a room," I poke, taking a seat beside Quincy.

Warren drops down in the last spot on my right. The four of us barely fit on this couch, which is Leah's excuse for always finding a lap to sit in, as if she needs a reason. Every one of us is a willing throne.

"What's tonight's movie?" Warren asks, tossing a handful of popcorn into his mouth.

"Flicka!" Leah blurts, full of a child-like glee. She practically bounces in Grady's lap.

He flushes, gripping her hip, already struggling. I bite back the coy grin on my face, scooting closer to Quincy.

Warren likes his personal space, not that there's a lot to go around at the moment, but I'll give him as much as I can.

The movie starts, and Leah is the only one fully focused on the screen. Quincy, eyes soft in the dim light, leans my way for a gentle kiss before curling into Grady's side. Leah immediately runs her fingers through his shaggy hair. The way he hums under her touch fills me with warmth.

Without fail, he's the first to fall asleep. That man can never make it through a movie. It has to be the way he thrives with our shared attention.

"You look lonely. Come here," Warren whispers, arm outstretched.

I fight the flutters in my chest and lay my head against him. I'll never admit it, not even on my deathbed, but he's secretly my favorite to snuggle with. Whether it's because I can't have him, or his constantly increasing comfort levels. It may be his dominance. Whatever the reason, when he asks, I obey. The duality makes my heart race.

Will we ever have sex? Doubtful, but moments like this are special.

A kiss against my head brings my body to life. I bury my face against him out of instinct. Realizing what I'm doing, I pull away, swallowing hard. My brows pinch together, hoping he can see the sincerity in the apology on my face.

We've come a long way in the past several weeks, but I don't know if he's *that* comfortable.

"Don't act shy," he murmurs just loud enough for me to hear. "You're too adorable when you get shy. Makes me want to bring out your naughty side." A low, slow growl rumbles in his chest, stopping my breath in its tracks.

Is he dirty-talking me right now?

"War." I drink him in, eyes dancing across his expression, unsure what I'm even searching for.

"Less talking." He slips his waistband down, and holy shit, he's hard—throbbing and glorious, looking at *me*. "Don't wake my brother. I want you to myself."

"Y-you want me?" I blink, mouth watering as his heated gaze locks with mine.

Holy. Fucking. Shit.

I have to be dreaming, that's the only explanation. Just gotta wake myself up before I come in my pants. No problem.

Warren swallows hard, doubt flickering across his face. "I do want you, but I... I don't think I can reciprocate. If that's too unfair, I understand." He runs his fingers through my hair. "I know you've wanted this. If my not being able to... touch you is a deal-breaker, we can forget about it. I won't be upset, promise."

Instead of answering, I bend down and take him all the way to the back of my throat.

A shuddering gasp escapes him. "Fuck, Parker." Raspy, louder than intended, his voice cuts through the room, waking Quincy and alerting the others.

Three sets of wide eyes snap to us, expressions equal parts shocked and aroused. I'm fairly certain Grady moans as he watches me trail my tongue over the barbells I've fantasized about time and time again.

The movie is paused a second later, I'm not sure by who, but nobody argues. Quincy slides his shorts off, shifting closer.

"Wait your turn, Q. Let me—" Warren moans when I change angles, taking him impossibly deeper. "God. Just let me enjoy this. Fuck." He grips my hair.

"Greedy bastard," Quincy jokes, sitting back to watch the show I'm putting on.

They're all enchanted, movie forgotten, as I wreck this man. I don't stop until he's a quivering mess, cursing my name with every bob of my head.

Last night blew me away. I'm pretty sure Warren will let me do it again, if his abnormally shy glances at breakfast were any indicator.

We're all at the stable now. Bridget has her second training session of the day coming up, and I'm dreading every minute of it.

"They really should be more careful," Warren says, making me jolt.

Hand over my chest, my attention travels to the corner of Tally's stall. Grady has Leah pinned against the wall, lost in each other. "We all make out in that corner, you know that." I quirk a brow.

He sighs. "Still, with the new cameras, I'm not entirely sure where the viewing angles are. Henrietta didn't give us the heads-up this time."

"You think she knows?" I whisper, scanning the area for any new lenses glinting in the rafters.

"Knows what, that Quincy and I are in on the plan to get the fuck out of Hartbrook? Away from her?" he asks, leaning against the wall, legs crossed at the ankles.

My mouth goes dry as I ogle his form. Conversation forgotten.

"Hey, Earth to Parker." He waves his hands, breaking the trance.

"Sorry, you're just hot, okay?" I quip back.

"You catching an attitude? I'll have to throat fuck it out of you." His voice drops with a raw edge.

The way my cock twitches is ridiculous. But his threat is a promise—a confirmation that whatever this is between us has transformed.

Breathe, Parker. Remember where you are.

"You can't talk like that here," I whisper-yell.

Tipping his head, he gives me a challenging leer. "What's wrong? You ashamed that you like sucking my cock?"

"War," I plead, wobbling on my feet.

"You're so easy." He chuckles, pushing off the wall to stalk toward me. "I'll stop being a tease, it's not fair, I know." He leans in, ghosting his lips over my cheek.

My hands reach for him on their own, but I'm quick to reel them in. "We're in the open."

Impossibly close as he whispers, "Quincy is in the bathroom waiting for you. I promised I'd get you revved up for him. He misses you."

Jesus, this is maniacal. These two will be the death of me.

Jaw clenched, I stare a hole into the floor. "You don't do this with Leah..."

"We do, there's a lot of free time when you're tied up with Bridget. We need to make sure you're taken care of, too." Softness overtakes him, as if he realizes just how much of our relationship I miss out on because of this training bullshit. "Go on, let Quincy make you feel good."

"W-will you come, too?" I avoid his gaze, immediately regretting the question.

"Is that what you need? I'm sure everyone will join if you're feeling particularly left out."

"N-no, it's okay. It's too risky here. We can get together tonight if you two are free. I... We haven't had a ton of time together as a unit in the last couple of weeks."

"Well, then, go get yourself a pick-me-up with Quincy, and tonight, we'll make sure you're fucked silly. All of us. I care about you, Parker, and I think the others get so caught up in everything that they forget you're under the most stress here. I'm an asshole, but I'm not *that* out of touch." He leans away, discreetly tilting his head toward the bathroom.

As casually as possible, I stroll over and open the door.

Quincy is on me an instant later. "I was starting to wonder if you were going to make it," he says against my lips. "You're working yourself into an early grave."

"Just shut up and make me feel good. Please?" I beg.

"So bossy, you're cut off from one-on-one time with my brother," he responds, voice light and playful.

"I love you, Quincy." My jaw ticks, breath catching. "Fuck. I-I didn't mean to say that here, not like this. I'm—"

His lips slam against mine, giving me every bit of reassurance I need to squash my regrets. His hands find the back of my neck, drawing us closer together. Languid and deep, he shows me his love without saying a word.

Still, when we separate, I open my mouth to apologize again, but he presses a finger to my lips. "Don't," he commands. "I love you, too. Okay? Don't freak out about letting it slip at a 'non-perfect' time. I don't give a shit about grand romantic gestures or believe in planning every detail of a relationship. I live for the chaos, and to see your practiced composure crack for me is *so* empowering. I couldn't have asked for a better time and place. I love the *fuck* out of you. Fuck anyone who judges us."

My face hurts from the stupid ass smile I can't fight. "You're all so good to me."

"You deserve it, but maybe tell War that you love him with a little more finesse." His eyes gleam with knowing mischief.

"I—"

"Don't have to explain it to me. I see the way your face shifts when he's around. Sure, your relationship with him is a lot different since he's sort of gray area gay for you. Honestly, he must love you too to do half the shit he does. I'm pretty sure in the beginning, he only put up with you to be with Leah, but that's not the case anymore. My brother would have *never* let another man touch his dick before you. So, you're doing something right." He presses me against the door, clicking the lock shut, kissing me like it's our last moment on Earth.

If this is the beginning of the end, I'm not complaining.

Thirty

Warren

Leah curls into me, humming softly as she dreams. It's not very often that she sleeps in, but I'm in no rush to wake her. Little moments like this are so rare for us. She's been training so hard, close to perfecting her routine on a level that shouldn't be humanly possible.

Parker presses himself closer against my back, and a smile splits my face. He grows on me by the day, the sneaky little shit. I'm not sure how he's managed it. I'm absolutely *not* into men, but he's my exception. His touch does something to me—freeing, unexpectedly pleasant. Nestled between the two of them, I could almost cry.

No.

I *am* crying.

What the hell? Warren Hart does *not* cry, especially over *feelings.*

I'm not allowed to get close to people. It's not convenient for Henrietta. I can't rightfully explain to a girlfriend why I need to seduce another woman because my aunt tells me to... Not that I would dream of doing that anymore.

Fuck Henrietta, fuck the Hart name.

"Your thoughts are deafening," Parker rumbles, scrubbing his chin against my shoulder. "Did I hear you sniffle? Are you okay?"

"Shh, don't worry about me. You'll wake everyone."

"T-too l-l-late," Grady yawns, lifting his head to look at me over Quincy.

"What's wrong?" my brother asks, eyes still closed as he presses his lips to Leah's shoulder.

"Nothing," I lie, as if they can't all read me like a book.

Leah tips her head to look me in the eye, hand moving to wipe away a stray tear. "War, talk to us."

Damn it, they're not supposed to notice.

"I guess this is happening," I grumble, letting out a heavy sigh. "I'm just... happy." My voice cracks around the word, realizing that this is the first time in a *long* time I've felt at peace with my life.

"I think we all are." Parker places his lips against my bare skin, and my heart jumps.

"I think—" I inhale through my nose, chin shaking while I fight the terrifying confession on the tip of my tongue. "No. I *know* that I love you." I may be looking at Leah, but I press myself further into Parker's hold. "All of you. Sure, Grady and Quincy are family, so it's different. And Parker—" I turn, admiring the adoration in his gaze. "—it's obviously not exactly the same as Leah, but I-I do love you. Somehow, some way, you've broken through and carved your name into my soul."

"That's the most romantic thing anyone has ever said to me." He swallows hard, eyes falling to my lips. "You've put in so much effort to accommodate me, and I just want you to know that I love you, too. I honestly have since you shocked me with that first kiss. I decided then and there that whether anything else ever happened, I'm in this with you."

"Kiss him already, so I can have my turn," Leah demands with a whine.

I bark out a laugh and catch the flicker of doubt in Parker's eyes.

"I guess I haven't made myself clear. Kiss the shit out of me right now, and *whenever* you want, going forward. I love you, affection included."

Noses brushing, he slots his lips over mine. We usually exchange quick pecks on the cheek. But this? The intensity he's meeting me with—tongues dancing together, stealing each other's breath in short gasps—kisses like this are a rarity. I can count all of the ones we've shared on a single hand.

Hopefully, after today, he understands how desperately I want to lose count.

It's a confusing thing; being in love with someone, while not being sexually attracted to them, but our whole situation makes it easier by the day. A situation I'm immediately reminded of as Parker pulls away.

My following pout is short-lived. Leah's mouth meets mine with as much love and passion as Parker's, showing me exactly how much I mean to her—to all of them. Her lips feel so right on mine that I don't want to separate, nearly whining as she leans back.

"I love you, too, War, and I love you, Q." She crashes into him and they get lost in one another in an instant.

The passion in this room is palpable. How dare Henrietta expect us to turn our backs on this.

Parker pulls me against him, resting his head on my shoulder—his favorite place. Grady's glimmering eyes drift over to meet his.

I swallow, gaze soft. "You're okay with your boyfriend *and* girlfriend loving both of us, too?"

Parker stills behind me. "How—"

I titter. "The bathroom door at the stables is *not* soundproof, just so you know."

"Fuck," he hisses, "I hope nobody else heard."

"You mean the whole *zero* people that ever come around?" Quincy jokes as he catches his breath.

"C-cameras," Grady speaks up.

Quincy's face goes stark white. "Shit, do you think they have audio recording capabilities?" Eyes bulging, he springs upward, running his fingers through his bedhead.

"Would she settle for less?" Leah asks. "Better yet, how do you not know? Doesn't she show you the footage?"

I roll my eyes. "That's rich. She barely trusts us to know they exist. Which, to her credit, is valid. Still, we've never been privy to the 'intel' she's gathered."

"It's fine, I'm not freaking out, there's nothing to worry about," Parker says in a tone that completely contradicts his words. "Well, gotta go train the mini-bitch. See you all at the stables." He pops up out of the bed like a jack-in-the-box.

"Parker," Grady says, wrapping him in a hug.

"I—I can't handle being caught." Parker's voice breaks, shoulders slumping.

"Hey," Quincy says, stepping next to them. "We all love each other *way* too much to let anything happen."

"You act like we can just stop her from kicking us out if she learns the truth," I add, immediately wishing I could take the words back.

Parker's brows crinkle closer together and Grady pins me with a frustrated scowl.

"Sorry, I just can't help but be the realist. I know it makes me an ass."

"It's okay, we're gonna focus on one day at a time, alright?" Leah stretches, grabs a pair of shorts and one of her cute little tank tops—mint-green and strappy.

I've never been so thankful that spring in Florida is so warm.

Right, focus.

"We're going to be okay. Let's go kick today's ass." She kisses each of us on the cheek and saunters out of the room.

"Damn, we're some lucky bastards." Quincy sighs, troubles forgotten.

"We really are," Parker agrees, looking at each of us. "I love you all so much, on a soul-deep level. No matter what."

Grady frames Parker's face with his hands. "N-no matter wh-what." He kisses him tenderly, sealing the promise.

Parker's lashes flutter, expression softening. "Thank you, all of you. I'll be back in an hour or two, depending on how this goes."

Leah feeds Tally another peppermint, giggling as she whinnies. Her love for this horse is precious beyond words. We're fortunate to share the space inside her heart.

"Once Grady gets Champ sorted, what do you say we all go get lunch?" She flashes an adorable grin at Quincy and me.

As if we'll ever deny her quality time.

Bridget's cackles fill the building, souring the sweet moment. I don't know how much longer Leah will be able to keep up the charade. If one of us doesn't get caught with our tongues down her throat, she's likely to go off on Bridget eventually.

I almost fuck up and reach for her, but remember the camera that can definitely see us.

As they grow closer, Grady steps out of the supply closet. He takes Champ's reins from Parker and leads him into the stall. Bridget is in rare form today, expression extra bitchy as she sneers his way.

I can practically hear Leah's blood boiling, ready to tear into her for whatever shit she spews this time. I like to lie to myself and pretend that she's gotten better at ignoring Bridget's antics, but the truth is that we've just done a better job of keeping her away.

That's not an option today. Their training session ended sooner than expected.

This is bad.

"Whatever the hell you keep doing to my horse, you'd better stop before I tell Mother. Useless idiot," Bridget snips.

My stomach twists, filling with heavy disdain. Parker's hands are clenched tightly at his sides, twitching like he might be the first to break.

Leah bristles next to me, and I'm powerless to comfort her, to do anything.

Quincy, ever the peacekeeper, does his best to diffuse without making anything too obvious. "I'm sure he hasn't done anything to Champ. He's not cruel and surely isn't dumb enough to compromise your training."

"I'm already on Mother's bad side because I have to wait for the next Olympics, I don't need the village moron interfering. Parkie is going to have to train me harder." She chews her lip in a way that is *supposed* to be seductive. Running her hand down Parker's chest, she presses herself against him. I'm pretty sure he holds back a gag as she purrs, "I think we should spend some real one-on-one time together so you can learn all of my riding techniques."

"If you ride a dick as poorly as you ride a horse, he'd probably rather rut into a jar of rusty nails," Leah spits, lip curled.

Quincy coughs to cover the snort that sneaks out. It takes every ounce of my willpower to keep my expression even. God, I love a feisty woman and she's one hell of a loose cannon.

"At least I'm not trying to whore myself out to the whole facility," Bridget quips with a victorious head wiggle.

Leah's back goes straight as a board, face shifting to a terrifying shade of red. "What the *fuck* did you just say to me?"

"I've seen you trying your hardest to get all of them to look at you. It's pathetic, honestly. As if any of them would sink to your level. Well, maybe Grady, if he could figure out how to talk to you."

Time stands still, we're all frozen in place. Well, everyone except Leah. I don't even see her move, it's so unnervingly fast. One swift swing and Bridget's nose makes a gnarly cracking sound as her fist connects.

But she's not done.

Before any of us can process what we just witnessed, a screaming Bridget is tackled to the ground.

Leah pins her down. "Joke's on you, I *am* fucking all of them. They love me, doesn't that make you sick with envy?" Her fist slams into Bridget's jaw, and Parker finally snaps out of it, grabbing her. "Put me down. Let me beat her senseless." She kicks her feet, arms flailing.

"Star," Parker begs, holding onto her with every bit of his strength.

We all rush to them an instant later, trying our best to calm her.

"She's not lying," Bridget says, voice muffled by her hand, but clear enough to understand the evident shock. "All of you." Her gaze drifts to each of us, watery and unfocused.

"I love you, and don't mean this," Parker whispers to Leah, just as she begins to settle in his hold. "She's crazy, don't believe her," he lies, voice filled with an unsettling amount of conviction. "You know you're the one for me, we're going to be great together, Bridget."

"Yeah, we just had to restrain her, that's all," Quincy adds, discreetly rubbing Leah's back.

Fuck I hate this. No amount of damage control can change the fact that this happened *right* in front of the camera. We may get off scot-free, but Leah? Her fate is sealed. You can't assault someone and still be welcome here, no matter who you are, or how much you're worth.

A somberness swallows the room as realization settles in. She's going to be kicked out, at the very least. If not arrested, depending on how petty Bridget wants to be. Knowing my family, she may as well start prepping for jail now.

"Well, someone walk her to her cabin to begin packing her bags. She's not welcome here anymore," Bridget orders. "Once Mother hears of this, you're done for, reputation soiled for good. Filthy peasant whore."

"Who the hell even talks like that anymore?" Leah spits. "I'll leave, don't you worry. But count your days, because I'm not going to disappear. Even if you press charges."

Grady and I take Leah by the arms and make a show of "escorting" her out of the stables. On the short walk to her cabin, my adrenaline fades and dread seeps into the cracks of my armor.

"What the hell were you thinking?" I ask as we walk through the front door. "What are we going to do now?" My blood pumps rapidly, ears roaring.

"I'm sorry, okay? I finally lost my shit, big deal." She throws her hands up, waving them around like a lunatic.

"S-sassy," Grady says, voice calm. "You... She'll k-kick you o-o-o—"

"So what? I know everything I need to kick ass at the World Cup." Her words practically slap him in the face. He recoils, brows furrowed. "I don't mean it like that, okay. You know I love you guys. Honestly, I don't even care about the Olympics anymore. If I make it, cool." Shrugging, she takes his hand. "But what we've built? It's beautiful. After the World Cup, we can start over. It may not be as prestigious as an Olympic medal, but it's a damn good representation of all of us. Determination, skill, willingness to put in the work and overcome adversity. Just, trust me."

"Forgive us for not understanding." I step next to them, tilting my head. "What difference does a World Cup showing make? You're about to be escorted off the premises and likely arrested."

"Just... help me pack. We'll worry about the details later. The timing sucks, and we need to have an actual conversation about this, as a group. But I'll give you the outline. I've been busy working on something."

I can't argue with her, there's no time. So I have to do the most terrifying thing ever and trust her. If she were anyone else, I wouldn't dream of it. But over the last several months, watching her every move, getting to love her and witness her tenacity up close. I do.

I trust her wholeheartedly to come through. Regardless of what her secret plan is, she's going to make this work.

"Let's get shit together then, and ice that hand."

Grady's nostrils flare, breath quickening as he lets her out of his arms. I fully understand his reservations, this could be the last time he gets to hold her. If we can't convince Henrietta that she was lying, we might very well be sent away for good—phones taken, contact and funding cut off.

This could be the end of our new beginning, dead in the water before it had a real chance. At least we got to know genuine love along the way.

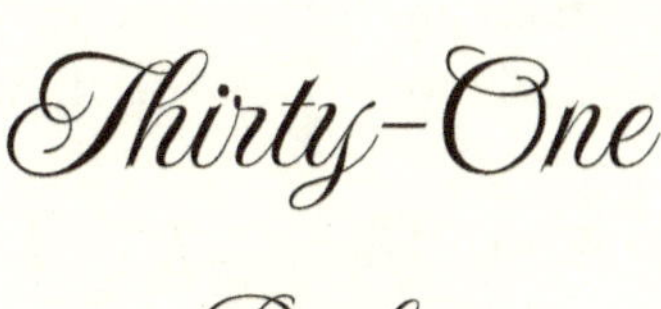

Thirty-One

Parker

Every part of me wants to be in that cabin. It's not fair. Leah is going to get arrested, all because I was too chicken shit to tell Bridget off.

I've failed us all.

"Mother will be here shortly with security. That filthy psycho will be gone before we know it, Parkie." Bridget throws herself against me, nose finally done bleeding. "Thank you for rescuing me from her, such a barbarian."

Breathe.

"Can you believe her audacity? Delusion is so dangerous," she continues, voice nasally.

Anything she says after is unknown to me. All I can focus on is the thundering of my heart. Quincy hasn't spared a glance in our direction, but he is occupied packing up Tally's brushes and gear. If Leah goes to prison, what will happen to her?

Things you never think about until you need to.

When Henrietta storms into the stable, every bit of color drains from my face.

"Bridget, my darling daughter!" she wails, rushing over to extricate her from my side. "What a monster! I should have known better than to let the riffraff in here." Her wrinkle-lined eyes zero in on me. "Jealousy makes people reckless, it seems."

Lump stuck in my throat, I nod. "Yes, Ma'am."

"Oh, Mother, Parkie came to my rescue. He's a hero!" Bridget places her hand over her heart, fawning over the version of me she's built in her mind.

Henrietta rights herself. "Is that so?"

My spine tingles. There's a challenge in her tone, daring me to keep up the charade. Does she know?

There's no way. We've been careful until now.

"He pulled her off of Bridget, the rest of us were too stunned to move." Quincy steps next to me. "Warren and Grady escorted her to her cabin so she could pack her belongings. I've secured all of her gear. Would you like me to load it into her truck? I figure the sooner we get her out of here, the sooner we—"

Henrietta moves faster than a woman her age should. The sound of her slapping Quincy registers before my eyes can process. My jolt doesn't garner a response, thankfully. She's too focused on Quincy. Grabbing him by the hair, she drags him to her level. "Don't you dare disrespect my intelligence, parasite."

"Mother?" Bridget tilts her head, otherwise unbothered.

To his credit, Quincy remains silent. This must not be the first time she's laid hands on him. My stomach twists at the thought.

Henrietta dusts herself off, arms tucked behind her back. "Nobody says another word until the others return." A clear threat. One not to be taken lightly.

She holds all the power here. We're on her property, in her stable. It would be her word against ours. She could do anything she wants to us. The implication settles like lead in my stomach.

Quincy's empty gaze stares through me. An understanding snakes its way into my mind. The three of them lived with this woman all their lives. This small taste of her evil has shown me how strong they really are.

In my silence, I try to convey the solidarity flooding my system. If he notices, there's no indication.

The door slides open and my heart stops beating.

Leah is done for.

Henrietta's face hardens, eyes dark in the brightly lit stable. "Ah, how nice of you to join us. Shame you won't be staying. I have several guards en route to ensure you leave this property and never return. Fear not, I'll allow you to gather your hell beast and go. I don't need a scandal, so we won't involve law enforcement, so long as you leave peacefully."

"B-but Moth—" Bridget stops her attempted complaint as Henrietta raises a hand.

"Hush, girl, this is no concern of yours." Henrietta stalks toward Leah.

Warren and Grady square their shoulders, prepared to... defend her?

Something happened in that cabin. What could she have said to them?

Chuckling, the old bag lifts her nose. "It seems you've got them wrapped around your grubby fingers. How cute. Don't mistake their alliance for an advantage. Play this smart. Leave this place and never return. No harm—" Her attention shifts to Bridget. "—Well, none that matters. anyway. No foul. Trust me, girl, you won't stand a chance in court. I have a powerful team on my side." The venom dripping from her words is sickening.

Leah puffs out her chest, jaw working. "Okay."

One simple word shouldn't hurt this badly. The devastation racking my body is physically painful. She's leaving. Just like that? No more fighting, no bargaining, not even begging.

Quincy reaches for me, lacing our fingers together. The simple act snaps the negativity from my mind, touch calming the swirling chaos. His attention is locked on Warren. There's a defiance in his eyes, determined and confident.

Leah, what is your game?

"Go on then, gather your things and leave us." Henrietta waves her off, returning to Bridget's side.

A dozen large men in suits enter the stable moments later, ensuring there's no resistance as Leah loads Tally into her trailer. She avoids direct eye contact, but there's the faintest smirk on her face. A silent victory that anyone but us would miss.

Knowing she has a plan does little to lessen the blow when her truck starts. Without so much as a goodbye, she drives off, leaving uncertainty lingering in the air.

"Office," Henrietta barks. "The four of you are *not* getting out of this mess so easily."

"Fuck," Warren mutters under his breath. His eyes flash with warning, darting to the security team.

"Don't even *consider* it," Henrietta seethes. "One wrong move and you know what happens." She prances toward our glorified courtroom, security detail in tow.

Bridget's face is overtaken by a disgusting simper, filled with evident giddiness from her mother's threat. She all but skips along behind her.

Warren moves first, laying a hand on my shoulder as he passes. Quincy follows close behind, nodding at Grady and me, face pained. I take Grady's hand, and he squeezes so hard I fear my fingers may break. This is like walking into an execution. Our execution.

Nothing good awaits us. The air is suffocating as we all sit silently, bracing for the raging storm.

Henrietta leans against the large desk, arms folded. "Well, who would like to explain themselves first?"

Quincy glues his attention to the floor, jaw clenched tight. Warren, while not speaking, stares her down, chest puffed. To my surprise, Grady takes on a similar stance.

"Well then. I suppose you're relinquishing your rights to convince me you're worth keeping around."

"What?" Bridget gasps. "Mother, what are you on about? She's gone."

"Stupid girl. She was only part of the problem. I raise the lot of you ungrateful bastards, and this is how you thank me? Plotting to leave?"

Quincy's leg bounces once before he's able to contain it. Every cell in my body aches to comfort him, but there's nothing any of us can do. The old bitch is on to us.

For once, I'm at a loss.

"But, Par—"

"Enough!" Henrietta backhands Bridget. The sound of her scream splits the air. Her nose gushes fresh blood, dripping onto the pristine marble floor. "You'd better clean that up when you're done being dramatic. How are you ever going to fill my shoes if you let a little harlot rough you up like this?"

Falling to her knees, Bridget cups her face to contain the mess she's making. Surprisingly, she's controlling her sobs fairly well, sputtering quietly in a heap off to my side.

She's had this coming, so I have no pity to spare. Sure, she's been raised and conditioned to be this way, but so were War and Q, yet they've proven their innate decency.

Bridget doesn't possess an ounce of kindness or compassion.

"Honestly, this is so predictable. I should have married into a smarter family. Maybe then I'd have *someone* worth passing all of this down to. Such a shame. Maybe I should have tried to bear one more child before Charlie's *unfortunate* death." The exaggerated pout on her lips and dry, condescending tone coating her words make Grady jolt to his feet.

Two of the guards are on him in an instant, holding him back mere inches from his mother's face. Anger isn't a strong enough word to describe the visceral, bone-deep hatred radiating off of him.

Sucking her teeth, Henrietta tips her head back to look into his eyes. "You look so much like him. What a disappointment. The lot of you could have had a great life, ruling over Hartbrook when I retire. But no. You can give a child everything on a silver platter, but a brat's a brat."

Rounding the desk, she sits and snaps her fingers.

The security team pushes Grady back into his chair. "F-fuck you," he snaps, fists clenched at his side.

"Whoa." Bridget gasps, blinking rapidly. Her bleeding has stopped, but Leah did a number on her face—eyes already puffy, bruising settling in.

If any part of this situation will be funny in the future, it's her crooked ass nose and swollen left eye. The time that has passed since Leah put her on her ass has been the quietest she's ever been in my presence.

Violence really is the answer sometimes.

"What was that? Did you find your voice after all?" Henrietta taps her nails on the wooden tabletop.

Don't react.

Jaw working, Grady's nostrils flare, brows knit together. "I hope y-you r-r-rot," he growls out.

I flinch as she stands abruptly, chair slamming to the ground as it topples. "Very well, if anyone is going to rot, it will be the four of you. I'll return when I feel like it, maybe then we can talk like civilized adults." She strolls out of the room, motioning for Bridget to follow. "I'll be tending to my daughter's injuries. think about your apologies carefully, and *maybe* I'll reconsider your punishment."

The door closes behind them, lock engaging with an ominous click.

Quincy collapses against Grady's side, sobbing like this is the end. It very well may be.

"Hey," Warren rubs his back. "Listen, I can't say anything, but just... trust in Leah. We'll be fine. Nothing will stop our woman. Be strong for her."

"Right," Grady agrees. "She's g-got us."

If only they could tell us more, because I could use a hint of certainty. Not that I don't believe them, but everything fucking sucks right now and all we can do is sit here and wait.

For how long? Who knows.

Grady takes my hand, wrapping his free arm around Quincy. "Believe."

"Okay," Quincy mumbles.

Looks like forever is off to a rough start. With any luck, it won't end before we get to enjoy it.

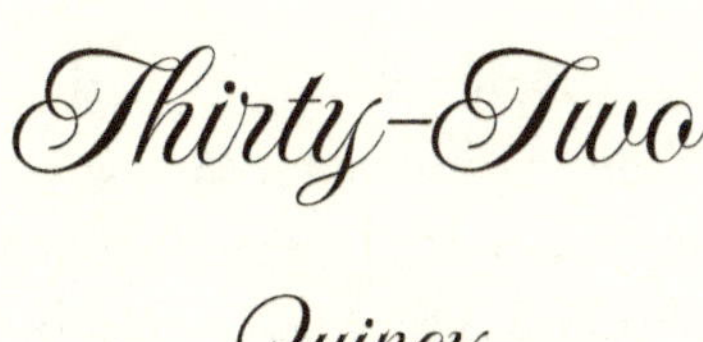

Quincy

We've been locked in this tiny room for at least four hours now. Every single stage of grief has racked each of our bodies. Well, except Warren. I know he can be a cold asshole, but his blasé attitude has my blood running scalding hot.

Sure, he claims it's because Leah shared something with him. But not knowing a damn thing about it isn't doing me any favors. I'm not built for this. Leah is worth it, though. I have to remind myself of that. Every man in this room is worth it. That includes me. They're not giving up, so I can't either.

I won't cave.

Parker is snoring on Grady's shoulder. It's adorable. They're almost enough to help me forget this room is a prison. Unease burns like magma in my gut. All I can think about is curling up in bed with my people. What a cruel fucking turn of events.

"War." My voice trembles. "H-how long do you think she'll keep us here?"

His jaw ticks. "I don't know. But it's okay. We just need to wait it out."

"Promise?"

He leans close, voice low. "Q. I swear. This room has a camera, so I can't say anything else."

Nodding, I melt against Grady, disturbing him for a second before he settles.

My attempt at sleeping through our time in isolation is short-lived. What must be mere minutes after I close my eyes, the lock unbolts. Every one of us jumps as the door flies open.

"So! Who has had a change of heart?" Henrietta steps into the room, hands on her hips. The resounding silence is very obviously not what she expected. Her entire demeanor shifts, eyes darkening, like a fox unleashed in a henhouse. "Well then. It appears that none of you were going to inform me that you've all been indulging in a disgusting group relationship with Ms. Porter." She prowls closer, looming over Grady where he sits. "I've watched the videos."

The small, lifeless office we're in goes deathly quiet. Our faces pale. At this point, it's officially an interrogation room, and we may as well be on trial for treason.

"V-videos?" Grady parrots with an eerie undertone, shrinking into himself.

"Oh, yes. The *videos.* Plural. I did not misspeak." Pointed, her tone delivers an unspoken explanation.

She's been aware of this for some time and said nothing.

What else has she heard?

I'm going to puke.

"So, let me rephrase." She circles the room, passing each of us a murderous look.

To his credit, Parker is handling his first-ever run-in with the *real* Henrietta well. Most people are fortunate enough to never meet the evil bitch that rules this place. He doesn't even flinch as she continues to berate all of us.

"Whom, might I ask, initiated this deplorable behavior?" She leans against the desk. Her perfectly manicured nails tap rhythmically against the top, clacking through the room in a maddening beat. The deja vu makes my skin prickle.

Only, Bridget isn't here this time to slap around.

An eternity of heavy silence passes. Our collective tense breaths echo through the room, the only responses she'll get from any of us. I nearly jump out of my skin as she slaps her hand against the desk.

"Very well, you had your chance. Pack your bags, you're not welcome here any longer. And Parker, if you think you'll ever train again, forget it. I'll be informing every facility in my network of your unprofessional behavior. As for the rest of you, well, you'd best find a way to procure some manner of financial stability, because the Hart accounts have already been deactivated. Pathetic men, driven to betray your own flesh and blood for some *nobody* hussy. She is very fortunate I pity her enough not to have her arrested for assault." Without so much as a second glance, she steps out of the room, door slamming behind her.

Parker is the first to break, crumbling to the floor. I move immediately to comfort him, Warren and Grady just behind me. As we huddle in the center of this purgatory, the sounds of our collective sobs and curses resonate off the walls.

"I fucking knew this was a bad idea, I'm sorry I f-failed," Parker sputters.

Grady frames his face with his hands, forcing him to look at us. "N-no y-y-you didn't."

"Don't you dare blame Leah for this," he fires back, fierce with devotion.

"Parker." Voice soft, I lay my hand over his clenched fist. "None of us blame her. It's a shitty situation all around, but it's nobody's fault. We'll figure this out together."

"He's right, and together *includes* a particularly feisty, pink-haired woman with a pretty impressive right hook," Warren adds, finally breaking his silence.

All of us snap our attention to him.

"Care to explain what the fuck that means?" I ask.

"I'm not entirely sure what she's planning, but she definitely made sure we'll be alright in the meantime. We talked at her cabin when I was helping her pack. She has a plan in motion. I don't know much, but she gave Grady and me the information for a hotel."

"Excuse you?" Parker straightens, surprised, but not particularly shocked by the news.

Warren heads for the door. "I don't know, okay? But we need to act fast before Henrietta changes her mind and ships off the three of us that she owns."

"He's right, if there's one thing Henrietta loves, it's power. She's upset and acting irrational. If we're still here when she comes to her senses, she'll likely have us sent to one of her time-out houses. I'm not particularly keen on going back to one of them." My skin crawls. I haven't had the misfortune of pissing her off in about three years now. The memories of that place are still a black smudge in my mind. It's mental torture, being cut off from civilization. Henrietta is smart about it. Never sending you away for too long, only enough to break your will, so you realize how much your livelihood depends on her.

"Well, let's go then. I have a car, all we need are some clothes. The rest will work itself out. Fuck everything else." Parker stands, holding his hand out to Grady. "I know it's not the glamorous escape I promised, but are you ready to run away with me, my love?"

The tension in Grady's shoulders releases, tears pooling in his eyes. "A-always." He stands and pulls Parker into him, stealing a quick, heated kiss.

Warren and I have very few possessions, so it won't take us long at all to get the hell out of here. A picture of our parents is the only thing I bring aside from a few changes of clothes. Nothing else here holds any significance. We can't even take our Jeep since it's *technically* hers.

The smallest bit of doubt pulls at Warren's face as we make our way to Parker's car. He's been stoic through most of this. Whatever Leah said is enough to convince him that she's got everything under control. Hopefully it's true. Not that I don't believe in her, that woman is as determined and loyal as they come. What worries me is his lack of one hundred percent faith. Warren has always been the smarter, survival-focused one. Some might call it the curse of being an older sibling, even in our instance, where he's only got a little more than a year on me.

The time doesn't matter. He's always let me find the joys life has to offer, while he sits back and keeps his eyes peeled, protecting me from the harsh realities of the world. Watching him fall in love with Leah has made me realize that he's equally terrified. Witnessing him come to terms with the way he loves Parker, too, was unexpected and beautiful.

No matter what happens, I'm going to flip the script. I need to be his protector in this.

All of us care, clearly. But I'm the only one who truly sees him. I know his struggles—everything he's endured—because I lived them, too. But he was my shield, weathering the worst of the storms.

Heart battered and bruised, he's lived a lonely life, forced to shut everyone out. Now that he's let people in, it's all going up in smoke before his eyes, and for once, he can do nothing more than swallow his fears and let someone else be the sponge.

I wrap my arm around his shoulder, and he leans into me. "I love you, War, we all do. This is going to work out. You know our girl. She's going to come through."

"She is." He sighs.

Parker takes our bags and loads them into the trunk. "We all good to go, boys?"

Grady nods, dropping into the passenger seat.

"Let's get out of here before we get kidnapped," I joke, but the truth peeks through.

Grady turns to give me a comforting look—one that tells me he feels it too, the looming uncertainty of what we'll do after those gates are in the rearview. Unlike Warren, Grady shows his thoughts on his face. Hope and excitement are abundant in his eyes, but the slivers of doubt and his fear are also easy to spot.

Parker slams his foot on the gas, peeling out of the drive with a final "fuck you" to this place. Once we're on the private drive, the weight of the world lightens. As dumb as it sounds, the sky seems bluer, the air easier to inhale. Troubles and worries be damned, the energy in the car is buzzing with our excitement.

We're free.

Maybe not how we planned, but we're out from under Henrietta's thumb. What a terrifying relief.

"She already cut our lines," Warren swipes at his phone screen. "I guess it's official, then. We're no longer Harts..." He stares out the window, jaw working.

Parker spares a glance over his shoulder. "You want to talk about it?"

"There's nothing to talk about. You witnessed the fallout. I'm just processing."

And he is. They'll get used to it in time. He's broody, always preferring his thoughts over talking in circles about things he can't change.

Parker wants to say something, it's obvious by the way he's holding the steering wheel—knuckles white from the force of his grip. "If any of you ever need to talk, just know that Grady is a great listener," he jokes instead.

Grady gently shoves him, causing the car to jerk.

"What?" Parker chuckles. "It's true. It's probably the reason I fell in love with you so fast. Nobody has ever heard me like you." His voice wavers under the truth. "You're all special to me for one reason or another. I know I talk a lot of shit, and I'm unserious more often than not. But you all get me."

Warren's posture relaxes. "You put so much weight on your own shoulders that you use humor as armor. I get it. Someone else here is just as big a goofball." He smirks my way. "That's what makes the two of you so unbearable together, but perfect for one another at the same time."

"And you?" Parker says, "Do you know why I love you?"

Warren leans forward, elbows resting on his knees. "Do tell."

"You're the rock, the one I can be serious and vulnerable with. Your energy is like a security blanket. Just be sure to let someone else do the same for you." They exchange a brief, but unmistakably tender, look in the rearview.

Warren swallows. "That's where Leah comes in. She's my anchor. The one who keeps my feet on the ground."

"I miss her," I cut in.

"It's been a whole seven hours," Warren deadpans.

"Yeah, but those hours were different. We don't know when we'll see her again. It's not like Hartbrook, where she'll be there to curl up between us at the end of the day. It's strange not knowing the next time I'll hear her voice, or be close enough to count her freckles."

"Or s-smell her sh-sh-shampoo," Grady murmurs, hands twisting in his lap.

Parker laughs dryly. "Or have her close enough to slap me when I say something out of line."

"We all miss her, okay?" Warren blurts, voice elevated in a poor effort to hide his pain. "And we'll see her again soon. She paid for a hotel, that's where we're going for now."

"What if she's there waiting for us?" I ask, mood-lifting at the idea.

"Doubtful, she said she's heading to Texas." Warren's face—soft with a slight twitch of his lip—gives away his disappointment.

"Well, we'll be in Georgia, which isn't Florida, so it's a start. Let's focus on the positives, okay?" Parker speaks up.

Grady smiles, taking his free hand to hold as he drives.

He's right. And if what she told Warren is true, our girl has been up to something. If he believes her enough not to freak out, then I'm going to accept that. This is my family, and I'll follow them to the ends of the Earth.

Or, in this case, Georgia.

Though it currently feels like the end, today is the start of our forever.

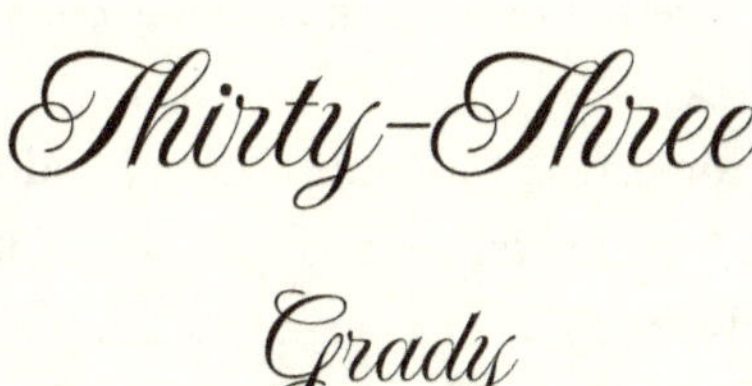

Thirty-Three

Grady

These three are getting on my last nerve. I love them all, but if they could stop moping, it would be appreciated. We're mere minutes from the hotel Leah set up for us, and you'd think we were about to walk into our executions by the solemn energy filling this car. Silence so heavy I wish Quincy would say something stupid just for the laughs he'd get.

Leah will come through. Her silent dedication is obvious to everyone, but not in the way it is to me. I sensed it the first time I met her. When she stood tall to tell me that she could unload her own tack and handle her own horse, others might view it as her being difficult. In reality, it was a show of her will.

A strong-as-steel will that is going to be our saving grace.

I don't need to know all the details of her plan to believe it'll work out. Olympic glory or not, she's going to make sure Parker gets his training facility and that Warren, Quincy, and I have jobs there, too. Nothing and no one will convince me otherwise.

"Well, Star's studs, we're here," Parker announces.

"*Never* call us that again." Warren shudders behind him, and I can't stop the chuckle that rushes out.

"What? It's accurate," Parker fires back with a coy smirk.

"That doesn't mean I'll allow it," Warren grumbles.

We grab our bags out of the trunk and make our way into the front lobby. The receptionist is an adorable older lady, frail and southern as can be.

"Lordy, welcome, fellas! You must be the handsome devils that little pink-haired sweetheart warned me about. I'll have to thank her for the heads-up if I see her again. She got y'all the best room in the building, and some gifts, they're in a bag on the stand next to the bed." She side-eyes us subtly.

"Bed" means there's only one, and she definitely has a knowing twinkle in her eye.

Key in hand, we head to our room. Inside, the first thing I do is grab the pink gift bag. An envelope is taped to it, pink with four adorable hearts drawn on the front.

As I peel it open, Parker reads over my shoulder.

To my team, my lovers, my everything,

I'm sorry. But only because this isn't how I planned our great escape. I know, I know, punching people is bad, but she had it coming. Anyway! The bag has a brand-new phone for each of you. I've already programmed my number in them, so grab whichever one, it doesn't matter. Text me when you get this, don't call. I may not be able to talk right away, depending on what I'm up to. I'll see you soon, just trust me. I've had some things in the works for a while now, and it's almost ready for the big reveal. All I need from you is patience. That's it.

Give me a few to iron out the last of these details, and we're in business, okay?

I love every single one of you so much it hurts,
Leah

Warren empties the contents of the bag onto the blanket next to me. "These are way nicer than the phones Henrietta gave us. How much do you think this all cost her?" His wide eyes travel across our faces until they stop at Parker—lips curled into his mouth, avoiding his gaze. "What aren't you telling me?"

With a swallow that gives too much away, Parker offers his best lie, "Nothing."

"Don't," Warren orders, stepping closer to him. As his lips find Parker's neck, I know he's not messing around. "I don't like being kept in the dark." He kisses his way upward, stopping just behind his ear. "We don't keep secrets from people we love; do we?" Voice low, he grabs Parker by the jaw, wrenching his face toward him.

Parker whimpers in his hold, licking his lips. His body trembles as Warren pins him against the wall.

Quincy, gaze heated and intense, speaks up from across the room, "Answer him," he demands, voice uncharacteristically gravelly.

I'm not entirely sure if he's turned on or pissed off, but my money's on the former.

Warren presses closer. The whine Parker lets out is filled with pure, delicious submission. We should focus on what to do now, but I'm powerless to stop this because I know Parker loves it. The way he can be vulnerable and reckless with Warren is freeing for him. So, as his yearning eyes dart to me, I nod, permitting him to let it out, as if he needs my approval.

But Warren is right, secrets don't belong here. While they aren't ours to tell, Leah won't mind. She's out there somewhere actively pulling strings in a grand scheme to salvage this. I don't think having their shock thrown into the mix will be helpful.

"Leah, she's not who she claims to be." Parker gasps as Warren's free hand glides down his arm.

"We're aware. Why do you think we were sent to watch her, to distract her?" He brushes the tip of his nose against Parker's, lips nearly touching.

Quincy, sitting in the chair at the foot of the bed, groans. This probably shouldn't be such a turn on, but Parker breaking for Warren, in a way he's longed so desperately for, is unfathomably arousing. I'm just glad Quincy agrees.

"Tell us what that means, and we'll all fuck you senseless tonight, isn't that right?" Warren turns just enough to catch our nods, then presses his lips to Parker's with dizzying intensity. When he drags his hand to the bulge in Parker's pants, I have to bite back my own desperate sounds.

"War," Parker says on a gasp, understandably caught off guard. All this time Warren has never touched him.

"Shh, just be a good boy for me." Reaching into Parker's waistband, he groans like a man who knows what he wants. "What's she hiding, Pretty Boy?"

By the crazed look on Parker's face, Warren isn't putting on a show. Slow, torturous, he strokes until Parker lets out a garbled moan, filled with astonishment and long-awaited relief.

"So hard for me. Do you like knowing I'll never touch another man's cock but yours? If you're a good boy, I might even let you come in my hand." After a few steady pumps, Warren stops, and Parker whines against him. "We'll get you off so many times you'll forget your name from moaning ours so much. All you need to do it tell me."

Quincy curses under his breath, gripping himself through his pants. This is going to be good. The thought of us using him until he's delirious has my cock straining against my jeans, ready for whatever the hell this is.

"A-answer." I hear myself say, having absolutely no clue what has possessed me.

He hisses, hips jerking as Warren strokes him again. "She-she's rich. Filthy rich. I don't know the exact number. Never cared to ask. Her money doesn't matter."

"That wasn't so hard, was it?" Warren growls, nipping at Parker's neck. "Now, here's what's going to happen. We're all going to fuck out our feelings because *god* do we have a lot of them going on. Then, once we're all sated, we'll talk about our situation." With a final kiss, he steps away and motions for us to join.

And do we ever.

"So, should we text her?" Quincy asks as he steps out of the bathroom. "Also, the next time we have some crazy gay foursome shit, I'm *not* the last to shower. There was precisely fifteen seconds of hot water left." He plops next to me on the bed.

"Are we not going to address the money situation?" Parker asks, half asleep, curled between Warren and me.

"No," Warren answers, "because you're right. Her money, regardless of how much, doesn't matter. She could be broke, and I'd cherish living on the streets as long as we're all together."

"Yeah, I don't really care, to be honest." Quincy shrugs. "I just want to talk to her so bad I could cry."

Same here.

"Well, it's getting late, but what's the harm?" Warren says, reaching for our phones off the nightstand. "I'll just make a group chat real quick."

Warren:

Hey there, Gorgeous. Come here often?

Leah:

You know, I'm not exactly sure which one of you this is. Have you all molded into one giant cheese ball?

I snort, smiling at my screen.

Parker:

Not quite, but after the way I just fucked all of them, we're pretty much fused into one person.

Leah:

Parker! ALL of them?

Quincy:

Technically, Warren only jerked him off a bit, then made Parker give him the sloppiest head, but still.

Leah:

WTF! I'm so sad I missed it!

Me:

I miss you.

Leah:

I know, Grady, I miss you too, you giant teddy bear. <3

Quincy chortles. "She clocked you, just like that."

Quincy:

When are we going to see you again? :(

Leah:

Based on the jokes and angst, this number must be Quincy. Which means Warren opened with a joke? No way!!

Warren:

Answer him.

Leah:

Yes, Boss. The World Cup is coming up and you all have an important mission.

The four of us exchange quizzical looks.

Parker:

And what would that be?

Leah:

Make it to Texas. I'll need one of you to get a bank account so that I can wire you money.

Me:

Are you in Texas already?

Leah:

No, silly, I will be tomorrow. I've already let the arena managers know my team will be a little late. Please don't rush yourselves, just be here in time for the show. Okay?

Parker:

We can be there tomorrow.

Warren:

We'll leave now.

Leah:

You all need some good sleep. Don't worry about me, I'll live through a couple of days without you.

Me:

We won't.

Warren:

I concur.

Quincy:

Yeah, if Parker thinks we can make it tomorrow, we're there tomorrow.

Parker:

We'll sleep for a bit in the hotel, then take turns driving. If we rotate shifts in a buddy system, we can probably even beat you there.

She doesn't respond. We're all glued to our phones like high school losers talking to their crush. I chew my lip, unable to look at the others because I don't need to. We're all tense, wondering if we've gone too far, done too much.

And then, after several painful minutes, a message pops up.

Leah:

Sorry, I definitely didn't just pull over to sob. You're all so freaking precious. I love you. Get me bank details so I can send gas money.

Parker:

I have an account. I'll get you my details. I love you, Star. Can't wait to see you tomorrow ;)

Quincy:

Be ready for us, Baby. <3

Me:

Good night, Sassy. See you when we get there.

Warren:

Sweet dreams, Gorgeous. It's the last time you'll ever sleep alone.

Leah:

I love you all, and I can't wait to get this mess over with.

Sniffling, Parker wipes his damp eyes. "Okay, sleep for a few hours, then we hit the road. Sound good?"

"I..." My face heats, heart hammering in my chest. Try as I may, embarrassment prohibits the words from leaving my mouth.

Parker slides next to me, gently raising my face to meet his easy eyes. "What's up?"

"He never learned to drive." Warren spares me the shame of having to admit the harsh truth.

"He was deemed 'unworthy' before driving age," Quincy adds, voice warm, understanding.

"Oh, that's not a big deal, you can just rotate co-pilot duties. We can work around it. Every few hours, we'll pull over and swap, and you'll just ride passenger every other time. Easy." Parker kisses my cheek.

I pull my head back, brows scrunched. "J-just l-l-like that?"

"It's that easy. No sweat at all. We love you, there's nothing to be upset about."

"He's right, we love you. You're so much more than what Henrietta made you out to be," Warren says, rubbing my shoulder.

Quincy claps, flashing a vibrant smile. "Exactly! We all are. We're never going back there, and have a whole future full of love to live. Let's sleep so we can get to it!"

This world is rough to navigate, but they always know exactly how to make it easier. The future gets brighter by the day.

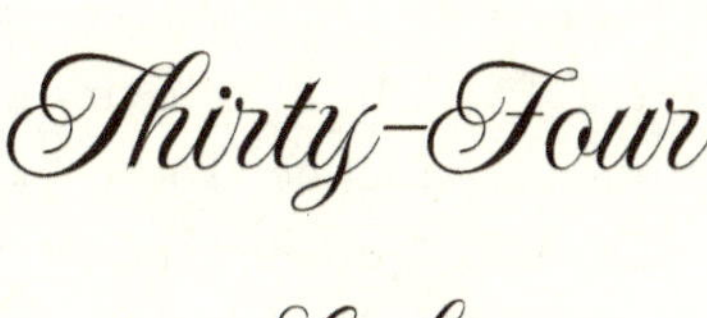

Leah

Who the hell let me do this? What the heck is happening to me? One night apart has made me a pathetic, almost blubbering mess.

I love every second of it.

It's new and, while I'm lonely and wish my men were here, I'm excited to be this gone for them. As desperately as I want to ignore everything and text them like an obsessed teenager, I have to get unpacked.

This place is large, extravagant in a classy way that Hartbrook could never dream of achieving. Some day, we'll have facilities like this. Warm, inviting, homey. All I have to do is push these doubts down and let my girl shine.

Sighing, I scratch Tally behind the ear. "No pressure, but we've got a name to build for ourselves. There's so much more at stake than I signed up for." A dry laugh breaks free. "It'll all be worth it, though." I press a soft kiss against her nose, reaching into my pocket for a peppermint.

Through the bustle of our competitors unpacking around us, I manage to find a sense of peace. Whether the Olympics happen or not, we've come this far. I'm confident in our abilities at this point. There's a ton of stiff competition waiting to take us out, but we've got this. I have to believe that all of the hardship—every sneaky training session, the stolen moments we used to practice this routine—they were all enough. We are enough.

"Do you believe, T?" I ask, braiding her mane.

A soft nicker rumbles out of her. For the sake of my sanity, I'm calling that a resounding "yes". Braid neatly in place, I toss her blanket on. It's new, something I had specially made for this event. Indigo with her name in a gorgeous blush-pink. She's regal, a true beauty among beasts. Not that there aren't a plethora of stunning horses here, but gosh, she's something else.

At this point, the guys have been radio-silent—no calls, no texts, nothing since last night. I can only assume they're still asleep. I drove through the night to get here and took a quick power nap. Not everyone can function on three hours of sleep, I know it's unrealistic.

I won't text first, desperation isn't cute. I probably won't see them until tomorrow, which is fine.

Totally, definitely fine.

Patience is my arch nemesis. But it's better than paranoia, that bitch trying to convince me they're never going to show. Surely they won't run away with the five hundred dollars I wired to Parker. That would be silly.

There is about a week until the World Cup. They won't miss it. I know they won't.

I haven't been entirely unproductive since I got here. The first thing I did when I made it—after getting Tally settled—was call my lawyer. The guys are going to lose their minds if my revenge plot works out. I can't wait.

I'm completely spaced out, filing Tally's things away neatly in the cubby of her stall when the sound of footsteps draws near.

A lot of footsteps.

They grow faster, heavier, more frantic. Before I know it, I'm hoisted into the air, squealing as the world spins. I don't know which one has me. They're all a blur.

"Put me down!" I sputter through my giggles.

People are staring, but none of us care. This time apart has obviously sucked for all of us.

As my feet hit the ground, I whirl to meet Quincy's playful grin. Powerless to stop myself, I lean up and kiss him. Not for long, I don't have time to waste. There are three more sets of equally delicious lips, eagerly waiting.

Grady pulls me from his cousin's arms and lifts me, claiming a kiss with a hum of satisfaction. I kick my legs, chuckling against him like we're in a movie scene. He sets me down reluctantly, almost possessively, only letting go at the last second. But he does.

When I approach Warren, he slides his fingers through my hair, gripping the back of my head as he pulls me in to a deep, demanding kiss—almost too steamy for such a public setting. My knees turn to jelly, stomach filling with flutters. I don't want it to end, but it must.

Pulling away, I beam at Parker. His smile is on full blast, arms open and waiting for me. "Told you I'd get us here in no time," he says, lips a breath away from mine.

"Shut up and kiss me, smart ass."

And he does, like a man savoring the last cupcake at a birthday party. His hands find my ass, lifting me to wrap my legs around him. I bite his lip, tugging gently as he pins me against the wall.

Doubts squashed, all my questions are answered. This is it for me.

They are it for me.

Still, what fun is it if I don't mess with them a little?

When my feet are back on the ground, I place my hands on my hips and put on my best "serious" face. "You're all in big trouble."

Not a single one of them believes me. But that doesn't stop Quincy from playing along. "I'll take any punishment you want to give me, so long as we're both naked." He waggles his brows.

"How about you all help me get the rest of this stuff put away, and we can go find some food? I'm starving." With an exaggerated pout, I rub my stomach.

"C-can we g-g-get steak?" Grady chews his lip.

"That's the most stereotypical thing you could have asked," Parker jokes. "It's a great idea, though. When was the last time any of us had a good steak?"

Grady's eyes fall as he fidgets with the hem of his shirt.

Warren rests a hand on his shoulder, squeezing gently. "I don't know that Grady has ever had steak. Not a real one, anyway."

Fire runs through my veins as I take him in. "Hey," I say softly. "Don't you ever feel ashamed for the things she robbed you of. We'll find a fancy steakhouse, the kind you've gotta get dressed up for, and I'll buy you as much steak as you can eat. Ribs, brisket, you name it." I lay my palm against his cheek.

He leans into it with a faint nod. "I l-love you."

Stepping onto my toes, I press a gentle kiss to his cheek. "I love you so much, don't ever worry about a thing."

"Well, seems like we need to buy some dress shirts then." Parker beams, leaning over to kiss his free cheek.

"A good meal sounds phenomenal. The dinners provided by Hartbrook were all bland excuses for sustenance," Warren grumbles.

"Hey! At least I made stuff," I retort, hands returning to my hips.

"Yes, however, a giant steak and some creamy potatoes, ugh. I'm salivating just imagining it." He tosses his head back with a dreamy, desperate groan.

"Jesus, he might legitimately fall over if we don't get a move on." Quincy pushes him and laughs.

He bumps into Parker, who swiftly wraps him up and lays a sloppy kiss on his lips. I expect Warren to shove him off, say something in warning. But that's not at all how it goes.

What happens instead is beautiful. Warren leans into him, face flushing, features softening. They're all at ease with our situation now. The transition happened so quickly that I hadn't even noticed until this moment.

A different type of warmth fills my body as I admire their love.

We're going to make it.

Olympics or not.

The details are negotiable. As long as they're in my life, we'll all win.

I'm still going to work my ass off to see my goals come to fruition. But in the instance that they don't, I'll be just fine. Having such a strong support system, bursting at the seams with unconditional love, behind me is more comforting than I could have ever anticipated.

Nobody else would ever drive halfway across the country in one day in order to reunite with me. None of my exes, not my parents, nor my brothers. Nobody has ever had my back like this.

Their devotion is the most precious thing. The sweetest part of it all is that I didn't even ask them to do it.

Their love has crept into the cracks of my soul and patched the fractures I tried so hard to keep hidden. The damaged and imperfect parts I convinced myself made me unlovable didn't scare them off like so many others.

This is the best day ever, and many more are ahead of us.

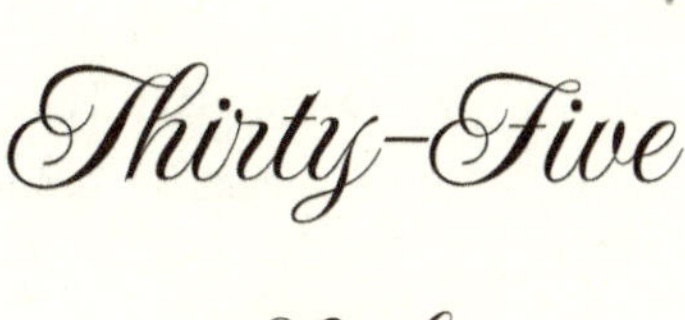

Leah

Eager to feel a sense of normalcy, we unpack the rest of my gear and Tally's supplies in a hurry. Easy jokes float in the air, tender touches as we pass each other bring beautiful smiles to everyone's faces. Each of them stops occasionally to kiss me, basking in the freedom to do so without fear of being caught.

It's so natural, being *us*, out in the open, no looming threats or looking over our shoulders.

Before I know it, we load into Parker's car.

I make quick work of finding a place nearby that sells dress clothes for big and tall men, since Grady's shoulders need their own zip code. When we pull up front, the standalone boutique almost feels out of place for the part of town it's in. Not that the surrounding buildings are particularly rundown, this place is simply spectacular.

Perfectly trimmed hedges, onyx doors shining in the Texas sun, windows spotless to allow perfect views of the immaculately styled mannequins inside.

Grady holds the door open, and we enter, immediately feeling out of place. The polished marble floors and golden etched shelves almost come off as performative, but the luxurious clothing on display says otherwise.

Warren turns to me, brow quirked. "These shirts are almost two hundred dollars."

"And?" I match his expression in playful challenge.

"The pants are, too," Quincy speaks up, holding a pair of navy slacks.

I stroll over to him, lay my palm against his chest, and lean in close to whisper, "Those bring out your eyes, buy them."

His mouth falls open, searching for a rebuttal.

They all come from money, except Parker, so I'm not entirely sure what their hang-up is. Based on how guilty Grady looks—staring at the price tag on the shirt he's holding—I can draw a few conclusions.

"Okay, here's the deal. Each one of you buys two or three full outfits. Don't look at the tags, just find things you like. I'm not gonna be a Henrietta and give you the bare minimum. Treat yourselves and don't feel bad about it. Get what you want for once. Enjoy a little autonomy," I announce, loud enough that they can't even think about ignoring me.

Like a shark drawn to the smell of blood, one of the personal stylists decides we're worth addressing, having undoubtedly heard my speech. She struts over, polished red-bottom heels clicking on the floor. Her veneer-clad grin is nauseating as she fixes her bleach-blonde hair.

"Why, hello. Welcome to Brighton Boutique. What a stunning collection of handsome men." She drags her predatory gaze over their bodies, slow as molasses.

Without missing a beat, Warren wraps his arm around my waist. "Yeah, we're lucky to have such an amazing woman to call ours."

She wavers, eye twitching. "All of you?"

I bite back a smile at the shock on her face, staring victoriously.

Parker steps to my other side, kissing my cheek. "Yup."

"I-okay. So..."

"So, her opinion is all that matters." Quincy flashes his perfect smile in her general direction, not bothering to give her his full attention.

"Very well," she grumbles, face scrunching with pure contempt. "If you need anything, I'll be around."

Grady snorts as she skitters away.

"I'm pretty sure you guys just cost her a hefty commission bonus for her 'consultation'. We're about to spend at least five grand in here. She was definitely going to up-sell us." I chuckle, but their faces don't reflect my humor. "What?"

"Five grand?!" Parker barks out, as if he can't fathom the thought. "For what?"

"Well, there are five of us..." I shrug.

Quincy tilts his head, eyes bulging. "You think we're going to spend a thousand dollars each?"

"No, I'm telling you to. Two or three shirts and pants will break a thousand easily, and then shoes are another story. Hell, we may get closer to seven grand." Clearly, my nonchalance is hard to understand, because they're all frozen in place, like gargoyles in the daylight.

"Leah," Warren eventually mutters, voice shaky.

"It's not a big deal." I smile and usher them back to the shelves. "I love this peach color for you, Parker. The way your eyes will pop against it like the ocean and coral." I sigh dreamily. "And this one for you, War." I hand him an emerald shirt with a navy paisley pattern. "Blonds look great in green, in my non-professional opinion."

He holds it up, turning toward a golden-framed, floor-to-ceiling mirror. My heart stops while I drink him in. By the smirk he gives me, he's well aware of the effect he's having on me.

Parker fans his face. "You have to get that one."

"You'll all need some basic white and maybe a powder blue, but these fun colors are a must. Q, let's find a nice mint-colored one for you. I think that'll make your complexion pop." We peruse a few options until the perfect one jumps out. I hand it to him and move on like a woman on a mission.

Last but not least, we travel to the big and tall section to help Grady. He stands before the rack, expression filled with wonder.

I love that we get to show him the world. One simple luxury at a time.

"What about this plum color? I think it will complement your eyes perfectly." I hand him a buttery-soft button-up.

Brushing his fingers over the fabric, he swallows hard.

"Go on, Hulk, hold it up for us." Parker's voice is soft, eager as I am to see.

Grady's face brightens, shoulders a little higher as he looks at himself in the mirror. Gentle and sincere, his smile could melt the coldest heart.

"Damn, if she doesn't fuck you tonight, I will." Parker bites his lip.

Shoving him, I hold back a snort. "We can take turns. You all owe me at least one orgasm."

"How about we go to the women's section, and *you* give *us* some eye-candy now?" Warren asks, hungry gaze gliding over my body.

"I'm thinking something simple, elegant, easy to take off." I wiggle my brows, and they nod in unison. "Perfect, easy as pie."

A sleek velvet evening gown—deep green with a corset top, sweetheart neckline, and a dangerously scandalous slit up the left side—jumps out at me immediately.

Polished dress shoes for each of them and simple black heels for me round out our haul.

Almost six thousand dollars later, and I'm satisfied with our bounty.

Fortunately, our hotel isn't far. Once we're all changed, I strongly consider ordering in. This dinner is going to be a test of my willpower. Every one of them looks delectable, and I'm a starved woman. But the rumbling in my stomach makes a valid point—actual food first, tasty men second.

Deciding that the high-end wine the steakhouse offers is a must, I spring for a limo rental. I don't want anyone feeling obligated to be the designated driver. Growing up, I had to do it too many times for my brothers and know *exactly* how lame it is.

I spend the entire ride switching laps to steal kisses and attention. Am I supposed to be wearing a seatbelt? Probably. But I'm just a girl in a limo with four gorgeous men who happen to love her. Who can blame me?

Pulling up to the front of a rather inconspicuous building, the driver gets out and opens the door. My guys let me exit first—I'm pretty sure it's to look at my ass, but I can't prove it—and file out behind me. Warren and Parker each bend an elbow, and I lace my arms through them. Grady and Quincy follow close behind.

I give them an impish grin as we enter the building. "I have an extra special surprise."

"Miss Porter, party of five?" the host asks over his tablet.

"Indeed," I respond with a nod.

"Right then, the balcony has been cleared for you. Follow me." He turns on his heel, guiding us to the rooftop.

The private terrace has an overhead trellis, scattered with flowering vines and fairy lights. Along the horizon, the setting sun is in clear view from the table we're seated at. Four sets of love-filled eyes watch me peruse the menu, like a queen, surrounded by my adoring retinue.

We place our orders and watch the sunset together, sipping the finest Cabernet this place has to offer. Before long, baskets of artisan rolls come to our table.

"How much is all of this costing you?" Parker asks, eyeing the second bottle of wine as our waiter steps away.

"Us," I reply simply, "and it's nothing. Never worry about money. I'm a little flashy sometimes, but not irresponsible."

"It's... your money. Feels strange having you spend so much on us. I looked this place up. The steaks are ten dollars an ounce," Quincy says, voice tight.

Grady stiffens. He ordered a massive wagyu tomahawk. I immediately decide not to tell him it costs three hundred dollars.

"You all come from a wealthy family, never having to worry about anything. Why is it an issue now?" I'm sure I already know the answer, but a small part of me needs to hear it from them directly.

"You think we ever had nice things?" Warren lifts a brow. "Quincy and I were just inconvenient baggage. Grady is still nothing to Henrietta. The spoiled life Bridget lives is so far removed from the way we were raised. Forgive us for having reservations."

There it is, the full truth. Suspicions confirmed. All the more motivation for me to destroy Hartbrook. Or, at least, beat them.

"Let me lay this out. Okay?" I straighten in my seat, squashing the anxious flutters in my gut. "*We* are a package deal. What's mine is yours, and that includes the seventy million in the bank." I pause, giving them each a chance to process the atomic bomb I just casually threw at them.

None of them says a word, but their expressions are deafening. Lips parted as they struggle to breathe in the thick, tense air.

"It's a shocking amount of money, I know. But there's no time to dwell on that," I continue without a second thought. "I trust you. Each of you." I slather a toasty piece of brioche with butter. "Don't try to fight me on this. We're all about to be business partners, as well as life partners. What kind of relationship would this be if I gatekeep *our* money?"

"B-but..." Grady sputters, eyes still bulging.

"Noooope." I take a big bite, groaning as my eyes roll back. "This is to die for, y'all had better get some before I eat it all."

"Leah," Warren speaks up, unflinching as I shoot him an annoyed look. "That's so much money and, realistically speaking, you barely know any of us."

"Yeah, what if this is some elaborate ploy by Henrietta?" Quincy offers.

"Then I'll live and learn. It's no more my money than anyone else's. I was just lucky enough to win part of a massive jackpot. I love you guys, so in the spirit of easing your worries, how does a joint account for all of us sound? One where I put a set amount in it each month, and that's it? I want you all to live for once. Spend the money, I make more in interest by the day, I'm really not that bothered."

"You're too good to us. We've done nothing to deserve any of this," Parker mumbles to his lap.

"You've all been there for me. That's more than my own family could be bothered to do, and I've spent millions on them. You've each supported my dream, shown up every time I've needed you, let me be *me,* and never once made me feel dumb for my unrealistic goals. Don't you understand that I value you far beyond whatever money I might spend?"

The moment it clicks for each of them is obvious. Their faces fill with warm recognition, silent devotion flooding the space around us.

The twisting in my stomach subsides. "I'd go bankrupt any day for the lot of you. So please, enjoy this dinner, enjoy the wine, and enjoy the life we all get to live together. Because I love you."

Grady moves to kneel at my side, wrapping his arms around me. "I-I love you t-t-too."

I fan my face in his hold, determined not to ruin my makeup. "Always the big softie." I chuckle.

"You're the most stubborn, difficult, ridiculous, perfectly amazing woman ever." Warren comes over and places his palm against my cheek as Grady keeps me close. "I didn't mean to upset you." His eyes sparkle, thumb stroking small circles over my skin.

"None of us did," Quincy agrees.

"Yeah. We're all just fucking windblown by the number," Parker mutters.

I laugh around my sniffles. "It's okay, my delivery could have been gentler."

Extracting myself from Grady, I give them all a sweet smile. "Let's eat some delicious food and then get freaky in the limo on the way back to our room."

A chorus of eager groans echoes through the cool night air.

Soon, they'll see just how much I mean every word I spoke tonight.

Thirty-Six

Parker

My blood is racing through my body so fast I might vibrate out of my seat. There have been a lot of solid runs today. She's got some fierce competition for sure. Two other teams have scored over eighty percent. Yesterday's practice was almost flawless—transitions smooth, on beat, perfect posture. She's got this in the bag. I know it.

If only the others were as confident.

"My stomach is in my throat," Quincy says, leg bouncing next to me.

Laying my hand on his thigh, I squeeze gently. "She's going to nail it. This routine is packed full of high-skill movements. I'm thinking she'll get close to a ninety."

Warren nudges me with his shoulder. "You've done a wonderful job with both of them. It's been amazing watching their progress."

Grady isn't here. I wish he could be, but as her officially registered stable hand, he has the most important job of all today. Fortunately, he's Tally's second-favorite person. His gentle nature is our secret weapon, one that is definitely going to secure the win today. Even on her crankiest days, he can butter her up until she's perfectly mellowed out.

The first notes of their familiar music begin, floating like promises on the slight breeze. I take Warren and Quincy's hands, gripping until my fingers hurt as we collectively hold our breath. This routine is seven minutes long. We're going to have to let it out eventually, but not until they hit the first pirouette.

On beat, they enter the arena in a stunning, collected trot. Moving in a half-pass to set themselves up for a beautiful flying change. The way Tally's powerful, elegant forelegs skip in time to the jazz composition of "Man I Feel Like a Woman" is entrancing.

They're at the top of their game today, going for gold, as always. A few more gait changes, and they're geared for the pirouette, perfectly on time. They're averaging above a ninety percent right now—beyond what I would have ever imagined.

"They're killing it," Quincy breathes out, relaxing at the nine point three that flashes on the screen when Tally finishes her rotation, polished hooves shifting the sand as she lands.

"Never doubted they would," Warren says, voice full of pride.

A piaffe for the ages, more flying changes done with the finesse people have come to expect from them, and a graceful extended canter to show off before they move into another series of tricky maneuvers. The second pirouette is a little looser than the first, but their overall score hardly changes.

"They're putting on a show-stopping performance," a man behind us mutters.

"Both of them have such natural talent, it's insane," his buddy says.

"I need to follow all her socials, she's my new idol," the young girl with them announces. She's about twelve, and the admiration in her voice is precious.

I smile to myself as Warren and Quincy squeeze my hands, silently cheering her on.

Hartbrook still claims all the credit for her training, so I have to bite back the sour taste that fills my mouth. When this is all said and done, whether she gets selected to represent the United States in the Olympics next year is irrelevant at this point.

I'll forever be her biggest fan, gold medal or not.

Well, I may have a few competitors, but I think they all love me enough to let me claim the title.

One last pirouette, a textbook transition to a near-flawless piaffe, and they've done it, finishing a solid routine with a ninety-one point seven two. Nearly breaking a world record at your first World Cup is one thing. Doing it in your rookie season is magic. Pure, untamed magic.

The crowd erupts with cheers and a standing ovation. The three of us join, finally able to release our anxious energy. We whoop and whistle, jumping and holding one another.

After the event finishes, the final scores have it. Leah and Tally claim first place. Seconds, that's all it takes before she's whisked away for a victory interview. Her first of many, if I have any say in the matter.

"Miss Porter, how does it feel to come out of nowhere and be one of the most well-known names in the dressage community?" the older woman asks, handing the mic to Leah.

"Well, I started this with a dream to qualify for the Olympics. I showed up every day, worked extra hard, and have my horse, Tally, as well as her breeder to thank. Her foundation was great. She had Grand Prix training before I purchased her, which set us up for a beautiful debut season. Thank you, Forrest Dream Friesians, for the partner of a lifetime." She flashes a vibrant smile at the cameras.

"We understand you've been training at Hartbrook. Surely, you're proud to study under Henrietta Hart and her dedicated team."

Her face twitches faintly, then shifts, a mischievous smirk taking over. "Actually, I wish nothing but the worst for Henrietta Hart."

Gasps echo through the arena. The interviewer sputters, "I-I beg your pardon?"

My heart practically implodes.

"Let me explain. Henrietta Hart charged me triple, knowing full well that I was a nobody. The fact that she did so with no faith and no intention of actually taking my training seriously is where the issue lies. However, I had the fortune of being assigned to the best trainer she had on her roster. She was just too stubborn to see his genius. Parker Jones, I love you. Thanks for doing everything in your power to see me succeed. Our hard work paid off."

"I—" the interviewer attempts to say something, but Leah grabs the mic from her.

"To anyone watching that has a dream, let it be known that my boyfriends and I are opening our own facility. And yes, let's get that out there now, I said *boyfriends.* Three of which happen to bear the Hart name, but have no ties left to Henrietta. They don't know it yet, but I've been working diligently for the past couple months to secure a location. If Alabama isn't good, we'll relocate, but for now, we've got about one hundred acres of land ready to go near a pretty neat Italian restaurant. We should be operational next year."

The poor interviewer looks like she's about to faint. "I-uh... Thank you, Miss Porter."

Me, on the other hand? I'm stuck in place.

"She bought us land?" Warren says, barely audible.

Quincy lets out a low whistle. "And claimed us in front of the world. You know Henrietta was watching that."

"I'm going to marry her." Warren sighs.

"Not if I beat you to it," Quincy quips back.

I roll my eyes. "None of us need to marry her to be a family. I also highly doubt she'd want to be a Hart."

"No shit, none of us do," Warren snips.

Quincy tilts his head. "What if we all take her last name?"

"She's not exactly close with her family. What if she doesn't like her last name?" I shrug.

"How about we go ask her?" Warren says in a way that silently calls us all ridiculous.

"Right, she should probably be part of this conversation." I motion for them to follow me out of the stands, now that the commotion has died down.

We find Grady in the stables, alone.

"She's at the h-hotel. S-said she needed to g-get ready." He scrunches his face dismissively.

His innocence is adorable. The rest of us immediately understand and help him finish up so we can go celebrate.

Once we're done, we head to the hotel and make a beeline for our room, stopping dead in our tracks at the sight that greets us.

Leah, scantily clad in lingerie that should be illegal, holding an envelope.

"Hi," She says, chewing her lower lip. "Hope you don't mind I made a little scene up there."

"Just a little," Warren rumbles, stepping up to her. "What do we have here?"

"Oh, nothing. Just the deed to our new property, the home of our soon-to-be training facility." She smirks, pressing her breasts together.

"You were serious," I say on a moan, claiming part of her space.

"Mmhmmm." She bats her eyelashes, pressing against my chest.

"Okay, is someone going to fuck her now, or do I have to thank her for all of us?" Quincy asks, already undoing his pants.

Leah chuckles, shifting to a gasp as I reach around to unclasp the bra of her little leather ensemble.

"Oh, we're going to make sure she's properly thanked." Nipping at her neck, I savor the heated sound she makes as I spread her out on the bed.

In a blur, every article of clothing in the room falls to the floor. There's not an ounce of restraint to be found here. Not tonight.

Grady kneels between her thighs, removing the little skirt, leaving the black fishnets on. "B-beautiful," he growls out, lips pressing softly against her hip.

Her shaky gasp sends a rush of blood to my dick, as if it had room for any more.

"We're so proud of you." Warren slides next to her, stealing a desperate kiss, swallowing her sounds as Grady's tongue makes contact with her clit.

His movements are well-practiced by now, swirling in a way she loves. I pluck at her nipple while he works, ghosting my teeth across her tender skin. In record time, she's coming undone, rasping out our names while Grady chases her orgasm.

"Damn, you're getting good at that, Hulk." I chuckle, and the bashful smirk he gives me goes straight to my painfully throbbing cock.

"Parker, please help me with our men." Leah breathes out, eyeing the impressive collection of erections in the room. "I need a minute, and really want to know what I missed out on in the hotel in Georgia."

I bite my lips, brows waggling at the three of them. "Well, boys, let's give our wife a show."

Her eyes widen, lips parting on a gasp. "Wife?"

"We'll talk about that later. For now, Parker has some more... important things to deal with," Warren answers, shifting to sit on the edge of the bed. "Come here."

Trembling with the need to obey his every command, I move to sit beside him. Without hesitation, I kiss him hard, gripping his cock with the ferocity he craves.

He hisses against my lips. "You're our naughty boy, aren't you?" He groans as I drag my thumb over his tip, collecting a bead of precum.

"He sure is," Quincy takes a seat next to him. "Show her how bad you are."

Leah breathes rapidly with undivided focus as I kneel, taking one in each hand. I alternate between using my mouth and steady strokes while they moan, loud and unrestrained.

"Oh my god, I can't believe this is my life." Leah lazily rubs her clit, eyes hooded. "Please, someone fuck him."

Grady is behind me a breath later, hand sliding up my back, leaving goosebumps in his wake. Unlike his cousins, he's tender and attentive. I quake each time he takes me. Not that I don't enjoy the sloppy, rough experience I get with Warren and Quincy, but something in the way Grady makes every time special does me in.

He starts with his fingers, getting me as prepped as possible while I take his cousins deeper.

Entranced, Leah moans, face flushed, and continues to work herself. As Grady begins to sink into me, I lean away from Warren and Quincy, letting out a garbled sound.

Leah slips to the floor and claims my lips, silencing my madness. "So bad," she whispers against me.

Grady grunts as he pumps deeper. When Leah slides her soft hand under me and takes hold of my cock, my eyes roll back.

"Fuck," Warren hisses, thrusting into my waiting mouth. He lets me drag my tongue along the barbells under his shaft once before driving into my throat.

Leah moans. "You're all so hot, it's so unfair that I get you all to myself." Shifting next to me, she opens wide to swallow Quincy.

I'm not even the slightest bit upset that she's stopped touching me. The squeaks she makes as he grabs the back of her head and hammers into her throat are erotic as hell. Grady bottoms out in my ass, reaching over to slip his hand between her thighs so he can work her clit.

Before long, the sensations become too much for her to bear.

She pulls free from Quincy's hold to catch her breath. "Please, someone fuck me." The needy whine that follows her words has Warren and Quincy springing into action.

Together, they lean me back, helping Grady position so that I'm sitting on him in reverse. He's deeper than ever, growling in my ear while I clench. Warren takes Leah by the hand, helping her lean forward so she's lined up with my cock.

I'm not going to survive this.

On her knees before me, pussy dripping and ready, she slides slowly down my length until I'm so deep I fear I'll hurt her.

Choking on a groan, Warren offers his cock like a delicacy, and she takes it eagerly.

Grady's movements push me into Leah further than I would have thought possible. Between them, I'm turned into a crazed sex toy. Moans bordering on screams erupt from me until Quincy approaches my side, silencing me with his cock.

My consciousness exists on pleasure alone.

Warren wipes tears from Leah's face, forcing himself into her until she chokes. "Fuck, this throat is heaven. Both of you are filthy sluts for our cocks aren't you?"

Leah tries to respond with a muffled moan, tightening around me. Grady pinches my nipple between his fingers, rolling his hips until I see stars.

It's too much, in the best way.

I plummet over the edge, shuddering as I come buried in Leah's silky perfection. I squirm on Grady's cock as she comes undone around mine. The aftershocks of my orgasm nearly wreck me as waves of his cum fill me.

Leah whimpers, nearly choking on Warren's release as it spills down her throat. The sight, paired with his frenzied string of curses, almost makes me come again.

Quincy is the last to fall, hissing, fist clenched tight in my hair while I swallow everything he's got.

We collapse into a pile of panting limbs and soft, satisfied chuckles.

"So, wife, huh?" Leah breathes out between her heaving breaths, head resting on my thigh.

Grady makes a huffing noise behind me that can only be interpreted as confusion.

"We want to change our names." Warren sits up on his elbows, addressing the room. "There's got to be a process. People do it all the time."

"We figured, if you want, we'll all be Porter's, like an unofficial marriage," Quincy explains, breathless, curled around Leah.

"S-sounds p-p-perfect," Grady replies.

I had no doubts he would agree. The man barely relates to his last name as it is. Our attention shifts to Leah, eagerly awaiting her response.

"I love it." She grins, eyes hooded over.

"That settles it then, first, we shower, then we sleep, and then forever begins." Warren gets up and extends a hand for Leah.

"Deal," she replies.

We all follow to the bathroom and exchange soft kisses and tender touches as we clean each other.

Once we're curled up in bed, the peace that settles in the air is nearly tangible. Understanding blankets the room—confirmation that this has all been worth it. Through all of the headaches and heartbreaks, we've come out on top. The Olympics aren't ready for the Porters, but they'd better be.

Because we made it.

All thanks to the pink-haired heroine curled up in the middle of us.

Epilogue: Leah – 4 years later

Heart thumping wildly in my chest, I wait for the final team to finish their performance. My people are watching at home, which is fortunately not all that far away since the Olympics are in LA this year. Sure, it's taken a bit longer to get here, but we made it.

I would have loved to make the team at the last summer games, but things got in the way. Namely, our fire-haired little girl, Sierra—who just turned three, with green eyes identical to mine. And our blue-eyed, brown-haired little boy, Devon—only a year younger.

As long as the team in the arena doesn't beat our score, Tally and I are taking home the gold for the United States. I close my eyes and breathe deep as they come to a halt. Eighty-nine point seven three percent, nowhere near our ninety-one point nine two.

Holy shit.

I can picture my men cheering back home. Surely, our staff is going ballistic right now. I wish I could have brought them. All of them, my husbands, our children, every single one of our trainers and stable hands. They've all become family over the past few years.

Someone has to train the next gold medalist, after all, and our trainers are the best in the world, thanks to Parker's guidance.

Several of them migrated from Hartbrook when it shut down. When my lawyer gave me the life-altering call that the private investigators found proof of Henrietta's involvement in her husband's death, well, it didn't take long to bring down an empire built on corruption.

Apparently, Grady's father didn't want to cut him out of the will. Henrietta couldn't have that, so she took matters into her own hands. A year of digging through files and offshore accounts, and they were eventually able to trace it all back to her. It turns out that I'm more petty than she bargained for.

As for Bridget? Well. She's fallen off the face of the Earth. Once Henrietta went away, she skipped out of town. None of us has attempted to find her, and she's not welcome anywhere near Magnolia Hollow. We've worked too hard to build ourselves up from the trenches.

This win is for *us*. Each person who showed up for me when I needed them, and those who continue to have my back, regardless of the long hours and exhausting amounts of practice.

As the medal ceremony commences, I make my way to the podium, wiping the tears from my face.

Most people would be in disbelief, shocked that they've come this far, but not me. Especially with the team I have on my side.

As I accept my medal, the only thing I can think about is getting back home to my family—the family I chose, since my own blood wrote me off. Tally will be excited to mingle with her friends in the pasture, soaking in the glory of retirement. My only goal going forward is to enjoy my life beyond this achievement.

Bittersweet? Maybe.

But what can I say? Plans change. Now I'm more focused on helping other people live out their dreams.

Keep up with Rii

Hi there! If you've made it this far, I must have done something right! If you want to stay up-to-date on my current and future projects **RiiFinley.com** has all my relevant links!

Thanks for reading!

About the Author

Rii Finley is a coffee-drinking, music-loving introvert. She finds joy in all kinds of creative outlets from painting and sculpting to writing (obviously). She loves animals and has two rambunctious boxer dogs. The Spotify team is probably concerned by how much of her listening time is consumed by Sleep Token and K-Pop (mainly Stray Kids).

Romance novels are her escape—her happy place—she's usually reading one on her phone in her down time.

If you love good banter and lighthearted humor in the midst of chaos, and prefer your books spicy and heartfelt, with a splash of darkness, you've found your new favorite author!

www.ingramcontent.com/pod-product-compliance
Lightning Source LLC
La Vergne TN
LVHW091250150826
845673LV00006B/1376